Mollie Hardwick was born in Manchester
where she worked as an announcer for the
BBC before moving to London to join the
Corporation's Drama Department. She
worked there on numerous plays for both
radio and television before going freelance
in 1963. With her husband, Michael, she has
written sixty books, many theatrical
adaptations and radio and screenplays.
An authority on Sherlock Holmes, Mrs.
Hardwick advised the BBC on its series about
the famous fictional detective and produced
a novelisation of Billy Wilder's film *The
Private Life of Sherlock Holmes*. She also
writes for *Woman* and *Woman's Realm*
magazines, works as a reviewer for *Books
and Bookmen*, and makes broadcasts
on books and drama for the BBC.
Mollie Hardwick's many books include
*Emma, Lady Hamilton; Mrs. Dizzy; Sarah's
Story* and *The Years of Change*, the latter
titles in the very popular UPSTAIRS,
DOWNSTAIRS series.

Also available from Sphere Books

UPSTAIRS, DOWNSTAIRS John Hawkesworth
ROSE'S STORY Terence Brady &
    Charlotte Bingham
SARAH'S STORY Mollie Hardwick
MR. HUDSON'S DIARIES Michael Hardwick
IN MY LADY'S CHAMBER John Hawkesworth
MR. BELLAMY'S STORY Michael Hardwick
MRS. BRIDGES' UPSTAIRS, DOWNSTAIRS COOKERY
BOOK

'The War To End Wars'

MOLLIE HARDWICK

SPHERE BOOKS LIMITED
30/32 Gray's Inn Road, London WC1X 8JL

First published in Great Britain by Sphere Books
Ltd 1975

Copyright © Sagitta Productions Ltd 1974

Set in Intertype Plantin

Printed in Great Britain by
C. Nicholls & Company Ltd
The Philips Park Press, Manchester

This book is based on the fourth television series of UP-STAIRS, DOWNSTAIRS, produced by John Hawkesworth for London Weekend Television Limited, and created by Sagitta Productions Limited in association with Jean Marsh and Eileen Atkins.

Rex Firkin was the Executive Producer, and Alfred Shaughnessy was Script Editor of the series.

The author wishes to acknowledge that in writing this book she has drawn largely on material from television scripts by the following writers:

John Hawkesworth
Elizabeth Jane Howard
Jeremy Paul
Alfred Shaughnessy
Rosemary Anne Sisson.

The author is grateful to them; and to London Weekend Television for the opportunity to attend rehearsals and recordings and to feel a part of the world that is UPSTAIRS, DOWNSTAIRS.

CHAPTER ONE

MR. HUDSON hoped he was not going to lose his temper again. The war, which on 4 August 1914 had seemed a solemn undertaking, a noble crusade in which Great Britain stood for the powers of good against the Kaiser and his evil agents, had turned in a very short time into an infuriating series of petty irritations. Himself of an orderly, well-disciplined nature, Mr. Hudson failed to understand why everyone could not be the same. If he was prepared to act as captain of the household at 165 Eaton Place, why could not his staff obey his orders with the military precision he expected of them?

Take this evening, for instance. He was determined that the regulation ordaining the blacking-out of windows should be enforced to the last detail. With the street lights no longer lit, the merest chink in the smallest window would be a beacon-light to guide the Zeppelins which were hourly expected. Yet, when he had supervised the ritual lowering of the kitchen window-blind, reinforced with dark green cloth, that idiotic girl Ruby had let the cord slip out of her hand so that the thing shot up again, exposing the full glare of the lighted kitchen to the enemy who might very well be cruising in the skies overhead.

'What *are* you doing, girrrl?' he had cried, his Scots accent, as ever, becoming pronounced in moments of emotion. Ruby quailed with terror under his glare, and Mrs. Bridges added her reproaches to his. 'Ruby, whatever was you thinking of? If anyone had seen that, they'd 've thought we was a nest of spies!' The blind secured, the snivelling Ruby was dispatched to lay tea. Mrs. Bridges looked after her.

'That girl! We ought to send her to fight for the Kaiser. That'd soon end the war!'

Rose and Daisy were admiring the blind in position, but Mr. Hudson was still not satisfied. 'Possibly,' he mused, 'we shall need to put drawing-pins at the side. "No inadvertent chinks" — that is to be the motto in this household.'

The two girls glanced sidelong at each other with the faintest twitch of a smile. The stage had not been reached when Mr. Hudson's fussiness would be as irritating to them as their carelessness was to him. Edward, too, grinned, though without letting Mr. Hudson see him at it.

When they marched upstairs in a well-drilled line Mr. Hudson's feelings suffered again. Richard and Hazel Bellamy were sitting in the morning-room and seemed surprised at the entry of their butler, the two maids and the footman.

'Yes, Hudson?' Hazel looked up from the curtain she was lining with black material.

'If we might draw the curtains, madam.'

'It's rather early, isn't it? We hardly need the light on yet,' Richard protested.

'I thought we had better make sure that the blackout is in order, sir, since I understand the street-lamps are not to be lit tonight.'

'Very well, Hudson,' said Hazel. With amusement she and Richard watched their staff move formally, like dancers in a pavane or acolytes in a mystic ceremony, Mr. Hudson to one window, the others taking up their places at his nod. Rose stood by one curtain, Daisy by another, ready to draw. They might have been sailors manning the rigging, waiting for the Mate's bellowed command. It came in the form of a crisp nod. Then, the curtains drawn, Mr. Hudson and Edward turned on the lamps.

'I trust we are not offending against the Defence of the Realm Act, Hudson,' said Richard, entertained. But to Mr. Hudson the question was a perfectly serious one. 'I will send Edward outside, sir, to make sure that there are no chinks.'

His duty done for the moment, he was able to return to his perusal of the map of Europe which he kept pinned up in the servants' hall. Mrs. Bridges, busy serving up boiled haddock, enquired how things were on the War Front.

'Not too good, I'm afraid, Mrs. Bridges. It would appear that the German attack has been halted on the River Marne, but Paris is still threatened, and there was a hint in *The*

Times today that the Belgians might not be able to hold Antwerp.'

Mrs. Bridges nodded sagely, though the statement meant little to her. Whatever Mr. Hudson said was bound to be gospel truth.

'Well,' said Daisy with her mouth full, 'I don't care what happens as long as Eddie doesn't get mixed up in it.' She shot her sweetheart a melting look across the table. It was amazing, and slightly galling to Rose, how pretty Daisy had grown since she and Edward had fallen in love. Gone were the wisps of hair straggling from beneath her cap, gone the tendency to draw a work-grimed hand across her nose instead of bothering to get her handkerchief out. She was really a very pretty girl, whose freshness and look of innocence suited her name just as the elder girl's belied hers. A camellia or an arum lily, Rose might be in flower terms, with her slender figure and fine-drawn face, looks inherited from her French mother; but anything so full-blown and flamboyant as a rose, never, unless it were the most graceful of white varieties. It was a pity, thought Mr. Hudson sometimes, that she had not married her Australian fiancé, Gregory Wilmot, especially after she had got as far as the ship with him; and then coming back in hysterics with a story about his being married already. A queer tale, a very queer tale indeed.

Mrs. Bridges was saying, 'If that there prescription comes in, that'll be time enough for Edward to go.'

Mr. Hudson laid down his knife and fork. 'I trust that, should the need arise, every true Englishman will enlist, without the need of – *con*scription – but in my opinion that time has not yet come. For the moment, Edward's duty lies here.'

Edward's face wore an enigmatic expression; almost as though he did not entirely agree with Mr. Hudson.

The next morning Edward was in attendance on three ladies. They were Hazel Bellamy, the Countess of Berkhamstead and Lady Prudence Fairfax, for whose Belgian Refugees' Committee meeting the morning-room had been set aside. They were discussing conscription.

'I cannot understand these people, as I said to Connie

Harcourt,' said Lady Berkhamstead, 'Naturally, one keeps one's butler and chauffeur, and for the sake of the horses one cannot part with one's grooms. *I* thought we should have sent our under-gamekeepers, but Henry said the poachers would become so tiresome.'

Lady Prudence eyed the befurred and bejewelled Countess with amusement. 'Your husband *is* a Justice of the Peace, isn't he?' she said. 'Perhaps he could sentence the poachers to enlist immediately.'

Lady Berkhamstead eyed her coldly. 'It is not a laughing matter, Prudence. We have given seven servants from our town house alone, and yet here are all these people with their houses full of able-bodied men, and refusing to part with them.'

Edward, who had been standing patiently by, ventured to interrupt. 'Excuse me, madam,' he said to Hazel, 'would you care for coffee to be served?'

'Yes, please, Edward.' He was turning away when Lady Berkhamstead's very loud voice recalled him sharply.

'How old are you?'

Edward, taken aback, stuttered. 'Me? Er – I – er – twenty-five, madam – my lady.'

'And you are not married?' she barked.

'No, my lady.'

As though he were no longer present, Lady Berkhamstead turned to Hazel. 'Mrs. Bellamy, you really will have to think about sending him to enlist. We all have to make sacrifices, you know, and it is up to people like us to set an example to the others.'

Hazel stared at her. 'Yes, I – thank you, Edward.'

After he had gone the conversation turned to the Belgian Refugees.

'Poor creatures,' said Lady Prudence, 'they're coming over in fishing-boats, dredgers – even colliers. Anything to get away. Most of them have left all their possessions behind, and have nothing but what they stand up in. It is too tragic. Imagine how we would feel if *our* country were invaded!'

'Dreadful,' said Lady Berkhamstead absently.

'How many are there?' Hazel asked.

'Five thousand at least, they say, and if the German advance continues they expect twice that number.'

'Good heavens!' Lady Berkhamstead put up her lorgnettes. 'Where on earth are we going to put them all?'

They discussed reception centres and the possibility of literally farming out the refugees in the country. Lady Berkhamstead, recalling that her husband had some cottages which might house some of them, fixed her eyes speculatively on Edward, who had returned with the coffee.

'And then,' said Lady Prudence, 'we must draw up a list of friends who are prepared to take the better class of Belgian into their home.'

'I should have thought the better class of Belgian would have relatives in England whom they could stay with.'

'My dear Violet, not all of them. Angela Carstairs was telling me yesterday of a most tragic case – a Comte and Comtesse who fled from their château with all their children and arrived at the reception centre absolutely penniless. They'd even left her jewels behind! We really must do what we can for people like that. Hazel, can we count on you to take in one family?'

Hazel hesitated. 'We'd like to do what we can, of course, but – we've very little space here. Georgina is in Elizabeth's old room, and the nursery is hardly suitable for—'

Lady Berkhamstead leant forward. 'My dear Mrs. Bellamy, we can hardly sit on committees like this, asking other people to help the war effort, unless we are prepared to do something ourselves.' Her glance at Edward conveyed even more than her words. Hazel steadfastly refused to notice it.

'Yes, of course. Well – I suppose we could manage to take in one family.'

Mr. Hudson had patriotically suppressed any private feelings he might have about the opening of 165's door to a parcel of foreigners. Calmly he directed operations in the kitchen, listening as Rose and Daisy chattered excitedly about the Scarlet Pimpernel and the suitability of giving the impending aristos Lady Marjorie's monogrammed sheets, while at the table Mrs. Bridges brooded on stuffed hare for the first meal. Then he proceeded upstairs to receive further orders from Mrs. Bellamy.

'Do we know how many to expect, Madam?'

'Well, Lady Prudence said that she would try to make it not more than three – but it might be a mother and father and one child, or a mother and two children.'

'Very good, madam. I've ordered the spare room to be got ready, madam, and Rose is putting a cot and small bed in the nursery.'

Georgina Worsley bounded in. Really, thought Hazel, it was alarming, when one had reached the thirties, to see the young appear at breakfast radiant as the dawn until which they had danced. Georgina's very blue eyes were sparkling, her dark luxuriant hair positively crackling with energy. Hazel's own pre-Raphaelite beauty still charmed the eye, but this morning she felt limp and washed-out; yet, unlike her young relative by marriage, she had slept all night.

Georgina kissed her. ' 'Morning, Hazel. 'Morning, Hudson.'

'Did you enjoy yourself last night?' Hazel asked.

'Oh yes! Billy said it was a last opulent evening before going off to the dreadful rigours of camp in darkest Kent. I thought I'd go and stay with the Fox-Bredons for a few days, and then I can see him.'

'In camp?'

'Yes, he says he can come over for dinner when he's tucked the men up in bed. Uncle Richard says we're going to have some Belgian refugees. What fun!'

'Yes. Oh, Hudson, I wondered if we had any toys in the house?'

'Yes, madam, there are some in the nursery cupboard which belonged to Miss Elizabeth and Captain James.' James Bellamy was always 'Captain James' now to Hudson, since he had left to join his unit at the outbreak of war; others might carelessly refer to him as 'Mister James' still, but not Hudson.

'I'll do that if you like, Hazel,' Georgia offered.

'Would you? Oh, thank you, Georgina.' She was just a little relieved that she would not, after all, have to spend any time in the room which should have been occupied by the child she and James had lost.

'I will send Daisy up to help you, Miss Georgina,' said Mr. Hudson.

When she had left, and Hudson was about to make his own stately departure, Hazel called him back.

'Hudson, do you happen to know if – if Edward is thinking of enlisting?'

Mr. Hudson's reply was shocked. 'Edward? Certainly not. I have explained to Edward that the time may come when it would be right for him to join up, but that for the moment his duty lies here – especially just now.'

'Yes. Thank you. That's what I thought.'

In the hall he almost collided with Edward, who had picked up the morning letters and was handing them to his master. Richard examined them, frowning. 'The post gets later every day. Oh, Hudson. I'll be lunching out but dining at home.' His face was disappointed. Again there was no letter from James. Mr. Hudson shut the door when his master had gone into the morning-room, and turned sharply on Edward.

'Edward, what were you thinking of, to put the letters into the master's hand, instead of presenting them on a salver?'

'I *was* going to put them on the salver, Mr. Hudson, but I didn't have time. The master—'

Mr. Hudson swept him aside. 'We are not going to get slapdash in our ways, just because there is a war on.' Edward looked resentfully after his retreating figure. He had heard the final sentences of the conversation in the morning-room.

In the servants' hall Rose and Daisy were gloating over a big, beautiful doll in Victorian walking clothes. 'No wonder she's in such good condition,' Rose said. 'Miss Elizabeth never was very keen on dolls. Someone might as well enjoy her.'

'And if it's a little boy he can play with the railway engine. Look, Eddie, hasn't the paint come up lovely?' To her astonishment, the usually amiable Edward snapped at her.

13

'What a fuss about a lot of blooming foreigners! I don't know why they can't stay where they belong.'

Rose was outraged. 'Edward! I'll bet if *your* country was being trampled underfoot by a brutal invader, you'd be glad of someone being kind to *you*.'

'It'll all come back on us, you know,' he grumbled, beginning to lay the table. 'All the extra work. If you ask me, the mistress should've consulted us first.'

They stared at him, Daisy with a trembling lip.

Georgina, waiting for her cab, was perched on the arm of the sofa, looking over Hazel's shoulder at the French conversation-book she was worriedly studying. 'I wish you were going to be here tomorrow, Georgina,' she said. 'I really only speak schoolroom French.'

'Won't Uncle Richard be here?'

'No, he has a meeting at his Club.'

'I'll try to get home early,' Richard promised. 'Anyway, they probably speak perfect English.'

Edward entered to announce the arrival of the cab, and listened impassively as Georgina chattered in the hall, gaily unleashing military secrets to all and sundry. 'And isn't it exciting? Winston has promised the Naval Brigade that if things get really bad in Belgium, he's going to rush them over to hold the line. Billy was afraid the war would be over before Christmas, and he'd never see any fighting, but now he'll be in action before anyone!'

The final preparations for the refugees had been made, writing-paper placed thoughtfully in the bedroom, and a vase of flowers elegantly arranged, and the nursery had been brightened with more. It was early evening, about the hour when Mr. Hudson had been told to expect the new arrivals; immaculate in white gloves, he was inspecting his staff as they stood lined up in the hall. Only Edward, in his new recalcitrant mood, protested. 'Not much point in us all being here, Mr. Hudson, is there? I shouldn't think they'd have much luggage.'

14

Mr. Hudson turned a quelling eye on him. 'Maybe not, Edward, but even if they arrive at our door destitute, they are our guests, and we shall behave towards them as we do to all guests in this house.'

Edward's ungracious reply was drowned by the sound of wheels outside, followed by the ringing of the bell. The moment had come. Mr. Hudson advanced to the door and opened it.

A flustered-looking woman, consulting a list, hardly looked at him. 'Mr. Bellamy?'

'This is Mr. Bellamy's house,' came the august correction.

An irrepressible gasp went up from the staff as the visitors were ushered in. Instead of the pathetic aristocrats they had expected, they found themselves staring at five people who could not be mistaken for anything but the lowest type of peasant. They were all bedraggled, dirty, and roughly dressed. The refugee organiser hurriedly introduced them.

'Madame Chargon.' A youngish woman with a strained, frightened expression and a great deal of coarse black hair coming down clutched tighter to a ragged child, who was asleep with her head hanging over her mother's shoulder. 'Celestine,' said the organiser. 'And this is Madame Huguot, her sister.' Madame Huguot was a witch-like creature with a rat-trap mouth and gimlet eyes.

'Monsieur Chargon, their father.' 'Oh *no*!' gasped Daisy to Rose. A big, burly old man with long once-white moustaches yellowed by nicotine, he smelt of beer, manure, foul tobacco and clothes that had been seldom, if ever, washed. Behind him trailed a boy of about seven, a sullen-faced child in ragged trousers and a soldier's jacket several sizes too big for him. Huge army boots covered his dirty bare legs, and round his head was a bloodstained bandage. 'And this is Jean-Paul,' said the organiser, and was gone before Mr. Hudson could clutch at her sleeve to ask if there had not been some mistake.

Hazel emerged into a hall filled with silent people, Mr. Hudson and his staff, dazed with horror, staring at the peasants, who stared suspiciously back, herding together like cows in a field.

'The – er – Belgian visitors, madam.' Mr. Hudson's voice was, for him, faint.

'Oh,' said Hazel. 'Yes.' The child Celestine, who had wakened, began to roar. Somehow Hazel managed to summon up a smile and some halting French.

'Er,' she began, 'vous êtes – er – bienvenues.'

The two women huddled closer together. Heavens, what do they think I'm going to do – shoot them? Hazel wondered. She beckoned them into the morning-room, murmuring 'Entrez – er – s'il vous plâit.' They shuffled before her, leaving the servants, who had been joined by an incredulous Mrs. Bridges and Ruby, open-mouthed, aghast. Rose was the first to speak.

'Mr. Hudson, *where are we going to put them*?'

'I don't know, Rose.' Nobody had ever seen him so much at a loss. 'We had better serve tea, then ask the mistress for orders as to sleeping accommodation.'

'Daisy!' Rose snapped. 'Go and put those toys away.' Daisy turned to go. 'And lock the toy-cupboard,' Rose called after her.

The scene of incongruity in the morning-room was one unmatched in the long history of 165 Eaton Place. Jean-Paul, skulking by the window, was eating one of the sandwiches he had grabbed from the plate Edward was handing round. His sister, who had been recently sick, was huddled on her mother's lap, while Madame Huguot sat jealously clutching a grimy bundle and her father sat gaping from one to the other, his filthy boots splayed out on the Persian carpet. At the table Hazel was pouring tea from a silver teapot, and beside each refugee stood a small occasional table bearing a cup, saucer and plate of delicate china. Rose approached Madame Huguot, who lacked a cup, with a full one, at the same time that Edward offered her a sandwich.

'If you'd like to put that on the floor—' Rose gestured towards the bundle. Madame Huguot clasped it even tighter, giving Rose a push which nearly capsized tray, cup and saucer. Rose deftly retrieved it with only a little tea spilt. 'No one's going to steal it, you know!' she said tartly, to be reproved by Mr. Hudson, and, very gently, by Hazel.

'I expect it's all she has in the world, Rose. She just wants to hold on to it.'

Edward, offering sandwiches to Madame Chargon, found himself hampered by the presence of Celestine. Hazel, as unobtrusively as possible, drew the child on to her own lap, stared at resentfully by Celestine's mother. Offered a sandwich, Celestine looked affronted.

'Mangez?' said Hazel. Madame Chargon, sandwich in hand, looked at it with disgust. Rose murmured in Hazel's ear. 'Excuse me, madam. I don't think you should have that little girl on your lap.' Hazel looked down at Celestine, who was scratching busily. 'Oh dear. I see what you mean.' She decanted Celestine on to the floor, where the child ate her sandwich with the maximum of mess.

'When she's had something to eat and a glass of milk, perhaps Daisy could give her a bath – with some carbolic in it,' Hazel suggested. Rose agreed, and proceeded with her tray to Madame Huguot, who looked at her cup of tea as though it were a cobra. Mr. Hudson advanced. 'Perhaps you should put the milk and sugar in, Rose. The – er – the Belgian lady doesn't seem to understand.'

The Belgian lady was glaring balefully at the cup. 'Qu'est ce que c'est que ça?' she enquired, the first words they had heard her speak. As nobody answered she took a mouthful, made a hideous grimace, and spat it out on to the carpet.

Richard arrived home, early, as he had promised, to find Babel itself awaiting him. From the morning-room came the high-pitched screech of feminine voices complaining in colloquial French that they were tired, that they didn't understand what was wanted of them, that the child was being frightened.

'What in the name of—?' The morning-room door opened. From it came an even louder noise, the servants shouting in English against their Belgian opponents, Celestine roaring. Mr. Hudson stood in the doorway, a broken man.

'Oh, sir,' was all he could say to Richard. 'The – the Belgian visitors – are – not quite what we expected.' At that moment Daisy rushed past them, holding the bellowing

17

Celestine and pursued by Madame Chargon, who, complaining in strident French, snatched her daughter and ran back into the room. fruitlessly pursued by Hazel.

Hazel abandoned the chase. 'Oh, Richard!'

'My dear Hazel.'

She was half-crying. 'I can't make them understand! The children are filthily dirty. Daisy's run a carbolic bath upstairs, and she's trying to get the mother to go up with them, but – my French isn't good enough.'

Richard patted her shoulder and strode into the centre of the battle. Edward was attempting to drag Jean-Paul towards the door, while Jean-Paul hacked at his shins with the army boots. Richard, who had been First Secretary in Paris, had no doubts about the excellence of his French.

'*Silence!*' he shouted; and an instant hush fell. '*Attendez ici.*' He joined Hazel in the hall.

'Oh Richard, the children are crawling with lice, and the others, too, for all I know. Their rooms are ready upstairs, but we thought if we could only get them to take baths first—?'

'*Upstairs?* It's out of the question. They're Belgian peasants. I can't imagine who let them into the morning-room in the first place.'

Mr. Hudson looked guilty and downcast. 'Obviously,' said Richard, 'they must go down to the kitchen and be looked after there.'

If Mr. Hudson had, in a morbid mood, set about designing his perfect nightmare, it would not have been unlike the scene he contemplated in his own servants' hall during supper that evening. Celestine had been fed with a spoon on her mother's lap, the larger part of her meal finishing up on the table-cloth or the floor, and Jean-Paul, having removed the last drop of gravy from his plate with a piece of bread, had then wiped his knife with it and laid both on the table-cloth, while his grandfather, relaxed, belched, pushed his chair back from the table, and lit a pipe whose contents could only be imagined, but which produced a smell something like a rubbish-dump on fire. It was too much for Mrs. Bridges.

18

'Mr. Hudson!' she burst out. 'We haven't had our pudding yet!'

'No!' said Mr. Hudson loudly. 'No smoking!' The old man's face was still uncomprehending. Mr. Hudson's guardian angel came to his rescue. 'Defense de fumer!' he said.

M. Chargon looked at him, then round the table at the disapproving English faces, philosophically knocked his pipe out on the chair-leg and spat on the floor. Mrs. Bridges swelled visibly and ejaculated like a jet of steam from an engine the word 'WELL!'

Her comments when Ruby found Madame Chargon holding Celestine out on the stone floor of the scullery are better imagined, as are Mr. Hudson's feelings as he sat in a hard chair while the Belgians occupied the comfortable ones and asked each other, loudly, continuously and monotonously, what these stupid English meant by their behaviour, their cooking, their appalling bread, their ridiculous number of servants for only two people, their failure to provide coffee. It was Edward, goaded beyond endurance, who looked up from his comic and snarled, 'Why don't you shut up?'

The women were silenced. but the old man, who had been looking sideways at Edward, replied with spirit. 'Et toi – que fais-tu? Tu es soldat, hein? Pourquoi pas? T'as peur?' To make his meaning quite clear he pointed an imaginary gun at Edward, made noises as of it being fired, and lumbering up performed a clumsy mockery of marching. The climax of the evening came when Daisy, restlessly pushing her cap about, suddenly paused and began to scream. Mrs. Bridges looked up.

'Whatever is it, Daisy?'

'Bugs! I got bugs in me hair! Nasty, filthy . . .' She yanked off her cap and began to scratch furiously, sobbing at the same time. Mr. Hudson put his head in his hands. He wished, very much, that he was lying beside his father in the little cemetery at Glenbryde.

Of course, there had to be a solemn conference. By unspoken consent, it took place later that night. Daisy's hair had been washed and de-loused, Mrs. Bridges had taken an aspirin, Rose was pale with anger and stress. They sat round the table in the kitchen. From the servants' hall came the stentorian rattle of M. Chargon's snores. Mrs. Bridges spoke.

'It's not right, Mr. Hudson. The mistress should have consulted us before she sent them down here.'

Edward nodded. 'I say charity begins at home.'

Mrs. Bridges continued. 'I wouldn't mind if they was grateful, but they're not.' All murmured agreement. Mr. Hudson, looking old and haggard. was for once helpless. 'It is a very trying situation, certainly, but I don't quite see what we can do about it,' he said.

Daisy, drying her hair, piped up. 'We could all walk out.' Rose, shocked, exclaimed '*Daisy*!'

'Well, we could. We could all give notice together.'

Mr. Hudson began to interrupt, but Edward, the new Edward, defied him. 'No, Mr. Hudson, I think the mistress should be told – it's them or us.'

Mr. Hudson glanced round at the mutinous faces, seeing agreement in all but Rose's. She flushed, looked down, then said 'Yes.'

It was Mrs. Bridges who took the initiative next morning. They had all slept on it, but a combination of M. Chargon's pipe, the two women's insistence on hanging up their imperfectly washed undergarments on a piece of string in the kitchen, and Jean-Paul's smashing of the jar of jam he had been surreptitiously eating under the table were too much for the fastidious cook. Without even bothering to put on a clean apron. she marched upstairs and confronted Hazel. 'It's more than flesh and blood can stand, madam.'

'Mrs. Bridges, Miss Georgina is coming back this evening. She went to school in Switzerland – she can talk to them – make them understand that they must behave themselves—'

'It's not a question of behaving. It's my kitchen, and either they go or I do.' She marched out.

Georgina, seized and briefed the moment she appeared in the house, looking enchanting in a Parma violet costume and a picture-hat to match, was not enthusiastic about tackling their difficult guests; but it was impossible to resist Hazel's pleading.

There was no need for her to worry. Her very English accent was perfectly comprehensible to the Belgians, who began to look almost human as she greeted them.

'Bon soir. Moi, je suis Mademoiselle Worsley, la nièce de Madame Bellamy.' She held out a comradely hand. 'Madame—?'

'Madame Chargon. Et ma soeur, Madame Huguot. Mon père, Monsieur Chargon.'

Georgina shook hands all round, then proceeded to introduce the servants by name, a ceremony which produced an instant warming up of the atmosphere. Mrs. Bridges hastened to unburden her mind of a problem.

'Miss Georgina, would you ask them why, when we give them a nice cup of tea, they spit it out on the floor?'

'Oh, I think I know that, Mrs. Bridges. Belgian people consider tea to be a sort of drug. They would think you were trying to poison them.'

Mrs. Bridges all but staggered. '*Poison*? Well, I never.'

Through Georgina's agency it was arranged that the Belgians in future should be given cocoa, a prospect which they welcomed eagerly. Then Ruby asked 'Why did they laugh when the little boy spilt the jam?' and Georgina put the question. Hazel had come quietly downstairs, and was listening. Georgina relayed the answer.

'They're sorry about the jam. But it was the first time Jean-Paul had been like a boy again – naughty – since he saw his father shot by the Germans. The Germans took all the able-bodied men in their village and stood them against a wall and shot them as a punishment for resisting the German advance. Madame Chargon's husband was lame, but they shot him just the same.'

There was a general gasp. Georgina asked Madame Huguot about her own husband, translating the reply. 'She says her husband was killed in the fighting in August. And her son too. He was in the army although he was only sixteen.'

'Only sixteen,' Edward repeated. Daisy shot him a glance. Then, without questioning, Madame Huguot began to tell the story of the burning of villages and raping of women which was coming ever closer to their own village. They

21

fled, M. Chargon and his wife, Madame Chargon and her two children, herself and her little girl. But a troop of German cavalry rode through them and scattered them, and when they reassembled old Madame Chargon was missing. 'They searched everywhere,' Georgina translated, 'but they couldn't find her. And the road was being shelled so they had to go on without her, for the sake of the children. Then the aeroplanes came again and dropped bombs. Madame Huguot was lying by the side of the road, with her little girl in her arms. And a bomb fell near, and Madame Huguot was knocked out. When she came to, she was lying ten yards away, and her little girl—'

Madame Huguot began to untie the grimy bundle she always carried.

'There was nothing left of her but . . .' The bundle was unwrapped now. On the shawl in Madame Huguot's lap was a tiny wooden sabot, a red hair-ribbon, still in its bow, a rosary, and a battered wooden doll.

The midday meal that day was a very different affair from the disastrous supper of the previous night. A loaf of French bread had been obtained, which Mr. Hudson cordially invited M. Chargon. as head of the household, to cut. Mrs. Bridges had actually allowed Madame Chargon to make the dumplings for the beef stew, and Mr. Hudson commented graciously on them as being très bon. Everybody dragged out any scrap of French they could remember; everybody except Edward, who was missing.

'I thought he was down here,' Rose said. 'He hasn't done his work in the dining-room.'

'Well, where is he?' asked Mr. Hudson. It was Madame Huguot who supplied the answer. 'Monsieur Edward? Il est sorti. Il y a une heure.' Seeing their uncomprehending faces, she pointed to the door. 'Sorti.'

'Gone out?' Daisy was alarmed. 'Where?'

At that moment the door opened, and Edward appeared, to cries of 'Wherever have you been?' There was a curious look on his face, half-ashamed, half-triumphant. A terrible suspicion came into Mr. Hudson's mind. 'Edward?' he asked, already knowing the answer to his unspoken question.

'I went to join up, Mr. Hudson.'

Nobody said anything. Then Daisy burst out, 'Eddie, how could you, without telling me first?'

'If I'd told you, you'd have tried to stop me.'

'Yes, I would! And so would Mr. Hudson and the master, if they'd known.'

'But I don't belong to them, Daisy. I don't belong to anyone – not even you. You wouldn't think much of me if I did.' Suddenly he looked older; taller, even.

'You'd better come and sit down, Edward, and have your dinner,' said Mrs. Bridges. She served out the stew and dumplings to everyone, the servants quietly shocked, the Belgians uncomprehending. To Mr. Hudson the food was tasteless. Edward felt the criticism that was being levelled at him.

'You see, Mr. Hudson,' he said, 'everyone kept saying what I ought to do. You and the master and Daisy said I shouldn't join up. And Lady Berkhamstead kept going on about how I ought to. And then there was—' He glanced at Madame Huguot. 'I never saw much point in the war – just a lot of foreigners bashing each other, but – when I heard about the things they was doing in Belgium . . . I'm sorry, Mr. Hudson. You've taught me everything I know, but – I had to do what I thought was right.'

An internal battle was going on in Mr. Hudson's mind. It was very hard to go back on one's stated opinions. He should put his foot down, upbraid Edward, hold him up as an example of arrant disobedience; he could fight back his own growing admiration for the young footman he had always regarded as a cheeky whippersnapper. He swallowed.

'That is what it means, Edward,' he said.

'Mr. Hudson?'

'That is what it means, to belong to yourself – doing what you think is right.' For the first time in his life as butler he had brought himself to admit that he might, on occasion, be wrong. Edward, in his way, knew it, and said, 'Thank you, Mr. Hudson.'

23

'What regiment did you join?'

'Oh, the Middlesex, Mr. Hudson – same as my brother.' His spirits suddenly soared. He turned to M. Chargon and imitated a rifleman. 'Bang, bang! Soldat. Moi.' The old man's face lit up. 'Ah, soldat! Boum, boum!'

Jean-Paul joined in the performance and everybody laughed.

The Belgians were going. Lady Prudence, horrified at the Bellamys' trials, had arranged for them to be transferred to a potato farm in Lincolnshire, the sort of place where they could feel at home. They were filing out of the back door, looking very different from their appearance on arrival. They were clean, the children had even been well scrubbed, they wore respectable second-hand clothes, and each had a present and a packed lunch parcel. Celestine carried a doll – not the Victorian lady from the nursery, but a simple, less destructible one – and Jean-Paul had the toy engine. As they went, they smiled back at their English friends and chorused 'Au 'voir! Au 'voir!' Their boots clattered up the area steps, the waiting wagon started off.

Mrs. Bridges turned back into her clean, orderly kitchen and sniffed. 'I really think,' she said to Rose, 'the mistress might have asked us first – sending 'em away like that. I'm going to miss them.'

'Yes,' said Rose. 'Funny, isn't it.'

CHAPTER TWO

THE war had been on for eight months; it was April 1915. With the exception of Mr. Hudson, No. 165 was manless. James Bellamy was with his regiment on the Western Front, Edward at a training camp in Essex, while Richard, dashing from committee to committee, was hardly ever at home, to Mrs. Bridges' disgust. Most of the time there was only the Mistress to cook for, and her appetite was disappointingly poor.

The atmosphere in the servants' hall was gloomy. Like the Three Fates, Mrs. Bridges, Ruby and Daisy sat knitting, Ruby's war-effort being a long, shapeless thing something like a woolly snake, growing steadily grimier as it progressed towards the floor; it was destined as a comforter for Edward, but Mrs. Bridges thought, and said, that she had never seen anything quite so uncomfortable-looking. Mr. Hudson, putting down his newspaper with a grim aspect, added some further pins to his wall-map of the Front. The news had been far from good in the past week. Zeppelins had raided the north-east and east coasts; the British transport *Manitou* had been sunk by Turkish destroyers in the Aegean, and the British submarine E15 had run ashore in the Dardanelles. Now, to crown it all, the Germans were using poison gas at Ypres, driving the Allies back with its deadly fumes.

'Terrible losses again today, Mr. Hudson,' said Mrs. Bridges. He shook his head bodingly.

'Aye. A hundred and two officers dead and missing; worse than Neuve Chapelle. Lord Wendover, Captain Mackintosh — eh, dear.'

Mrs. Bridges sighed. 'I pray for Captain James every night.'

The indicator board buzzed to inform them that someone was at the front door. Daisy, glad of an excuse for activity, went to answer it.

'If you ask me,' Mrs. Bridges went on, 'we're getting beaten this time, and no mistake.' Mr. Hudson rallied. 'Mrs. Bridges! That's tantamount to defeatism. We're holding our own — we have a firm grip on Hill 60 — there have been many successful counter-attacks. Look at our advance on Notre Dame de Lorette—'

'Wasn't that where we lost all them thousands of soldiers? And every day this week you've moved that row of pins back. Don't look like a victory to me.' She knitted furiously, as though her needles were transfixing the Kaiser like small bayonets.

'That gas,' Ruby said, 'it's not fair. It must smell awful. It's a wonder to me it doesn't go off bang.'

'It is not common coal gas that the Germans are employing, Ruby,' Mr. Hudson explained, 'but a chemical asphyxiant. The Huns have forgotten one thing — the prevailing wind is west to east, and once we have *our* gas — woof!'

He was interrupted by Daisy, pale-faced. 'There's a telegraph boy outside, Mr. Hudson. I – will you come and see?'

Without a word he was gone, leaving Mrs. Bridges with her hand on her bosom, woman's age-old reaction to shock. She and Ruby exchanged glances. Was it Captain James? Or even Edward, killed or injured in manoeuvres? They hardly dared think.

Mr. Hudson had to force himself to enter the morning-room with the ominous envelope on his salver. At the door he coughed. Hazel looked up from the khaki scarf she was knitting for James.

'A – a telegram has arrived, madam – from—'

'The War Office?' Mr. Hudson admired her for putting their fear so swiftly into words.

'From France, madam.' She took the telegram and sat with it in her hand, while the butler hovered anxiously. 'Thank you, Hudson. That will be all,' she said, and reluctantly he left the room. Whatever the news might be, she would receive it alone. There must be no scenes in front of the staff. With shaking fingers she tore open the envelope, and her face suddenly lightened. 'Hudson!' she cried. 'Come back!' But there was no need to shout; Mr. Hudson had his ear pressed closely to the door, and practically fell into the room. Her face told him the news.

'Oh, Hudson — Captain Bellamy — Captain Bellamy's coming home on leave!' Hudson beamed, aware that a scuffling in the hall meant that Daisy had been listening and had dashed down to the kitchen.

'Well, madam, that *is* good news. When is he expected?'

'Army post office, Boulogne, it was sent from — it doesn't say when he's due.'

'May we presume the Captain will be here in time for dinner?'

Hazel hardly heard him. 'Oh, yes. I do hope so . . .' Suddenly her legs gave way under her and she subsided into a chair, her face crumpling. Hudson tactfully withdrew. Alone, she could give rein to the tears that shook her, tears of reaction, of relief; of guilt, in some curious fashion. There had been so many bitter words said between her and James, more storms than sunshine in their four years together. Things had got worse and worse, until last summer she had decided that their marriage was over. Then the war came; and one didn't leave a man who had gone to serve his King and Country. So she had stayed, helping Richard to keep up the morale of the household, knowing that James was glad to be at the Front, not missing her; perhaps, just a little, missing Georgina.

But to have lost him would have been terrible. She mopped her eyes and told herself not to be a fool.

Mrs. Bridges had ordered Ruby to broach the treasured, illicit hoard of tins, and bring some sardines from it. 'Sardines on toast — they've been Captain James's favourite savoury ever since he was only a little mite.'

Mr. Hudson looked severe. 'Sardines? With Sir Geoffrey Dillon coming to dinner, and a very important general?'

'I don't care if it's Lord Kitchener himself, he'll just have to lump it. Why, whatever is it, Ruby?' For Ruby was at the door, gasping and trying to say something. They all gasped as a soldierly figure strode past her, a smart young warrior in khaki, with a suitcase. Could it really be Edward, transformed? He acknowledged their united cry of welcome with a salute and rattled off his new title.

'049202 Private Barnes E., 12th Battalion the Middlesex Regiment, the Duke of Cambridge's Own.' Then, having established his glory, 'I got a forty-eight hour pass.'

They crowded round him, admiring his uniform, his bearing, his neat small moustache. 'You do look really well, Edward, I'll say that,' commented Mrs. Bridges. Daisy was almost too full of adoration to speak; she held tight to his arm. 'It's the delicious army cuisine,' he said. 'We just marched from Colchester to our new camp at Codford, on Salisbury Plain.'

Mr. Hudson was impressed by his former footman's translation, but felt a little out in the cold personally. He broke up the admiration society with a chilly recall to duty. 'Well, now. We've got a dinner party to prepare for. But if you'd like to stay for supper, Edward, I'm sure you're welcome.'

Edward's disappointed face was too much for Mrs. Bridges. 'Supper! He'll stay here as long as he likes. His old room's always ready. You just put your case up there, Edward. You're always welcome here.'

Mr. Hudson protested feebly that Edward had parents in London, to be told that Dad was building camps at Folkestone and Mum was with Aunt Ivy at Watford. There was nothing for it; Edward was going to stay. Looking pointedly at his watch, Mr. Hudson began to issue instructions for the dinner.

'I'll give you a hand, Mr. Hudson, if you want,' Edward proffered, backed up by Daisy. 'We *are* short-handed – you were saying so only this morning, Mr. Hudson, with Rose away in Scotland with Miss Georgina.' Mr. Hudson gave in.

'Shall I go and put on my livery?' Edward asked, to be quelled by Mrs. Bridges. 'You'll wear the King's uniform, my boy, and if them upstairs isn't proud of you I'll eat my boots.' Ruby clapped her hands. 'And Captain James is coming on leave, too!'

'There you are,' said Edward. 'That's war for you – you've got the house full of heroes.' Daisy picked up his suitcase and began to lead the way upstairs. Out of sight of the others, she turned him towards her and put her arms round his neck. Mr. Hudson, following, saw, and froze with disapproval, and the merest touch of envy.

Half an hour later another embrace was taking place in the morning-room. James, the worse for travel and lack of sleep, held Hazel in his arms, looking down at her as though she were unreal, touching her hair and her face. The same James who had left in August, tall and dashingly handsome, but perhaps the boyish look had faded, a little. It was a man who had come back to her. She broke from him and poured a drink.

'Thanks. Come and sit here with me.' He looked round the room, as though seeing it for the first time, just as he had looked at her. 'Extraordinary,' he said. 'It's just like coming back from school. All those people bustling about in the streets — buses and motor-cars — theatres — everything so clean and shiny — and umbrellas. I'd forgotten what peculiar things umbrellas were.'

They both laughed. Then Hazel said 'Was it — very horrible?'

'Horrible? Yes, I suppose that's the right word. But it's enormously exciting as well. Each time you go into action it's a new adventure. It's hard to explain. But you're all keyed up with your own men, and friends all round you. The danger doesn't seem real . . .'

The door opened, and his father stood there, frozen with astonishment.

'James!'

'Hello, Father.'

'What a lovely surprise! Why did nobody tell me?'

'I did try to get you at the House,' Hazel said. Richard rubbed his hands with anticipation. 'We must make some plans. You couldn't have come back at a better time, James. We've got Geoffrey Dillon and General Frankie Nesfield coming to dine — Geoffrey's got himself well into the thick of it as Northcliffe's lawyer — and of course you know about Nesfield.'

'He has a certain reputation in the army,' James said drily.

'Don't underestimate him. He's the power behind the throne at the War Office, and he's on our side.'

James smiled. 'I'm glad to hear that.'

'No, no, I mean politically. He'll be damn useful when we get back in, which won't be long now by the look of things. There's a terrible stink about the naval losses at Gallipoli. Winston made a cracking speech a couple of months ago about "open piracy and murder on the high seas", and now he and Fisher are hardly talking to each other. Lloyd George's Munitions Committee—'

James, at the risk of being impolite, got up. 'Father, talking of stinks, I haven't had a proper bath for a very long time – two weeks, to be exact, in a brewery in Armentieres. I think I'll get out of these things.'

'Of course, my boy.' Richard looked after him affectionately. 'Well, Hazel? Glad to see him?'

'Yes. Very glad.'

The dinner had been a resounding success. Mrs. Bridges's sardines had gone down well not only with James but with the guests: General Nesfield, an upright martial figure in uniform, grey of hair and moustache, and the impassive Geoffrey Dillon, penguin-like in evening dress. General Nesfield congratulated Richard on Edward's appearance. 'Nice to see your footman in uniform, Richard – very patriotic.'

'But not too patriotic, I'm happy to note,' put in Dillon. Richard looked puzzled. 'You don't follow the Royal example in banishing all alcoholic refreshments from your table.'

Richard was enlighted. 'Oh, the ban on wine, spirits and beer in the Royal households? No, indeed. I was delighted when the Government dropped those ridiculous proposals for dealing with the drink trade.'

General Nesfield sipped his port with relish. 'It would take more than a war to make me sign the pledge,' he said. Hazel rose and departed, not without a slightly anxious glance at James, who, tired and unused to rich food and drink, was already almost through his second glass.

Left alone, the men talked animatedly of the Second Battle

of Ypres, in which James had taken part; the deadly new gas, surges of thick yellow smoke paralysing the whole of the line from Steenstraate to the east of Langemarck, held by the French Division, the sudden, terrifying onslaught of French African troops, and the gallantry of the Canadian Division's left flank as the French line crumbled.

'Well,' said the General, 'our own gas is ready, and better than theirs.'

'I don't think it will have much effect on the war in the end,' James said.

'Not much about gas in the newspapers, General.' said Richard. Dillon shrugged. 'Don't blame the papers, blame the Censor. It's official policy to give the public pap. If you want to see how the war's going don't look at the headlines, look at the casualty lists.'

'What do the troops think of the newspapers?' Nesfield asked James.

'They just laugh. "Our brave boys at the front", all that stuff. I just happened to see tonight's papers' report of our little show between Ypres and Hill 60. "German attack smashed – successful counter-attack drives back weakened enemy." Well, as you know, General, we're the ones who were smashed if anyone was, and they drove us back a good mile.'

'Surely there's nothing wrong with the men?' Richard asked.

James was becoming flushed and voluble. 'Nothing at all. They're better than the Bosche, tougher, braver, better soldiers. What remains of the professional British Army is being squandered by a lot of amateurs who don't know their job.' He turned to the General. 'I don't mean the generals, sir, I mean the politicians, the people who are meant to be running this war – only they haven't realised that it's a new sort of war, more like siege warfare than anything else – a war of barbed wire and machine-guns and artillery – guns, more than anything else.'

'We had the guns at Neuve Chapelle,' Nesfield said.

'We ran out of shells on the second day. The first Grenadiers lost twenty officers and three hundred men and gained

31

two hundred yards,' James answered bitterly.

Richard joined in. 'And what did Asquith say at Newcastle? I read a statement the other day that our armies were being crippled by our failure to provide the necessary ammunition. There is not a word of truth in that statement.'

'Probably drunk, as usual.' said Dillon.

James was in full flow. 'If I might give you an example, General; when the Germans attacked last Thursday they plastered us with shells – heavies, mediums, everything they had – from four ack emma until seven, when their infantry attacked. There was very little left of our trenches or our wire – not one single British gun of any sort supported us. I think it was about two-thirty when the Blues made their counter-attack that one solitary howitzer started to fire – one six-inch "how", obsolescent since the South African War. I saw it later, when we were relieved, and I also saw the battery commander sitting on a limber in tears. That's a fine way to win a war.'

The others were silent, impressed. James shot his final bolt. 'I tell you this, gentlemen. If any politician went up anywhere near the front at this moment he'd be torn limb from limb.'

The General shook his head. 'It's an enormous problem.'

James rose. 'If you'll excuse me – I only got back this evening.' He left them, and a buzz of praise broke out behind his back.

'Well,' said Dillon, 'the Government may not have provided any ammunition to blow up the Germans, but James has certainly provided us with plenty to blow up the Government. Northcliffe will be delighted.'

Richard looked worried. 'I trust you're not going to quote him, Geoffrey.'

'No, indeed. Impressions of the second battle of Ypres – eyewitness account by a gallant officer just back from the Front – splendid stuff – anonymous, of course. No names, no packdrill.'

Next day was beautiful. The trees in Eaton Square were jewelled with young leaves, the sun was warm, the sky blue. There might not have been a war on at all. And Edward and Daisy (who had been reluctantly given the afternoon off by Mr. Hudson) were cuddled up together in a cinema, watching the epic *Jane Shore* and sharing a bag of sweets. The film was getting sadder and sadder. King Edward was dead, Jane had been sent away from Court by his brother; now she was being made to walk barefoot through the City, carrying a lighted candle, as a penance for her sins. Large glycerine tears rolled down her cheeks. Daisy began to sniff in sympathy.

'Cheer up, love.' Edward offered her his handkerchief. 'Like to go?'

She shook her head. 'No. I must know how it ends.'

'Oh, she dies. There's a picture of her outside, dying in the snow.'

Daisy looked horrified. 'Ooh, I couldn't bear that.'

'Nor could I. Come on, cheer up. Let's go out and buy a ring.'

Daisy sat up straight; the last of the sweets went on the floor. 'Buy a *what*?'

'A ring. For your finger.'

She turned a startled face to him in the flickering gloom.

'Oh, Edward, are you — are you — you aren't, are you?' He nodded, and her sniffs turned to real tears, as copious as Jane Shore's. Cries of 'Shush!' were heard, and Edward went scarlet with embarrassment.

Mrs. Bridges was in the middle of a lecture to Ruby on the perils of talking to strange men, when two lots of footsteps came clattering down from the street, accompanied by the laughing voices of Edward and Daisy. They rushed in, hands clasped. and Edward struck an attitude.

'I have an announcement to make. Private Edward Barnes, bachelor, and Miss Daisy—' He stopped and looked blank. 'Peel,' said Daisy, giggling.

'Peel. We'll have to have wedding bells, then — when Edward Barnes marries Daisy Peel, a spinster of this parish.'

Everybody reacted typically. 'Well, bless my soul!' cried Mrs. Bridges, throwing her arms round each of them in turn and kissing them heartily, while Ruby copied her, round-eyed with excitement. Mr. Hudson kissed nobody.

'I'm surprised, Edward, that you should make such an announcement, even in jest, before you have permission.'

'Who from? My mum and dad knew of my intentions.'

'The master, Edward, and the mistress.'

'My master's the King,' Edward retorted cheekily, 'and I haven't got a mistress — not yet, any rate.' Mr. Hudson drew himself up to his considerable height and prepared to blast Edward off the face of the earth.

'Even though you seem to have forgotten that you were employed in this house for many years, and therefore, I would have supposed, owe *some* small sense of loyalty to the Bellamy family, you presumably remember that Daisy is still employed here as an under-housemaid.'

Edward was unsquashed. 'I don't see why we should ask anyone — except my company officer, so we can get dependant's allowance.'

Mrs. Bridges sized up Mr. Hudson's degree of antagonism, and decided she must drop a hint to Edward. 'You wouldn't want Daisy turned off without a reference, Edward.'

'Who cares? There's posters in every street saying women are urgently needed for war work — and a lot better paid than they are here.'

Mr. Hudson let his anger and resentment have full play. '*Edward*! You have changed in the army, and considerably for the worse, so it seems. Now I come to think of it, I remember when you first came there was a streak — a nasty wee streak of insolence there.'

Edward sighed. 'Oh, Mr. Hudson. Things are changing, can't you see that? The war's changing everything.'

'I do not see that. And I grieve to think that all these years that I have spent trying to instil in you some sense of propriety have been completely wasted.'

Again Mrs. Bridges thought fit to intervene. Proper nasty Mr. Hudson was being, and it wouldn't do for the poor young things to get into real trouble with him. 'Edward didn't mean it like that, did you, Edward?'

'No, no, I didn't. Daisy and I were going up to tell the family. It was just the way Mr. Hudson pitched into me without – well, I've enough of it in the army without Mr. Hudson starting.'

Daisy squeezed his arm sympathetically; her brave soldier sweetheart.

The bell rang. 'Front door, Daisy,' ordered Mr. Hudson.

'I'll go,' said Edward. only too pleased to escape. But Mr. Hudson assumed an air of injured pride mingled with heavy sarcasm. 'No, no. You are a soldier home on leave. Just sit down – smoke, if you will – enjoy yourself.' And he stalked out, back to his own pantry, where everything was still as it had been, his possessions all ranged neatly, nobody answering him back or questioning his authority. He had forgotten how, as a young man, he himself had challenged the authority of a butler over a matter of injustice. It was a very long time ago, after all.

The official request for permission to marry was made by Edward after Mr. Hudson had thoroughly briefed James and Hazel Bellamy on the matter, intimating delicately that the Captain might just like to throw in a few words of warning on the rashness of marrying. Uncomfortably James tried to do so, but he was so sorry for the young pair who stood nervously before him, Daisy with her cap very straight, her fingers twitching to reach out for Edward's hand, Edward looking sheepish, that he gave a very poor performance of one in loco parentis.

'Er – what division are you in, Edward?'

'18 Division, sir – fifty-fourth brigade.'

'New Army? Well – in the late summer, or autumn at the latest, you'll be coming out to join us in France – and we're very much looking forward to having you, have no doubt of that. There's plenty of fighting to do – and if you're married it'll not be so bad for you – but it'll be pretty hard on Daisy. I know – unfortunately, one of my more depressing jobs as an officer is to write to the dependants of the casualties in my squadron.'

Daisy, who had been looking thoroughly frightened, sud-

35

denly spoke up. 'I think, sir — whether we was married or not it'd be just the same.'

James shrugged. He had come to the end of his brief-notes. Hazel helped him out. Smiling, she said 'Well, you both have our blessing, and I hope you'll be very happy together.'

They thanked her, shyly, and went out.

'Poor wretches.' James poured himself a whisky. 'Let them have what happiness they can get.'

Mr. Hudson re-entered with a letter. 'Excuse me, sir. This came by special messenger while you were out.'

'What sort of special messenger?'

'A boy scout on a bicycle, sir.'

'Oh, War Office. Thank you, Hudson.'

Hazel watched his face change as he read the letter. 'What is it?'

His voice was angry as he read it aloud. ' "You will attend War Staff Course number four at the Staff College, Camberley, prior to being posted · to Headquarters 11 Corps, B.E.F. (New Formation) as a General Staff Officer, Grade 3." Well!'

'Oh, James, that's wonderful!'

He glared at her. 'Nothing wonderful about it. I'm not going to join the Yellow Brigade — sitting at a desk in shiny boots, covered with red tabs, miles behind the lines. Not on your life.' Savagely he crumpled the letter up and poured another drink for himself.

Colonel Buchanan's office at the Regimental Headquarters of the Second Life Guards was as dignified as the figure sitting at the rosewood desk. The Colonel's dark hair had begun to grey rapidly after the First Battle of Ypres, where he had left an arm; he looked tired and stressed, conditions belied by his upright carriage and the defiant flare of his scarlet sash. An array of ribbons on his breast now included the DSO.

James, in the visitor's chair, was uneasy. There were conventional greetings before he brought out the thing he had come to say.

'To be quite honest, Colonel, I'm not very happy about this posting to the staff.'

Buchanan glanced down at a typewritten letter. 'Quite frankly, I'm rather surprised to hear you say that. I thought you'd be delighted. I imagined that it was the result of a successful piece of judicious string-pulling in high places.'

James went red. 'It was nothing of the sort, Colonel. I would never think of such a thing.'

'It's quite usual these days, I'm sorry to say. I apologise if I misjudged you. It certainly wasn't at my recommendation.'

'In that case, Colonel, I would be glad if you would ask for the posting to be cancelled and allow me to return to regimental duty.'

Buchanan surveyed his visitor. James began to feel that the interview was not going the way he had expected. 'Yes, I see,' the Colonel said at last. 'In fact, I've taken the trouble to discover the source of this letter.' He tapped the sheet of paper. 'The Military Secretary was ordered to make this posting personally, by a very senior and influential officer on the General Staff. I'm sorry I can't reveal his name to you.' James's face was shocked. 'So I couldn't possibly alter it, even if I wished—' There was a long pause before he said 'Which as a matter of fact I don't.' Before James could answer he had produced a copy of the *Daily Mail*. 'You've seen this, I suppose? Article in yesterday's *Mail*?'

'No, Colonel.'

Buchanan opened the paper. ' "News from the Front. Household Cavalry Captain home on leave reveals grave shortage of artillery at Ypres." ' He tossed the copy to James, who looked at it with distaste.

'We – I don't read the *Daily Mail*,' he said.

'Nor do I,' Buchanan barked at him. 'But apparently the King does, and he's not very pleased, to put it mildly. This has been brought to my attention in no uncertain way.'

'Really, Colonel,' James said earnestly, 'I haven't been talking to reporters. I honestly believe this has nothing to do with me.' But a dreadful suspicion was growing in his mind; he had been talking to somebody, if not a reporter. What had he said? Had Dillon passed it on? He felt very cold inside.

Buchanan was openly angry now. 'Well, I *do* believe it. You are the only officer in the Household Cavalry on leave who took part in the battle. That is an eyewitness account – it tallies more or less exactly with other reports. Your father is a distinguished Conservative Member of Parliament, and I'm sure that you are neither so misinformed or so naif as not to know that just at the moment the Conservatives are throwing every brickbat they can lay their hands on at the Government, to try to force a Coalition.'

James's head was down. 'Yes, Colonel. I did know that. And – whoever wrote it – the facts in this article are true.'

'That's not the point,' Buchanan snapped. 'Officers in the Household Brigade do not indulge in politics in any form, as you know damned well – and I don't in the least enjoy losing my name to Buckingham Palace any more than I enjoy sitting here in this office while the regiment is fighting in France.' He glanced down at the stump of his left arm.

James knew the worst now. 'If someone picked up something I said in private, I'm exceedingly sorry, Colonel.'

Buchanan piled on the agony. 'I've had a report of this last show from your commanding officer. He singles you out for special praise. You're almost certain to be mentioned in despatches – might even have been in line for a medal. As it is, you're damned lucky I'm not going to ask you to transfer to another regiment. So take your staff job and be thankful.'

James knew himself dismissed. He rose, saluted, and left the office.

The news was taken at No. 165 in a very different spirit. Mr. Hudson gleefully revealed to Mrs. Bridges that Captain James's uniform jackets had all gone round to the tailor's to have red tabs attached to them. 'The Staff, Mrs. Bridges, the General Staff – and the strong likelihood of a brevet majority if you ask me.'

'Well, that's the best news I've had since Christmas. Well, I never did!' She sat down suddenly.

Upstairs a blazing row was taking place. James was shouting at his father.

'I blame you! You and that slimy Dillon, using me and

abusing my good name in the rotten cause of building your own little Empires.'

Richard tried to keep calm. 'I agree that Dillon should never have quoted you, even anonymously as he thought, without consulting you first – but you must realise that this article will probably do more for the troops in France—'

'*And* for the Party.'

'You've done your stuff, James – you've been in the thick of it from the start, and there's certainly nothing dishonourable in accepting a staff appointment. Rather the opposite, I should have thought.'

'Honourable?' James blazed back. 'To be labelled one of Nesfield's bumboys and looked on by everyone as one of his private army of spies? Damn Nesfield, damn Dillon!'

The door opened. 'Sir Geoffrey Dillon,' announced Mr. Hudson.

Dillon was purring. He purred congratulations to James on his 'plum job', and, apparently unaware of the tenseness of Hazel, of Richard's troubled face, and of the white anger of James, produced a draft of *The Times* main leader for the following day. 'Listen to this,' he said. ' "A Government incapable of fighting a war, hampering our brave soldiers, thanks to the obstinacy of the War Office in ordering shrapnel shells instead of high explosive." The Liberals'll never survive that kind of attack. It's Asquith's death sentence.' He beamed at them over his spectacles. James managed to say, 'Excuse me. I'm going away in the morning. I've a lot to do.'

Hazel followed him out. 'Where are you going?'

'I've suddenly realised I've got to get away – somewhere, anywhere away from this muck, or I'll go mad.'

'Yes,' she said. Her eyes looked a question. 'Do you want—?'

'I think I'd rather go alone, if you wouldn't mind.'

She watched him go up the stairs. It was happening again; things were coming between them, the happiness of reunion fading into a memory.

The other soldier in the house had had a poor evening, too. Feeling unwanted by everybody except Daisy, Edward had gone out to the pub to look up old friends. It was his last night of leave; he was entitled to a bit of lively company. But none of his particular mates were there, and the beer tasted as flat as Edward felt. He slipped in and went to bed, thoroughly depressed.

He was half asleep when the click of the door-handle and the pale glow of a candle roused him. Daisy was in his room. in her dressing-gown, the soft ruffle of her nightdress showing at the neck, her pretty hair flowing over her shoulders. Edward gaped. 'Daisy! What's the matter?'

'Ssh! Nothing's the matter.'

'What is it then?' They were both whispering. Daisy sat on the bed. 'I'm going to spend the night with you,' she announced. Edward's reaction was one of horror.

'They'll skin you alive if we're caught.'

'We won't be. It's quite safe with Rose being away. We might not see each other again for ages.' She bent and kissed him, but he fended her off. He was a very worried young man.

'Daisy, I been thinking. Perhaps Captain James is right. Perhaps I oughtn't to have asked you to marry me. It isn't fair. I haven't got any money put away, and I'm more or less bound to get wounded – or something – the way this war's going. If you had a baby you'd be chucked out of this place sharp, whatever they say now.'

'That's my business, isn't it. I can look after myself all right, and a baby as well if necessary. Oh, come on, Eddy, cheer up. You asked me to marry you and I said Yes and I've got a ring to prove it. Anything else, and it'll be breach of promise. Now move over, I'm cold.'

Edward moved over.

CHAPTER THREE

THE baker's shop in Elizabeth Street, Belgravia, was a model of its kind. Spotlessly clean counters held appetising goods, everything that could be polished had been polished; a delicious savour of new bread wafted in from the bakery. The name displayed on the shop-window was ALBERT SCHOENFELD, but his customers and staff called him Mr. Shonfield. Everything was English about Albert but his accent, in which a trace of German lingered. He was fortyish, stocky, serious-minded; his wife Maria, dark, thin and intelligent, and his young son, Wilfred, an ordinary English schoolboy.

Maria handed over to Daisy the Bellamy household's allowance of bread. 'Take care of those loaves, Daisy. They're precious like gold nowadays. I can only bake two days in the week with flour and coal so scarce.'

Daisy was peering critically into her basket. 'Here, these ha'penny buns have got smaller.'

'And dearer,' said Albert. 'They're a penny now. What can you expect, with quartern loaves up to eightpence ha'penny?'

'You're lucky to have them, my dear,' put in his wife. 'You can't get these buns anywhere else in London.'

'How d'you manage, then?'

Albert laid a finger to his nose. 'Special methods, Daisy, same way as I got your hot cross buns at Easter.'

Wilfred appeared from the back of the shop, with a request for tea, and was shooed back by his mother. Albert looked after him fondly. 'He wants to join up in the Army – at ten years old, I ask you.'

Daisy, who was missing Edward very much, replied, 'Hope he doesn't have to. Hope it's over soon.'

'It will be. No doubt of it. Already we're pushing Fritz back. Wilfred loves to play soldiers. I give him some for his birthday.'

'It's my birthday next week — Wednesday.' Daisy made a tempting face at him.'

'*Is* it? Then you must have a cake. You leave it to me.'

'Oh, thanks, Mr. Shonfield! You shouldn't trouble.'

He strolled to the door with her. 'How's Edward getting on?'

'All right. I get nice cheerful letters, anyway.'

'From the Front, eh?'

'No — Codford Saint Mary. That's his camp on Salisbury Plain.'

'Tell him to stay there.'

'I will!' They smiled at each other.

Mrs. Bridges was pleased to see the loaves, but took amiss Daisy's report that Mr. Shonfield had said he was doing them a special favour. 'A favour, eh? So I should think, considering we've had our bread from him since I can remember.'

Mr. Hudson had been listening with a frowning brow. 'We want no favours from Mr. *Schoenfeld*, thank you.'

Rose looked startled. What was this fancy pronunciation? You never knew, with Mr. Hudson. 'Why not?' she asked. 'Best bakers round here.'

'I like Mr. Shonfield,' Daisy said. 'He's ever so nice and kind to me.'

'I've watched him grow up,' Mrs. Bridges recalled. 'From a young lad, when his father first come over here and started his shop.'

'Exactly so, Mrs. Bridges.' Mr. Hudson's voice was steely. 'When his father first came over here as a German refugee.'

'I don't think I quite get your meaning, Mr. Hudson. You was here too.'

Rose laughed. 'I get his meanin'. I read a leaflet. Mr. Hudson thinks Mr. Shonfield, being of German origin, is going to start poisoning the bread.'

Daisy laughed, and Mr. Hudson turned on her. 'This is no laughing matter, I assure you. As long ago as last August all enemy aliens were obliged to register at their nearest police stations.'

'Enemy aliens?' Mrs. Bridges had heard the term, but it

didn't seem to apply to the Shonfields. Mr. Hudson elaborated.

'German people living and working over here. The Government have since seen fit to intern thousands of aliens in special places; but many more are still roaming free.'

'Why?' asked Ruby, with confused visions of herds of cattle.

'Because they're cunning, Ruby.' Mr. Hudson's tone was very like that of the preachers of his Scottish childhood, discoursing familiarly of the Devil. 'They change their names. I read in the paper that a city firm called Sieburg Brothers had changed their name to Curzon Brothers. And a man called Rosenheim announced in *The Times* that he was to be known in future as Rose.'

'Nice of him,' said that lady.

'But,' said Mrs. Bridges, 'Albert Shonfield hasn't changed his name. Why isn't he in one of these "special places"?'

' 'Cause he's a naturalised Briton,' Rose answered sharply, 'born and bred here, and as patriotic as you or I are.' Mr. Hudson talked her down.

'That's not the point, Rose. If his father were still alive, he would already be interned. *Some* of us may pronounce it Shonfield for convenience. But the name and spelling are German.'

Rose, collecting the tea-tray she had been preparing for upstairs, raked him with a withering look from her fine eyes. 'Better off dead then, isn't he.' She swept past him, and he turned back to the still captive audience of Mrs. Bridges, Ruby and Daisy.

It was Daisy who conveyed his dreadful warnings upstairs, as she helped Georgina to dress for dinner with one of her young soldier friends.

'Spies?' said Georgina. '*Spies?*' Daisy met her eyes in the mirror, nodding knowledgeably. 'Yes. There's been cases of signalmen bein' overpowered and trains sent down the wrong lines and comin' off the rails, and Germans have been caught on the east coast signallin' to German submarines, and carrier pigeons have been found in German homes, ready to fly off with messages, and bombs have been found in the trunks of

43

German governesses.' Hazel, entering with a pair of gloves for Georgina, heard the last bit.

'Who's been telling you about German spies, Daisy?'

'Mr. Hudson, madam. He's read about it in the newspapers, and he's told us we've all got to be on our guard.'

'Well, I've read these stories too, and I think they've been rather exaggerated. You put all that out of your head, Daisy.'

'Yes, I will, madam, but Mr. Hudson says the papers don't tell you enough. He thinks they're muzzled, like dogs to stop them biting. I thought the war was happening in France. It's horrible to think it's over here, right under our noses, and we can't see it. Will that be everything, miss?'

'Just my bag.' Daisy handed Georgina the dainty object of satin and sequins which was to accompany her to Covent Garden. 'There, miss. And Mr. Hudson said we was to beware of tennis courts, madam. In German people's houses. 'Cause they're really gun-platforms, he said.'

'Yes. All right, Daisy.' Hazel's expression was very thoughtful.

At breakfast next morning Richard was glooming over the bad news from the Dardanelles. 'Looks like a major blunder on our part,' he observed, 'if these latest reports are to be believed.'

Hazel looked up sharply. 'And are they? How much are the newspapers telling the truth about anything these days?'

'Well, it's not in our best interests to be told the literal truth. It would only cause alarm and confusion. That's why we have a Press Bureau.'

'Propaganda is more important than the truth, then.'

'Of course it is—the right sort—to keep up public morale. And remember, people rely on their newspapers nowadays more than ever before. We must make the best use of them.'

Hazel drained her coffee-cup. 'Like filling them with German atrocity stories.'

'Well . . . It's what people want to read. It stiffens their determination to beat the enemy. I believe it's justified.'

'But Richard, people are being roused by these loathsome stories to a point of uncontrolled hysteria! It spreads to other things. We've got everybody looking for spies under their beds. It's ludicrous.' Rose was standing by, and at a look from Hazel began to collect the breakfast-things.

'The Government's always denying rumours about spies,' Richard said.

'But no one believes them. Why should they? People know they're not being told the truth. So they believe what their imagination tells them. And soon, if we're not careful, they'll start to act. Stupidly, from fear and ignorance.'

Richard turned to Rose. 'What do you think about all these spy stories, Rose?'

'I don't believe them, sir.'

'Not the ones Hudson has been telling you,' asked Hazel.

'Hudson?' Richard's eyebrows went up. 'Is this so, Rose?'

'Yes, well, sir, Mr. Hudson's always had this bee in his bonnet about spies. Long as I can remember. He thought Alfred was a spy.'

Hazel dismissed her, and looked reproachfully at Richard. 'You see? *She* may not believe them, but the others do, downstairs.'

Richard was becoming irritated. 'What are you driving at?'

'I think you ought to know the state of morale in your own home, Richard. Hudson's been spreading horrible stories.'

'Then you'd better have a word with him.'

Later that morning Mr. Hudson was summoned to the morning-room. He went with no anticipation of what he was going to hear; with no particular anticipation at all, indeed. He was in a remote, curious mood, and it was an effort for him to concentrate on what Hazel was saying.

'I'm reluctant to criticise your conduct in the servant's hall, Hudson, which is your own concern, and I know this war is upsetting you a great deal, but — I've heard Daisy telling Miss Georgina stories of so-called German spying activities, which she heard from you. She was recounting them in a way that clearly alarmed her, probably alarmed Miss Georgina, and certainly alarmed me.'

'They're alarming stories, madam.'

'Not in that sense, Hudson. I was alarmed that you should be spreading these stories, which for the most part aren't verified—'

'But madam, the newspapers—'

'Yes, I know about the newspapers.' Hazel remained standing, feeling more capable of dictating to her formidable butler in that position. 'And I know about certain types of magazines that seem to be printing the pictures and stories people want to see. For instance, that Scottish nurse, the one that was supposed to have been tortured in Belgium—'

'You mean Nurse Hume?' Mr. Hudson asked eagerly.

'Yes. It was proved there wasn't a word of truth in it. Nurse Hume volunteered for service, but never in fact left Huddersfield.'

'That was later reported, madam.' Hudson's voice was sceptical.

'But you don't believe it. Neither do Daisy and Ruby. I heard them talking about it while they were packing the parcels for the troops this morning. Don't you see how irresponsible talk *can* affect innocent lives? The Germans are human beings, exactly the same as ourselves. If we don't believe *ourselves* capable of such horrors, how can we believe it of them? The servants have been unsettled by these stories, Hudson, and I want that to stop. Do you understand me?'

Mr. Hudson's face was like granite. 'Yes, madam. But you will allow I can't alter my own feelings. And I feel, strongly—'

She cut in. 'Of all your alleged stories, there has been only one single spy caught and convicted – Carl Hans Lody.'

'With respect, madam, there was also the barber in the Caledonian Road.'

'Yes, you're quite right, I forgot the barber in the Caledonian Road.' Mr. Hudson was surprised to hear the edge of sarcasm on the Mistress's gentle voice.

'I will curb my tongue, madam. I'm sorry. I appreciate there are gullible young minds . . .' Suddenly fury seized him. 'They ought nevertheless to realise the utter savagery and brutality of those pigs, the Huns, madam!'

Hazel's eyes flashed. 'You go too far, Hudson.'

'They are inhuman monsters, madam.' shouting.

'They are human beings, Hudson, like us. T̶
inclined to inhumanity or cruelty than we are.
let us have no more talk of spies or atrocities
Do you understand?'

'If those are your orders, madam.' Their icy glances met; then Hudson turned and left the room.

It was a few days after this that Britain and America were plunged into gloom by the news that the famous Cunard liner the *Lusitania*, steaming on a placid sea under May skies, only a few miles off the Irish Coast, had been attacked by two torpedoes. Only a few boats and rafts could be lowered in time to take off passengers. Those who perished with the ship included the rich and famous, but Mr. Hudson was reading to his awed hearers of the simple human tragedies that had occurred.

' "Many hundreds of people were hurled into the sea. There were no ships near at hand. Parents held up their children in the water, till both sank from utter exhaustion. One mother held her baby above her till rescue came, but the cold had killed the little one before it could be taken out of the sea. Rich and poor, millionaires and labourers bravely met their doom. Close on twelve hundred souls perished, and Germany proclaimed herself by the act the Enemy of the Human Race." ' He looked round for effect. The women were silent; Ruby gave a noisy sob. A knock at the door startled them all.

Albert Schoenfeld stood there, a large basket on his arm, a hopeful smile on his face. People had not been very pleasant to him that morning; he hoped it was not going to be the same here. 'Hello, Rose,' he said over-heartily. 'Some extra loaves for Mrs. Bridges. And a surprise for Daisy — a cake for her birthday.'

Daisy recovered her spirits in a twinkling. 'Ooh! Of course, you promised. Thanks, it's lovely. I'll get a candle for it.' As she bounced off Albert greeted the others. Mrs. Bridges' reply was wary; she glanced at Mr. Hudson before uttering it, and

...ped obviously at the Union Jack badge on Albert's ... The candle was fixed on the cake, and lit, to cries of ...'any happy returns'; but Mr. Hudson said nothing. He turned his back and walked out of the kitchen, leaving them to it. A few moments later he returned, wearing hat and coat, and stalked past them, without even acknowledging Daisy's offer of a slice. They were uncomfortable after he had gone, banging the area door after him.

'Not hungry, I suppose,' Rose said.

Several hours later Mr. Hudson came back. His mien was dejected, his usually straight shoulders stooped. Rose viewed him with annoyance. Wasn't there enough going on without *him* turning moody? Impatiently she pounced on him. 'Where you been, Mr. Hudson? The master's been asking for you. There's Mr. Bonar Law and Mr. Arthur Balfour upstairs! I had to let 'em in myself and show them into the study.'

'Oh, my goodness!' He threw off his coat. 'Have they been served with tea?'

'Yes, and Mrs. Bridges sent up those nice pastries Mr. Shonfield let us have.'

Mrs. Bridges, too, was concerned. 'Now then, Mr. Hudson, what have you been up to? Going out and leaving us like that. Was it Albert Shonfield upset you? Was it, now?'

'No, he didn't upset me,' Mr. Hudson snapped back. 'I wasn't upset. I just went out for a wee walk, that's all.'

'Walk? Where to?'

'Nowhere.'

'You must have gone *somewhere*. You been up to something. What was it?'

Mr. Hudson drew a long exasperated breath. 'If you must know, I went down to the Recruiting Office at Scotland Yard.'

'You never .... oh, good gracious me!'

He smiled a wintry smile. 'You can breathe again. They wouldn't take me.'

'I should hope not, indeed. At your age!'

'There's plenty of men my age serving—'

'You wouldn't last a second.'

'Thank you,' he retorted icily.

'Well, I'm sorry, Mr. Hudson, but whatever made you think of such a thing?

'The same as makes every decent man think. The desire to do one's duty to one's country.' He waved *The Times* at her. 'The enemy has been repulsed at Ypres. Lord Kitchener has asked for another three hundred thousand men, to make the final push for victory.'

'That may be, but if we've come down to asking the likes of you, we're in a pretty sorry state – and I mean no disrespect, Angus, you know that.'

He sat down heavily. 'But what can I *do*, Kate? I can't knit socks for the army, like you. I feel of so little value, when there's Captain James and young Edward, both in uniform.'

Mrs. Bridges patted his arm. 'You never mind them. You're as much a man as them, in your way. And as much use, believe me. You got to have some men stay at home. You could join the Specials, like Mr. Murphy the butcher, who got turned down for his varicose veins – Special Constable, he is now.'

Mr. Hudson's gloomy face lightened. He would do anything, anything to erase the memory of that humiliating moment when at the medical examination his eyesight let him down. He had thought things were going so nicely; the M.O. had even seemed to believe he was thirty-eight.

Fortunately the atmosphere upstairs was one of cheerful excitement. The Liberal Government, after nine and a half years, had finally collapsed, and Mr. Balfour's visit had been to ask Richard to undertake the post of Civil Lord of the Admiralty in the new Coalition Cabinet. As Mr. Hudson served champagne to the master, the mistress, and Miss Georgina, he listened with approbation to the good news. When the ladies had gone to dress he hovered.

'May I offer my sincere congratulations, sir. I know how pleased the staff will be.'

'Thank you, Hudson. It's been a long wait, but worthwhile in the end.' Mr. Hudson continued to hover.

'Er – might I ask your advice about something, sir? I too have been looking for some contribution to make to the war effort. And while I realise that the army is out of the question, it did cross my mind that I could be of some use as a Special Constable, sir.'

'A Special, eh? That's interesting. What kind of hours would you have to be on duty?'

'I haven't yet fully investigated, sir, but I believe it would be shifts of four hours at a time — and only on certain evenings of the week.'

'Do you think you can still manage the household?'

'Yes, sir. I won't let anything interfere with that.'

Richard heard the eagerness in Mr. Hudson's voice. 'I don't need to tell you the Specials are having a rough time of it at the moment — all this anti-German rioting. You might just come back with your head broken.'

'I know the danger, sir. I can look after myself.'

'Yes, I'm sure you can. We shall have to consult Mrs. Bellamy, of course, but I can't see any objection.

Hazel, to his surprise, was furious. Richard had gone over her head, undermined her authority over the servants, allowed the key member of the staff to go off and 'play at policemen . . .' Richard had never seen her so angry. But it was too late to reverse his decision. The servants' hall knew. Within two days Mr. Hudson had signed on as a Special, and set out proudly on his first stint of duty, impressively kitted out in great-coat and bowler hat, and armed with a truncheon and a whistle. With amused affection, the women watched him go.

It was late that night when the knocking came to the door. Daisy and Ruby were knitting, Rose tidying up, and Mrs. Bridges was asleep in her chair. The imperative, regular banging woke her and startled the others.

Rose set off towards the door, but Mrs. Bridges called her back. 'Don't open the door, Rose. Might be anybody — Mr. Hudson shouldn't leave us on our own, at night-time.'

But Rose was already there, staring aghast at the tragic little group huddled in the area: Albert Schoenfeld, dirty and blood-stained, Maria dishevelled, her hair down, and Wilfred pale and trembling with shock.

'Oh my goodness!' she said. 'Oh, come on in. Mrs. Bridges! It's Mr. Shonfield...'

Mrs. Bridges panted into the kitchen, clucking with horror when she saw the state of the visitors. 'Good gracious, Mr. Shonfield, whatever's happened? Ruby, get some water to bathe those cuts. Daisy, pull up that chair for Mrs. Shonfield. You sit here, dear, that's right. Here, boy, you sit here, by your mother.'

Maria Schoenfeld began to weep quietly, but Wilfred was white and silent, looking at the blood on his hand from his gashed forehead. As the girls attended to their wounds, Albert began to talk, stumblingly.

'They came to our shop – a whole crowd of people – broke the windows, beat us and stole everything – then they set it on fire. We had to run for our lives.'

'What sort of people?' asked Mrs. Bridges.

'English people,' Maria said bitterly through her tears.

'They call us horrible names,' her husband went on. 'I see faces in the crowd I serve. My customers. I tell them, I am not German, I hate what the Germans do. They think we are spies – they think because of the name . . . It's German, how do I deny it? But I am a naturalised British subject. I have all the same rights as you do. I speak – a little with an accent because I live in a close community with German people, from my father's time. My son Wilfred – he is second generation, and still they beat him . . .' He broke down, burying his face on his hands.

Mrs. Bridges patted his shoulder. 'There now, there now, Mr. Shonfield. You're quite safe with us.'

When Mr. Hudson returned the Schoenfelds, bandaged and cleaned up, were sitting round the kitchen table finishing bowls of soup. He paused on the threshold, staring. 'What's this?'

The five women all began to tell him together. 'They thought they was spies,' Mrs. Bridges said.

'Who did?'

Rose answered him. 'People like us. English people.'

Albert's pleading brown eyes met Mr. Hudson's. 'We came

51

here for refuge, Mr. Hudson. We could think of nowhere else.'

Rose came forward and helped Mr. Hudson off with his unwieldy coat. 'Did you have a good patrol?' she asked.

'Yes, what did you do?' This was Ruby. 'Did you go up the Fire Tower, Mr. Hudson?'

'I was shown the Fire Tower, yes, Ruby . . .'

'Then what?' asked Daisy.

Hardly able to take his eyes off the Schoenfelds, Mr. Hudson replied absently, 'We were detailed to guard the Battersea Power Station.'

'Did anything happen?'

'No, things were quite peaceful, as it turned out.'

'Thank goodness you weren't near poor Mr. Shonfield's shop,' said Mrs. Bridges, not altogether tactfully. Mr. Hudson was thinking that that was exactly where he should have been, and he saw the thought reflected in Maria's eyes.

'What were they expecting to happen at this power station, Mr. Hudson? Were they expecting it to be attacked by German spies?' Her husband laid a hand on her arm, but she went on. 'I want to know why the Special Constables are guarding peaceful power stations, when they could be out in the streets stopping ordinary British people behaving like savages.'

'She is upset,' Albert apologised. 'There were Special Constables there, I saw them – doing their best to bring order, and sometimes they are hit on the head by the regular police in mistake.'

Mr. Hudson addressed Maria without any great compassion in his voice. 'I think you'll find, Mrs. Schoenfeld, that after these riots which I must confess to knowing nothing about – we will spend more time patrolling the streets. And – I don't, obviously, wish to defend what has happened, but you must realise this great wave of hostility – misplaced as it may in some cases be – is largely the result of the sinking by a German submarine of the neutral American liner, *Lusitania*.'

Maria smiled coldly. 'Ah yes, the *Lusitania*. You have

clearly not been told what we have been told about the *Lusitania*.'

'Maria—'

'No, Albert. You have not been told, Mr. Hudson, that it was carrying women and children, and Americans, yes — and concealing arms and Canadian troops below?'

There was a horrified silence before her husband spoke. 'It is exaggeration, propaganda. Don't talk like that to these people. They are our friends. They have taken us in, when we needed help.'

'Arms and Canadian troops?' repeated Mrs. Bridges. 'We'd never do a thing like that, would we, Mr. Hudson? The British, I mean.'

'No, Mrs. Bridges, we would not. But it's what one would expect the enemy to say of us. To justify the frightful deed.'

Rose broke in. 'Where are they going to sleep, Mr. Hudson? Wilfred's almost dropping.'

'He can have Edward's room,' Daisy said.

'Yes, and Mr. and Mrs. Shonfield can have ours. You and me can make do down here.'

Mr. Hudson raised his hand. 'Just a minute, Rose. You're making rather too many assumptions. I shall have to consult the master.'

He came down with a triumphant face. 'Mr. Bellamy says you are to go to the police, and report the damage to your property.'

Albert and Maria looked at each other. Wilfred was asleep with his head on the table. 'And what then?' Maria asked.

Hudson gave his nearest impression of a shrug. 'It may be considered safest for you to be interned. The camps are quite well run, Mr. Bellamy believes.' It was a version of what Richard had said.

'What happens to the boy?' Maria asked sharply.

Mr. Hudson hesitated. 'I would assume he goes with you.'

'Or to the workhouse?'

Albert turned to her. 'No, Maria, they wouldn't separate us.'

'No? Well then, if you are so confident, let us not waste

53

any time.' She got up stiffly, and touched Wilfred on the shoulder. 'Come on, Wilfred.'

Mr. Hudson forced himself to say 'The master has said you may spend the night here.' (And the mistress had said 'The wife and child can have my room.')

'We have to go anyway,' Maria said indifferently. 'Why should we inconvenience you further?'

'Liebe, don't be stupid,' said Albert. She turned on him.

'Who are you calling stupid? You are the stupid one, with your stupid English badge. Can't you see you fool nobody? They don't want you, these kind people, you make them feel uncomfortable. Look at them, staring at us. Even your son they don't trust. So – let them take their bread from English bakers – if they can find any!'

Half-lifting, half-dragging Wilfred, she led the way out. Albert followed her, with a last look back at Mr. Hudson.

'Well,' said Rose, when the door had slammed, 'I'll bet you're glad to see the back of them, Mr. Hudson. Who knows? They might have burnt the house down during the night. Come on, Daisy, Ruby – it's late.'

He was alone with Mrs. Bridges. He began to bustle about, collecting things, looking for his spectacles, backing away towards his own confines. But she remained, looking at him with pity and reproach.

'You didn't manage that very well, did you. Why are you like this, Angus? You've changed, you know. This war's done something to you. Those poor people! Harmless. Wouldn't hurt a fly. And the little boy with that nasty cut on his head.'

'You don't understand,' Mr. Hudson muttered, moving a pin on his war-map for no particular reason.

'No, I don't,' she said. 'Good night.'

CHAPTER FOUR

IT was a perfect day; one of those warm golden days of late September. The news from France was good. There had been a great Allied advance; after twenty-five days' bombardment, British forces had penetrated German lines and captured Loos and Hill 70. Over twenty thousand prisoners had been taken, and eighty-eight guns. And at 165 Eaton Place excitement reigned, for it was the wedding-day of Daisy and Edward.

Rose, who had been in a bustle of preparations since early morning, had torn herself away from the bride-to-be in order to attend on Georgina. As she entered the bedroom Georgina hurriedly put away in a drawer the letter she had been reading, but not before Rose had seen it, and had noted the pinkness of Miss Georgina's cheeks. Hanging up some dresses she had brought in, she said innocently, 'There was a letter for you this morning, Miss Georgina. From France. Did you get it?'

Georgina went on wielding the hairbrush she had hastily picked up, drawing it in long strokes through the glossy dark curls. 'Yes, I did, thank you, Rose.'

'That's all right, then. It was on the hall table.'

'Yes. I went down early in my dressing-gown.'

Rose refused to give up. 'Oh, I see. Well, it's nice to get letters.'

'Yes. It is.' Georgina was not going to give away anything about her precious letters from James. Rose could think what she liked. Never a day passed in Georgina's life without a dinner or a dance in the company of young officers; boys who went off to the Front happier for the memory of her beauty and the hint of promise in her eyes. Sometimes her photograph was in the pocket of one of them when he was blown to pieces, and the stricken mother would write to Georgina under the impression that she had been the Only Girl in her son's life. And still Georgina had managed to remain heart-free; why should one, as she told herself, become vulnerable by allowing oneself to fall in love? Yet, with James, it was somehow different. She had always admired him, had led him on a little. Things were not well between him and Hazel. Since he had gone to France they had written to each other in warmer terms than they had used before. 'Love' and 'dearest', and rows of kisses . . . Darling James.

Rose knew when she was beaten. 'What will I put out to wear today, miss?'

'Let me see. What am I doing? Harrods this morning to buy some gloves, lunch with Harry Gurney at the Queen's in Sloane Square, then the Duchess of Somerset's Bazaar for the Wounded, with Harry and Rupert and Angela; bring them back to tea here, then to the station to see Harry and Rupert off tonight . . . Yes, I think my beige dress, Rose. And my fawn coat.'

'Very good, miss. So you'll be busy this afternoon, then.'

'It sounds like it, doesn't it?'

'Only Daisy was hoping you'd see her in her wedding-dress before she left the house.'

'Oh dear, I'd forgotten. It's today, isn't it. Oh, I'd love to see her in it. Where is she?'

'Only upstairs, miss, slipping it on for me to take a tuck in the skirt.' She darted out and called up the stairs.

Georgina sighed. 'I do hope she won't mind me missing her wedding, only it's these friends of mine, they're going to France tonight.'

'Yes, miss. So's Edward.'

A tap at the door heralded Daisy, pink, excited and nervous in the pretty, simple tunic dress of spotted net, embroidered with pearl beads. It had been a combined effort on the part of Daisy herself, Mrs. Bridges, Rose, and even Ruby.

'Oh, Daisy, it's *lovely*,' Georgina said. 'How clever of you all. Turn round and let me see the back. You ought to start a shop, Rose.'

Daisy, having been sufficiently admired, went back upstairs. Rose, kneeling at her feet with a mouth full of pins, reflected that the last weddings from 165 had been Miss Elizabeth's and Captain James's, and look how *they'd* turned out. Daisy and Edward might be luckier — touch wood.

The wedding in the Pimlico church went off without a hitch. Edward's parents were there, and his old granny, while on the Bride's Side of the church Mrs. Bridges, Rose and Ruby sported their best hats. Mr. Hudson, a figure of imposing gravity, gave the bride away, and Edward was sustained by his friend Charlie Wallace, who showed an unfortunate disposition to giggle.

At the celebratory tea the atmosphere was less gay than it might have been, for the shadow of Edward's departure hung over it. He himself tried to pretend that he was in the best of spirits, and Daisy was so relieved to have come through her ordeal that she talked and laughed more than usual. There was confetti all over the floor and the wedding-party; the scent of the carnations in the men's buttonholes mingled with the rich spicy odour of bride-cake. Mr. and Mrs. Barnes were unable to relax in unfamiliar company, while Edward's granny was frankly asleep. After a particularly long silence had fallen Daisy asked, 'Well? Isn't anyone going to make a speech?'

With one accord they all looked at Mr. Hudson, but he shook his head. 'I think,' he said, 'it is customary at a wedding-feast for the Best Man to get to his feet and address the assembled company.'

'Course it is.' Edward jogged Charlie's elbow. 'Up on your feet, Charlie.'

'What, me?' Charlie looked horrified.

'Don't force him if he's shy,' said Mrs. Bridges kindly.

Daisy giggled. 'He's not shy, are you, Charlie? Wasn't shy with me. Not in the vestry when we was signing the register.'

A barrage of teasing followed her revelation that Charlie and she had had a bit of a kiss and cuddle while Edward's back was turned, all among the choirboys' surplices, and the party livened up considerably. But the hour of parting was growing nearer every minute.

Upstairs, Georgina was entertaining to tea her friend Angela Barclay and two young Grenadier officers, Captain Martin

Adams and Second-Lieutenant Harry Gurney, both, like Edward, due to return to France in the evening. The prospect did not diminish their appetites, and Georgina summoned Rose to bring some more teacakes and jam.

'By the way,' she asked, 'how did Edward's wedding go off?'

'Very nicely, thank you, miss. No hitches.'

'Who's Edward?' Angela enquired.

'Our footman. He got married this afternoon to our under-housemaid, and he's off to France this evening.'

'First time out?' This was Martin Adams.

'Yes.'

'Poor old chap. Like Harry.'

'Don't rub it in,' Harry Gurney pleaded.

Georgina sighed. 'Poor Edward. Is he very nervous, Rose?'

'A bit, miss.'

'Tell him not to worry,' Martin said to Rose. 'It's not all that bad.'

An idea struck Georgina. 'Martin – would *you* tell him? Yourself? Tell him not to worry. Would you?'

Martin looked surprised. 'Well – all right. If you insist.'

When Rose had been despatched to fetch Edward, Martin said 'What am I supposed to say to the chap?'

'Well,' said Angela, 'don't frighten him. Tell him it's all rather fun.'

'Is that fair?' Harry had a very strong conviction that it was not going to be rather fun.

'Why not?' Martin asked. 'Anything to keep him cheerful on the boat and in his cattle-truck going up the line. Once he gets there he'll be too busy to get a shock.'

If anything could have made Edward more nervous than he already was, it was being sent for Upstairs to be addressed by officers. Standing before them and the young ladies in his stiff, unfamiliar uniform, he was as uncomfortable as Martin was in the rôle of mentor, unable to concentrate on the toasted teacake he had been enjoying.

'Well, it was just to tell you,' Martin said after an awkward pause, 'it's not really too bad out there. Not all the time.'

'No, sir.'

Martin warmed to his subject. 'You get short, sharp bursts in the trenches, which are pretty good hell. Patrols, working-parties, occasionally a trench raid and plenty of shelling and mortaring. It's just luck then. All you can do is keep your head down and say your prayers.'

Edward had turned clay-colour. 'Sir.'

'But you do get out of the line into billets for rest periods, even do a bit of training. That means a comfortable game of cards, kick a football, drink a bit of cheap wine. If your rest area hasn't been evacuated you can talk to the French people, go out with the girls and – that sort of thing.'

'Martin!' Georgina protested. 'He's only just got married.'

Edward managed to smile. 'That's right, miss.'

'Don't forget to mention what you told me about inspections by visiting Generals,' Harry reminded Martin.

'Oh yes. You have to be cleaned up for them, and shaved, rifle well oiled. That usually means you're going into a big attack. Still, it's not really too bad out there. At least you're with your friends, and you can have a good laugh – every now and then – with a bit of luck,' he finished lamely.

He had been just about as disastrous as he could, with the best of intentions, and Edward was terrified.

The departure platform at Charing Cross was milling with people. A platoon of infantry had just joined the throng of officers and other ranks saying goodbye to their 'ladies, wives and women'. The windows of the leave train were crowded with the heads of those who preferred to be at one remove from their dear ones. It made it just that bit easier not to give way.

Edward was one of these. He and Charlie Wallace were hanging out of their window, while Daisy stood on the platform, longing to cry and knowing she must not. Edward was being falsely hearty.

'If the old engine runs out of steam we shan't get to Folkestone, eh, Charlie? So cheer up, Dais. You never know. I'll write you a nice long letter every day, that's a promise.'

Daisy could only nod.

It was very hard thinking of something to say. Edward

improvised wildly. 'Here, I bet Mr. Hudson will miss me, having to clean the silver himself now, not leave it all for me to do on my weekend leaves. And don't you let Rose take advantage, while I'm out there. She'll have you running up and down them stairs all day, if I'm not there to . . . Here, come on, no need for that.'

Daisy was weeping into her hands, her best straw hat askew. 'Dais, cheer up. Come on, train'll be going soon. Look. There's Miss Georgina with her friends, down by the bookstall. They look cheerful enough.'

They did indeed. They were laughing and smoking; the girls were pretty (Georgina had decided on a delicious dress of lilac check); the two young men dressed for war. Acrid steam swirled round them as they chatted vivaciously about a house-party to which Angela had been invited. Suddenly the conversation died, and Martin said almost angrily, 'How I hate going back off leave. After a fortnight of clean sheets and eatable food it's such a damned awful shock to one's system.' Angela's hand crept into his and squeezed it. Harry's eyes sought Georgina's. Then Martin said, 'Well, come along, Harry. All aboard.'

In the last agonising minutes Edward was getting desperate. 'I'll tell you what, Dais. Why not pop off home, eh? Don't wait for the train to go. You skip off. Go on. We've said goodbye. Here, perhaps Miss Georgina wouldn't mind taking you home in her taxi. You could wait for her by the exit.'

Daisy shook her head. Her pretty face was swollen with crying.

'Oh, I couldn't. I don't want her to see me like this, Eddie. Still, I will go – before the train goes. If you don't mind.'

'Yeah. Well. Give us a kiss, then.' She stretched up and they clung together for a moment. 'Take care of yourself,' Edward said unsteadily. She nodded and fled.

The whistle blew, and to a chorus of goodbyes the train began to move. Waving and cheering, those on the platform watched it slide out of the station, then began to disperse.

The empty roadway beside the platform was empty no longer. A convoy of Red Cross ambulances and a mobile soup kitchen had arrived, and a throng of people — military police, V.A.D.s, and volutary helpers.

'Come on, Georgina,' said Angela, 'or we'll never get a taxi. Don't stand there gawping. It's only a hospital train.'

'I know. You go on. I'll get a bus home. I want to stay.'

'You won't like it.'

'I want to stay.'

Angela shrugged. 'All right, if you must. I'll telephone you tomorrow.'

The train was in. From within it emerged a stream of wounded men. Some could walk, with sticks and crutches, though heads or eyes were bandaged; some were borne on stretchers; some were helped by nurses to the wheel-chairs waiting for them; some could not be moved until the two M.O.s had inspected them and given directions. Georgina was so appalled, yet fascinated, that she failed to hear the rumbling clatter of a trolley bearing cocoa and buns until it had almost knocked into her. The pusher of the trolley, a large lady wearing a Red Cross armband, addressed her loudly.

'Excuse me, dear, but you're really rather in the way unless you want to help.'

'Oh, could I?' said Georgina eagerly.

'Yes, you can. I'm short-handed tonight. Mrs. Duffy's just lost her son at the Front, so you can help hand out mugs of cocoa to those wounded if you're game. The stretcher cases first.' She filled two tin mugs with steaming cocoa and handed Georgina a packet of cigarettes. 'Offer them each a fag.'

Georgina delivered them, getting smiling thanks from the men, and returning for more. This time she managed three mugs, and then three more. She paused by a stretcher on which lay a very young soldier. He was deathly pale, his throat heavily bandaged. Georgina knelt beside him. 'Would you like some hot cocoa?'

He could neither turn his head nor speak, but his eyes focussed on her. He pointed to his throat and tried to say something.

'I'm so sorry,' Georgina said quietly. 'Could you manage a cigarette?'

Somehow he found the strength to nod; she put a cigarette in his mouth and lit it for him. He gave a feeble puff or two, then strained to talk; but in the noise of the station it was hard to hear what he said. She bent over him.

'Thanks . . . for . . . the fag . . . miss. Nice . . . face . . . Blighty.'

'That's right. Blighty.'

She got up and returned to the trolley. 'He couldn't manage the cocoa,' she told the Red Cross lady. 'So I gave him a cigarette. He's only a boy — almost too young to smoke. Still, he's puffing away happily and so pleased to be back in dear old Bli . . .'

As she turned her head to look at the boy, the M.O. and a nursing sister were gently covering his face with a blanket. Two stretcher-bearers approached and bore him away.

Georgina's eyes filled with tears, not unnoticed by the Red Cross lady, who said tactfully, 'I expect you'd like to go home now, wouldn't you. Thanks for your help.'

But Georgina was not just another shocked Society girl. She managed to say, 'Do you know if there's anywhere on the station — where I could sign on for war work?' The older woman nodded. 'You want to be a nurse, don't you. Well, V.A.D. Headquarters is at Devonshire House in Piccadilly. Tell them you want to volunteer for hospital work.'

'Thank you,' Georgina said, and turning away disappeared among the swirling crowds.

Rose was surprised and not a little shaken. 'Well, *I* couldn't do it, Miss Georgina. I never could stand the sight of blood, not since I was little.'

'They say you get used to it very quickly,' Georgina replied, admiring the fit of her new V.A.D. uniform, a dark blue cloak and cap over a white dress. Hurrying off to catch her omnibus she collided into Mr. Hudson in the hall.

'Good morning, Hudson. How do you like my uniform?'

'Very smart indeed, miss.'

'I'm starting my nurse's training today, as a V.A.D. at

Guy's Hospital. Perhaps one day I'll nurse at the Front.'

Mr. Hudson's eyebrows soared. 'Indeed, miss? I was under the impression it was necessary to be twenty-three or more for a young woman to nurse in the war zone.'

'Oh, it is. But when the times comes I shall lie about my age. Everyone does. That sort of lie is considered patriotic, not at all wicked.'

Hudson was well aware of the fact.

The servants' hall approved, on the whole, of Georgina's action.

'I think she's got a lot of pluck,' Rose said, 'not being brought up used to it. I couldn't do it — not bandaging up horribly wounded soldiers and seeing them all in pain and that . . .'

A sharp dig in the ribs from Mrs. Bridges reminded her that Daisy was listening, wide-eyed with alarm. 'Oh, sorry, Daisy,' she said. 'Anyway, she's not been brought up to scrub floors.'

'There's lots of young ladies doing war work now, Rose,' said Mrs. Bridges, 'driving ambulances and helping in the factories, doing the men's jobs what's away at the Front. Dukes' daughters and all sorts.'

'I reckon she's lucky,' Daisy said. 'Being able to go off and do something to help the war, not like us, just sitting here. I'd like to do war work, I would.'

'Your war work's knitting socks for Edward and helping me keep this house dusted and cleaned,' Rose said sharply. Mr. Hudson began to discourse upon the privilege they all enjoyed of serving in the household of an important member of the Government. They all listened respectfully, but there was something about Ruby which put her ever so slightly outside their circle. She was unusually neat; her hair was capless and, for once, tidy; she wore a flattering high-necked blouse, and in her large dark eyes was a wary, secretive look. As Mr. Hudson reached his peroration she summoned up enough courage to say, 'Mr. Hudson, would it be all right for me to get me hat on, please?'

'Get your hat on, Ruby?' She might have been asking for a king's ransom. Rose explained. 'It's Ruby's afternoon off,

Mr. Hudson. Daisy and me said we'd wash up, so she could get off while there's still a bit of the day left.'

'Very well. Where were you intending to spend your afternoon off, Ruby?'

Ruby did not quite meet his eye. 'I'm going for a walk, Mr. Hudson.'

'Where?' asked Mrs. Bridges.

'Kensington Gardens. I'll take some bread and feed the ducks.'

'Mind you don't get talking to no soldiers.'

Some three hours later the servants' hall seethed with drama. Ruby, still in her neat clothes, sat by the table, calm and mutinous, while Mrs. Bridges wove circles around her, raging, and Rose and Daisy watched from the wings. Mr. Hudson appeared on the scene as Mrs. Bridges was saying, 'That's enough of your lip, my girl. I say it's not accepted and that's that.'

'What is not accepted, may I ask?' he enquired.

'Ruby's notice.' Mrs. Bridges was scarlet with fury. 'I've told her.'

Mr. Hudson turned his gaze on Ruby. 'Is this the fact, Ruby? Speak the truth, now.'

'I am speaking the truth. I'm giving notice because I've got work outside.'

Mrs. Bridges broke in. 'Sneaks off on her day out, without a word to no one, and signs on for work in a munitions factory down the river, then comes back, bold as brass, to announce that she's leaving the master's service.'

'She can't do munitions work part time, you see, Mr. Hudson,' Rose said. 'They have to sign on for full employment.'

Mrs. Bridges drew a deep breath and launched out. 'And how do you suppose I'm going to manage without a kitchenmaid, eh? It's bad enough with Edward gone and Daisy and Rose doing half his work, and you out evenings on air raid duty. I can't manage the meals in this house, upstairs and downstairs, not without a kitchen-maid. And if Ruby chooses to walk out on us at a time like this . . .'

'I'm not walking out, Mrs. Bridges,' Ruby said patiently. 'I'm going to help make shells for the artillery, like it says on the posters. They want keen and willing girls . . .'

'Keen and willing girls!' Mrs. Bridges snorted. 'And they pick you. They must be hard up.'

Ruby continued, impervious. 'I saw a poster asking for girls to work in a factory. Down by the Docks. So I took a tram down there and the lady took me on. It's putting gunpowder into the shells, you see. You have to wear special gloves and masks. It's at Silvertown, near Woolwich, and you get good pay — 34 shilling and ninepence a week.'

They all stared at her, this new, independent, well-paid Ruby. It was Mr. Hudson who spoke.

'I think you'd better come upstairs, Ruby, and see the master. Tell him what you've told me.'

'Yes,' broke in Mrs. Bridges, 'and I think I should come too, as the injured party.'

But Mr. Bridges' storming did not even ruffle the surface of Richard's calm acceptance of Ruby's resignation. In Hazel's absence, at the bedside of her sick father, he took and held to his firm decision.

'Surely you can see, Mrs. Bridges, that I cannot possibly in my official position in the Government refuse to allow one of my servants to give notice and volunteer for war work. If I did I should be strongly criticised. I know it's hard on all of you downstairs, and Mrs. Bellamy and I will do our best to avoid putting too much strain on the household during these difficult days. I'm sure we can manage. We'll just have to try, shan't we.'

Though choked with fury, Mrs. Bridges managed to reply, 'Very good, sir.'

CHAPTER FIVE

IT seemed as though the war had been going on all their life-
times. They were managing without Edward, without Ruby.
James was in France, Georgina, incredibly, a conscientious
V.A.D. darting to and from her spells of duty, Mr. Hudson
sallying forth four nights a week to act as a Special.

Daisy was frankly mutinous. Since Ruby's departure a lot
more work had fallen on her shoulders, for no more wages.
One morning Rose found her poring over a newspaper cutting.
'That's from Mr. Hudson's paper!' she said.

'He'd finished with it. Here look. I thought I might do
that.' Rose took it.

' "Young ladies wanted to work as conductorettes on the
buses." Daisy!'

'It's good wages. Anyway, see what it says – "Take the
place of a man at the Front." '

'I've told you before, your place is here,' Rose said firmly.
'Specially just now, with Captain James coming home on
leave.'

James brought back with him his familiar aura of discontent.
In the drawing-room before dinner he viewed with disfavour
the trim figure of his father in full evening-dress.

'Do you always dress for dinner?'

Richard smiled. 'Only on special occasions – such as your
coming home. It pleases the servants.'

James stared at the fire. 'When I was in the trenches I was
simply delighted to be coming back to England and find
everything going on just as usual. But now that I spend my
time sending other men to their death, it drives me mad.'

Richard nodded. 'I can understand that.'

Suddenly James faced him. 'Father – there's something I
must ask you. You've *got* to pull some strings.'

Richard did not need to ask what strings. 'I'm in the
Admiralty, James, not the War Office.' He poured two glasses

of sherry and handed one to James. 'In any case, I strongly disapprove of using one's influence in private matters. And I think you might consider how Hazel would feel.'

At that moment she entered, smiling. 'What were you saying about me?'

James improvised. 'Just that we wondered how much longer you'd be.'

Hazel was disappointed. She had taken special pains to look nice, and the two men stood there glowering, lost in some argument, not noticing her appearance. More than ever she felt like a cypher in the establishment. 'I don't think that's what you were saying.'

Richard said, 'James wants to get back into the front line.'

'Father!' James stared reproachfully. 'That was a matter between the two of us.'

'I think it concerns me as well,' Hazel said: '*I* certainly don't want you to go back into the front line.' She could see that James was in one of his black moods, uncaring how he hurt her or anybody else, luxuriating in his own unhappiness. 'I suppose you'd rather have a husband who was a shirker?' he said sarcastically. She looked at him.

'How do you think I'd feel if you went back to get killed, when you didn't have to?'

His cold stare conveyed that he was quite uninterested in the state of her feelings. Pouring a sherry for her, he asked, 'How does Georgina like her work at the hospital?'

'Oh, she's doing splendidly,' Richard replied. 'Enjoying every minute of it.'

Georgina was not enjoying at all the particular minutes she was spending just then. Her vision of smoothing the brows of romantic wounded soldiers had dwindled into stark reality: in the general hospital ward where she was doing her training she was washing the neck of a woman patient. A sharp admonition from the head nurse, a formidable young person whose unofficial title was Strings, caused her to upset the basin of water over the patient's bed-sheets. Nervously she apologised, but the patient, Mrs. Carbery, a cheerful Cockney, was far from offended.

'You didn't ought to be doing that for me, miss. It's not fitting, a lady like you.'

'I'm afraid I'm not very good at it,' Georgina said.

'I should hope not, indeed! Whatever next? Here, give me that, miss.' She passed the wad of cotton-wool swiftly over her face and neck, and dried herself. 'There we are. I'm clean everywhere it shows. That's good enough, ain't it, eh?'

Georgina surveyed with dismay the extremely damp bed, but she had barely started on it when Strings called to her, 'Clear all that up, Nurse, and then you can come and help me with the dressing.'

Obediently Georgina went off to the pantry with the basin and towel, followed by Strings' sharp voice. 'And disinfect that basin well. Don't want the whole ward to get septicaemia.'

In the pantry she tipped the water into the sink, then looked round for disinfectant. It was on a shelf above her head; she poured some into the basin and carelessly left the bottle uncorked on the draining-board. Rushing back into the ward she almost collided with Strings, who handed her a kidney-basin.

'Put boiling water in that, and a few drops of iodine.'

With difficulty Georgina found the iodine bottle among a host of others, and in her haste poured a large amount of it into the basin. 'Oh dear!' she cried, and 'Oh no!' as she simultaneously knocked over the disinfectant bottle, which fell with a resounding crash. A pool of brown liquid poured out of it and to Georgina's horrified eyes seemed to cover the floor. There was no time to mop it up — Strings was calling her. She dashed back to Mrs. Carbery's bedside, to see Strings removing from Mrs. Carbery's ulcerated leg a singularly nasty-looking dressing. But the nastiness of the dressing was as nothing to the nastiness of the sores to which Strings invited her to apply boiling water. Georgina felt a wave of nausea and faintness overwhelming her; she fought it, aware of String's appraising glance. The re-dressing of the leg seemed to take hours instead of minutes, but she survived. When it was over she wheeled the trolley into the pantry, and stood with closed eyes, pale and shaking, by the sink.

That night she was sent for by Matron. It was a discouraging interview.

Straight-backed and daunting behind her desk, Matron surveyed her V.A.D. with dislike.

'Shut the door, Worsley,' she said. 'Your cap is crooked.'

'I'm sorry, ma'am.' Under Matron's steely eye Georgina felt she was beginning to shrink like Alice in Wonderland after drinking from the magic bottle. After an awful silence Matron spoke. 'Tell me, why did you join the V.A.D.?'

'Because I wanted to nurse.'

'And why did you want to nurse?'

This sounded more promising. Eagerly Georgina began, 'Well, I was at the railway station and I saw some wounded soldiers . . .'

'And you thought you'd like to nurse them, no doubt.'

'Yes.'

'And wounded officers, no doubt. I must tell you that you have been sent here entirely against my wishes. I am short-staffed, because many of my nurses are in France, but the last thing I want is to have a lot of society women playing at nursing in my hospital. As long as you *are* here, I shall expect you to make yourself useful and to obey the rules.'

'Yes, ma'am,' Georgina murmured.

Rose and Daisy were changing the sheets on Georgina's bed. 'Though it's hardly worth it,' said Rose. 'She's only slept in these once, and she won't be using it.'

'Still, better have it ready for her, just in case.'

'I don't know why she has to sleep at the hospital, anyway.'

'She has to be up at six,' Daisy said. 'And they go to chapel before breakfast.'

'Sooner her than me. What, every morning?'

'And she has to wash, and scrub floors, and make the beds . . .'

The incongruous vision was too much for their gravity. 'I wonder if she'll stick it?' said Rose, when she had finished laughing.

' 'Course she will. Why shouldn't she?'

'All right, I know Miss Georgina's your pet, but . . .'

'She isn't! There, that's done. Here, Rose. With all the family out for lunch I thought we might ask Mr. Hudson if we could go out directly after our dinner — go to a picture show. It's *Tillie's Punctured Romance* at the Bioscope. I could do with a good laugh.'

'I can't,' Rose replied tersely.

'Oh, come on, Rose. I don't like going by myself. I know Eddie wouldn't like it. Soldiers keep trying to pick me up. Rose?'

'I'm already going out. I've asked Mr. Hudson, and he says it's all right.'

'You are? Where?' But Rose had already left with the used linen. 'Rose!' Daisy called after her. 'Where are you going?'

There was no reply. It was teatime when Rose returned.

Richard's brow was clouded. Something to do with James again, Hazel guessed, rightly.

'The Prime Minister says he's heard that James is going round everyone he knows — including many of my friends — demanding to be posted to a front-line regiment. And then he expects me to pull strings to help him! Even if I approved of pulling strings — which I don't — James and I haven't always seen eye to eye, and to ask me now to . . .'

Hazel kept her eyes on her sewing. 'You mean, if you loved him more, you'd be more inclined to send him into the trenches?'

'No, of course not. Hazel, what an extraordinary thing to say.'

'I'm sorry. But *I* find it extraordinary that so many people seem to think that sending, or not sending someone to die should be considered to be a proof of love.'

Richard paced to the window, returned to the hearthrug, and sat down opposite her. After a moment he said, 'You have to love someone very much and be very close to them to be able to face the prospect of their dying. I envy those parents who are so close to their sons that they know that, no matter what happens, the relationship will continue, even after death. I know that if I lost James I should lose everything. So, in that sense, yes, sending him to the trenches would be a proof of love. But it isn't one that I feel able to give.'

Hazel looked up. 'I'm sorry, Richard.'

'That's all right. One should speak the truth now and then. We tell too many lies — especially in wartime.'

Georgina entered the room as though borne on a high wind, out of breath and still in uniform.

'Georgina!' Hazel moved towards the bell. 'Did Hudson see you come in? I'll ring for some more tea.'

'No, thank you. I had tea at Gunter's.' She took a deep breath. 'Is it true that James is trying to get sent back to the front line, and that Uncle Richard is helping him?'

Richard stared. 'Who told you that?'

'Derek Benton-Smith. Viola Courtney — you know she's nursing with me now — I went to Gunter's in a taxi with them, and Derek said James had been to see his uncle, but he said that you'd be able to pull more strings than he would. Is it true?'

Richard and Hazel exchanged glances. Hazel said, 'You know that James is unhappy at being on the Staff . . .'

'But at least he's *safe*! What were *you* thinking of doing — helping him to kill himself?' They had never seen Georgina so angry. Richard almost shouted at her.

'Behave yourself, Georgina! I think Hazel has James's welfare at heart rather more than the rest of us.'

It was a fair indication of Georgina's feelings for James that this thought had not occurred to her. She stammered an apology, but Hazel put an arm round her. 'It's all right. We all want to keep him safe.'

At that moment James himself entered, his face brightening as he saw Georgina. 'Georgina, how splendid. I thought they were never going to release you from that prison of yours. Are you out on parole?'

She laughed. 'If that means having tea at Gunter's . . .'

'Is that what you've been doing? Would Matron approve?'

'I'm sure she wouldn't.' There was a tiny, awkward pause before James asked, 'Well, don't I get a kiss?', and a hesitation before Georgina said, 'Welcome home,' and stretched up to give him a cousinly peck on the cheek. It was a pity their first reunion had to be in public. He kept his arm round her waist. Mr. Hudson was at the door, beaming.

'Excuse me, sir. Will you be in for dinner?'

'No thank you, Hudson. We'll all go out and celebrate. Georgina, are you going to look very fetching in your uniform, or are you going to change?'

Her face fell. 'Oh, I can't come, James. I have to go back.'

'Back? Where?'

'I'm on duty at six o'clock. Goodbye, Hazel. Goodbye, Uncle Richard. As if it were an afterthought she kissed James again. 'Goodbye. Have a nice leave.'

Very clearly disappointed, James turned to Hazel. 'Well, it looks like you and me,' he said ungraciously.

'Oh, James, I'm sorry. I *must* go to the canteen at Charing Cross this evening. I tried to get out of it, but we're expecting two trains and a hospital train, and since Prudence has a bad cold . . .'

'Oh, don't apologise,' he flung at her. 'I can quite see you're all much too busy. I'll go and find someone else to have dinner with.' At the door he turned for a parting shot. 'I really don't know why I bothered to come home at all.'

Downstairs they heard the slam of the front door. Mrs. Bridges sighed. 'I don't like to hear raised voices with Captain James on leave.'

Daisy nodded. 'I think the mistress ought to give up all her canteen work and that while he's home. I know *I* would if it was Eddie. What do you think, Rose?'

Rose, who had been staring into space with her cold teacup in her hand, gave a slight start. 'Hm?'

'I'm sure Rose is thinking,' Mr. Hudson pronounced, 'as I am, that we have no business to be criticising our betters. Now since there is no upstairs dinner tonight I suggest we get cleared away quickly, and . . .'

Suddenly Rose put down the teacup and said, 'Mr. Hudson?'

They all looked at her. 'Is something wrong, Rose?' he asked.

'No, Mr. Hudson. It's just that I thought I ought to tell you — I've taken a job.'

If a pin had fallen in the ensuing silence it would have sounded like a bomb. 'A *job*?' Mrs. Bridges lowered her spectacles. 'You've got a job here.'

Rose avoided her eye, and Daisy's. 'I'm going to be a conductorette.'

They all spoke at once. 'A *what*?' 'Rose, you haven't!' 'A conductor on an omnibus?' Mr. Hudson made it sound like 'A waitress in a brothel?'

Mrs. Bridges almost wailed, 'Oh, no, Rose — out in the streets, taking people's money, and a lot of nasty, drunken men . . .'

'Everybody else is doing their bit. Why shouldn't I?' Rose retorted.

'It is quite understandable, Rose,' said Mr. Hudson, 'that you should wish to do your bit, but it is not something to be rushed into. The war won't last for ever, and giving your notice is a very serious step.'

'I won't have to give notice. I've talked to the mistress. It's shift work, you see. I can go on living here and do my work in between. It says all about it here.' She handed a newspaper cutting to Mr. Hudson, at the sight of which Daisy went crimson with anger.

'Rose, that's mine. *You kept it*!'

'What if I did?' Rose got up, pretending nonchalance, and began to carry crockery into the kitchen. The look Daisy gave her receding back was sufficiently malevolent to have scorched the clothes off it.

It was late when Hazel got in, tired and cold after her spell of duty at Charing Cross. She was surprised to find James in the house, by the morning-room fire. He indicated a thermos and a plate of sandwiches.

'I thought you might like some hot coffee and something to eat.'

'Oh, I would. We didn't even have time for a cup of tea.' She knelt by the hearth, warming her hands at the meagre fire. James handed her a cup of coffee, and sat down beside her. 'I'm sorry I lost my temper,' he said.

'I'm sorry I've spoilt your leave.'

'You haven't. *I* have. I feel like a leper, going about in these things.' He touched the scarlet tabs. 'I'd rather be in plain clothes.'

'And have a lot of madwomen coming up to you and giving you white feathers?'

'Why not?'

'Oh, James.'

'I'm a soldier! You forget that because when I met you I'd left the army. But I never felt at home in the City. I'm a soldier.'

'James, what on earth does that *mean*?'

He stared into the embers. 'It means that you're prepared to put your life on the line. You have a relationship with your fellow soldiers which you don't have with anyone else. You know you'll be out there together getting shot at. You depend on each other, and in the end, if you have to, you die for each other. It sounds sentimental, but you *are* . . . a band of brothers. And to think that I'm sitting there, miles behind the front line, while they're up in the trenches, my own men and my brother officers, getting blown to pieces – half the time because of orders *I*'ve given . . . But I don't expect you to understand.'

If he had troubled to interpret the look in his wife's eyes he would have seen that she understood very well.

The following morning Colonel Buchanan, in his office at Regimental Headquarters, was going through papers with his adjutant, Captain Hanning. Suddenly he glanced at his watch. 'What time is Mrs. Bellamy coming?'

'She's probably here now, sir.'

'What on earth does she want?'

'I don't know. She's been at the barracks all morning, helping the wives with their allotment papers.'

The colonel mused. 'James is on the Staff already. What's the betting she wants him promoted or posted to G.H.Q.? All right, wheel her in.'

Though he would much rather have got on with his work he greeted Hazel politely.

'Awfully good of you to help us out like this. The wives

have enough problems without being baffled by incomprehensible forms.'

She nodded. 'I'm horrified to find how many of them can barely read.'

'Yes, it's a problem. Now, what can I do for you? The adjutant told me that a room had been set aside for your ladies. I hope it's comfortable?'

'Yes, thank you. I didn't want to talk to you about that. I wanted to talk about James.'

The colonel's reply was chilly. 'Oh.' He was not going to give her any help, though he could see how much effort it was costing her to make whatever request she had to make. She summoned up all the courage she had.

'He wants to be posted back to the Regiment.'

'Oh?' The fierce, bushy eyebrows went up.

'I think he's too proud to ask you personally.'

'Then, if you'll forgive me, Mrs. Bellamy, I think *you* should be too proud as well.' It was said as cuttingly as he knew how, but she stood her ground. 'Oh no. It's different for me. I want what's best for him.'

'But he's on the Staff.'

'He hates it. And he loves the Regiment.'

'Does he indeed.'

She brought up every argument in James's favour. 'You don't understand about that dinner-party. It was the very night he came back on leave. He hadn't had any sleep for forty-eight hours, and he was exhausted. James was tired, and he drank a lot of wine. If he said some injudicious things . . .'

'He certainly did,' put in Colonel Buchanan grimly. 'I'm afraid you must understand that there was a great deal of resentment, and that the King was extremely angry.'

Hazel brushed the King aside. 'Yes, but now could you please ask for him to be posted back to the Regiment?'

'The Regiment is in action in France.'

'Yes, I know. That's where James wants to be.'

'You *know*?' He frowned, and rose to his feet. 'I'm sorry, Mrs. Bellamy. James's posting is a military matter, and I really cannot discuss it with you. We're most grateful for all the work you are doing for the wives' welfare. Do please let me know if there is any help I can give with regard to that. Philip! Mrs. Bellamy is just going. Goodbye.'

'Goodbye.' Hazel's voice was small and quenched. She went without a backward look of appeal. When she was gone the colonel, who had been standing by the window, turned and snapped out at his adjutant, 'Has she got a lover?'

Captain Hanning looked startled. 'Hazel Bellamy? Not as far as I know.'

'The woman wanted me to get her husband sent back into action.'

'How extraordinary. There'd be trouble from General Nesfield if you did. I imagine he'd take it quite personally.'

The colonel sat down, stroking his chin thoughtfully. 'Yes. I expect he would . . . Damn it all! James is an officer in His Majesty's Household Cavalry, and if some damned general at the War Office chooses to interfere I think the Colonel-in-Chief would like to know about it, don't you? Nesfield doesn't hold all the cards. An ace can be trumped by a King any day.'

The three young society girls in the training ward were thankfully finishing off the evening's duties. Angela Barclay had fainted, half-way through dressing Mrs. Carbery's repulsive sores. Georgina took a visitor's chair into the pantry and sat Angela on it while she recovered.

'You'll have to give it up, you know,' she said.

'Oh no, I can't.'

'But you . . . you'd never be able to stand it.'

'Yes, I will. I'll get used to it. Georgina, I *can't* give it up. I had such awful quarrels with my mother before she'd agree. She said I'd never stand it, and that I was too scatter-brained to be any use. I can't go back home . . . I'm all right now, really. I'll come back and help.'

Georgina pushed her back. 'No, you sit down for a bit. We'll finish the dressings.' When she got back into the ward Viola Courtney, beautiful, serene and confident, was putting the last touches to the bandages. Georgina looked on admiringly. 'Very good. You're much better at it than I was.'

Viola rose gracefully. She had had her uniform specially tailored for her, and it showed. 'Oh well, I think it's so second-rate not to do things well. I believe in showing that you *can* do them, and then deciding whether or not you want to.'

Georgina saw with concern the high flush on the face of her patient, and the feverish eyes; but Mrs. Carbery, ever cheerful, smiled up at her.

'Hello, dear. Nurse, I should say. I thought for a moment you was Beatrice. My eldest. You got a look of her. She was here last night, wasn't she? Looking after me.'

One didn't contradict a patient over a pleasant delusion. Georgina smiled. 'I'm sure your sister will bring her to visit you when you're better.'

'Oh yes, I'll be better soon. I feel ever so funny – like as if my head was floating.'

'We've been giving you some injections. And the doctor drew some of the poison out yesterday, so . . .'

'Yes. My Beatrice told me that this morning – or was it you, miss? You've got ever such a look of her. I feel better when you're here.'

'I'm glad.' Georgina stroked back the hair from the damp forehead before leaving her bedside. Viola was looking at her neat fob watch. 'Goodness, the party! I hadn't noticed what time it is. Derek and Bruce will be at the gates with taxis. Bruce said they'd have two, so that we could change in one while they rode in the other.'

Angela had emerged from the pantry, still very pale. 'I don't think I'll come, I just feel a bit . . . I think I'll go to my room and lie down.'

'All right.' Georgina glanced at Mrs. Carbery, now dozing but still hectically flushed. 'I suppose I shouldn't come, really. She's rather poorly.'

'Oh, nonsense. We're off duty,' said Viola.

Georgina was still not happy. 'You're sure we can get back in time?'

'We'll arrive at the gates on the stroke of ten – like Cinderella.'

'Well . . . it *would* be nice to go to a party again.'

77

But they were not back in time. When they reached the hospital the gates were closed. Georgina went back to Eaton Place, and arrived in the ward next morning refreshed after a night in her own bed. She greeted the head nurse brightly, but got no greeting in return, only 'Matron wants to see you.'

Georgina looked round the ward. Mrs. Carbery's bed was empty, stripped, the folded blankets neatly piled on it. 'Where's Mrs. Carbery?'

Strings continued to prepare medicines at the trolley, without looking at Georgina. 'Your patient died during the night. Septicaemia and endocarditis. She was asking for you. The night people came to your room to fetch you, but you weren't there.'

Georgina stood before Matron's desk, resigned to her fate. Matron was looking her most formidable.

'You left the hospital last night, and did not return until this morning.'

'I got back just after ten, but . . .'

'You know perfectly well that the gates are shut at ten o'clock.'

'Yes, ma'am.'

'Where did you spend the night?'

'I went home. I'm sorry, Matron. I know it means I'm dismissed.'

There was an agonising pause, as Matron sifted through the papers on her blotting-pad, knowing full well the value of suspense. Then she said, 'Lady Viola is leaving anyway. Apparently the Duchess is opening a convalescent home for officers in Somerset. We can hardly compete with *that*. And Miss Barclay is really not suitable for the work at all.'

It was easier to plead for someone else than for oneself. 'Oh, Matron, she does so much want to make a success of it. You see, her mother didn't want her to . . .'

'I am not interested in the private lives of my nurses.' Another pause. 'She can stay for a little longer. We'll see how she gets on. As for *you*,' she fixed Georgina with a steely eye, 'you have the makings of a nurse. Try to keep the rules in future.'

Georgina could hardly believe her ears. 'Yes, ma'am.'

Matron had another surprise for her. 'Have you thought of applying to go and work in a field hospital in France?'

'Oh no. I'm not nearly good enough.'

A faint smile hovered on Matron's tight lips. 'Well. That's a beginning.'

That evening a transfigured James burst in on his father and Hazel. 'The most wonderful news — you'll never believe it!'

Richard looked up sharply from his papers. 'My dear boy, what is it?'

'I'm going back to the Regiment. They're forming a special Machine Gun Corps, and we're to be attached to the Guards Division. I didn't tell you, but the colonel sent for me this afternoon.' Hazel carefully did not look at him. 'I'll be with my friends — well, all that are left. Don't worry too much, Hazel. There'll be quite a long period of training first. It's quite a new thing, you see. The colonel was very nice about it. Said I was just the man they needed to take it on.'

'Well done, James,' said Richard. Hazel smiled.

Hudson appeared behind in the doorway, bearing champagne and glasses. 'I thought we'd have champagne to celebrate,' James said, quite impervious to his father's modified enthusiasm or to Hazel's faint, secret smile.

'So in the end nobody had to pull any strings, after all,' said James. 'I must say I'm glad.'

CHAPTER SIX

THE passage of several days had done nothing to mollify Daisy's feelings towards Rose. She had made no effort to overcome her resentment, but had let it smoulder on inside her, constantly feeding it the fresh fuel provided by constant brooding, itself deepened by the strain of overwork and tiredness.

The presence in the kitchen of a Mrs. Ganton, temporarily replacing Mrs. Bridges, didn't help. An urgent message from Mrs. Bridges' sister in Yarmouth had brought the news that the house there had been hit by a shell during a warship bombardment. The sister herself was unhurt though badly shocked, but her husband had been injured in the head. Mrs. Bridges had obtained willing leave to go there immediately.

Mrs. Ganton was a pleasant enough woman, but strange to the household. It fell to Daisy's lot to find things for her, deal with tradesmen and assist with numerous kitchen tasks which were normally outside her province.

Neither was Mr. Hudson's current mood doing anything to brighten Daisy's vexation with life. The duties of a Special Constable, so eagerly taken up, had added hours of work to his already considerable load, making him unjustly irritable and more than ever critical, especially towards the end of the day.

'Have you not finished brushing the master's hat?' was his first remark as he entered the servants' hall that May evening, frowning to see Daisy languidly stroking the brush across the black nap. 'Get a move on, girl. Mrs. Ganton needs you in the kitchen to make a salad for the mistress.'

He went out again, followed by Daisy's sharpened scowl. 'I'm not a blinkin' valet!' she told herself out loud. 'And I'm not Mrs. Ganton's blinkin' kitchen maid.' She took out her ferocity physically on the hat, doing wonders for its appearance as a result.

The area door opened and the hated Rose entered, smiling

and pert in her bus conductorette's blue uniform with white piping to the collar of her hip-length coat and the brim of the round hat. A brass hat badge and an oval brass number plate on her left breast completed the decoration, and a calf-length skirt completed the outfit. She looked happy and fulfilled; though, like everyone else doing two jobs, she carried stress marks about her eyes and she was paler and perhaps a little thinner in the face. She ducked her head and called through the open hatch into the kitchen.

'Evening, Mrs. Ganton.'

'Evening, Rose,' came the cheery reply.

Rose sighed wearily but contentedly, undoing the chinstrap of her hat as she sank into a chair.

'Phew, what a day! Stifling on that bus – even upstairs in the fresh air. Still, it's a lark. The people on that East End run, Daisy – you should hear their language.'

Oblivious to the younger girl's mood she stretched a booted leg towards her.

'Give us a tug. My feet are dropping off.'

The look Daisy gave her in response quite startled Rose.

'No, I won't. Sorry, I'm not your ladies' maid, Rose.'

'Eh?'

'Ever since you became an omnibus conductorette you been carrying on as if you own this place. Every night, asking me favours. You're not like a servant any more.'

The rebuke Rose was about to utter was interrupted by the front door bell and Mr. Hudson's distant summons to Daisy.

'Not like a servant?' Rose snapped back. 'I'll have you know I'm serving my country and this house – equal. I'm doing a full day's work, then I come back to another day's work, clearing up after you. So don't you be cheeky.'

Daisy let her feelings have their head. 'Oh, you *poor* thing. Well, I have to do *four* days' work – my work, your work, Edward's work, *and* Ruby's. And Mrs. Ganton don't know where things are kept.'

She got up abruptly as the doorbell shrilled again. 'Nobody helps me. My legs are dropping off – and my arms. And look at these hands. They're all wrinkled, and scabby, and old. Look!'

She thrust them into Rose's face. Rose recoiled and pushed them away, as Mr. Hudson came in, shirtsleeved and carrying his heavy constable's coat.

'Daisy, did you not hear me calling? The front door, girl.'

Daisy was too far gone in anger for discretion. 'It's not my place to answer the bell, Mr. Hudson.'

The butler stared. 'Not . . .? If I tell you it is, it is, my girl. Off you go now. Look sharp.'

His look and tone made even the rebellious Daisy obey.

'She's having a brainstorm,' Rose said, with difficulty removing her boots for herself, showing more of her legs in the process than Mr. Hudson thought it proper for himself to see. He turned away, struggling into his own uniform.

'Yes, Rose. I rather fear it's her marriage affecting her. She simply is not mature enough to handle the strain of an absent husband.'

'Nor a present one.'

'Well, that remains to be seen, Rose.' He fought tremendously with his shirt collar, the near-strangulation rendering speech difficult. 'We're . . . all under a strain, but it's up to all of us to . . . pull together . . . with the master's important work. We must make sure we keep up to the mark.'

A last fierce wrench got the collar secured. He picked up his coat again, as Rose, bootless, got up and hobbled slowly across to the table. Her exhilaration was gone now. Both looked what they were – overworked people under the stress of war.

The aftermath of breakfast had been cleared away. Mrs. Ganton was out doing her shopping. Mr. Hudson and Daisy were upstairs, about various tasks. The kitchen was deserted, the long table scrubbed and bare. A repeated knocking at the area door went unheard.

At length the door opened and a khaki-clad man peered hesitantly round it. He stepped into the kitchen and stood looking at surroundings he had known only briefly, two years before.

He was a well set-up figure approaching his mid-thirties, light-haired and his pleasant face deeply tanned His tunic arms sported sergeant's stripes. One of the arms moved unnaturally stiffly as he took off the broad-brimmed felt hat, caught up at one side.

He moved through into the servants' hall, just as Daisy, clutching a wicker basket of linen topped with a pile of newspapers came down the stairs. She gave a little gasp of surprise.

'Who are you? What d'you want?'

He, too, was a bit startled, and rather embarrassed.

'Sorry. Nobody heard me knocking.' He gesticulated. 'Back door.'

'Give me an awful fright,' she said, putting down the basket. (Not a bad looking feller! Aussie, from that hat and the way he spoke.)

'Sorry,' he grinned. 'I, er, used to know someone who worked here. A Miss Rose Buck . . .'

Daisy sniffed. 'Still does.'

'She does? Well, I'm on a bit of leave, and I just thought I'd come and look her up . . . And the rest of the staff, I mean.'

'I know you!' Daisy said, connecting at last. 'I've seen your photograph. You're Gregory.'

'Gregory Wilmot. That's right. Is . . . Rose here?'

'She's a bus conductorette in the daytime. Gets back at six.'

He grinned. 'That's where we first met – on a bus.'

'Rose said it was a tram. You sat on her cake.'

'Oh, yeh – it was a tram.' His broadened grin forced her to smile back, despite herself. 'What's your name?'

'Daisy.'

They shook hands formally. Gregory crinkled his brow. 'I remember the footman – Edward?'

'I'm Edward's wife.'

'You are? Oh, yeh, I liked Edward. Is he . . .?'

'The Middlesex Regiment. At the Front.'

Gregory glanced down for a moment and fidgeted with his hat. 'Oh . . . well, you mustn't worry too much.' He brightened again, for her benefit. 'Mrs. Bridges still here, with her famous cakes?' Daisy nodded. 'And Mr. Hudson?'

83

'Yes.'

'I had a bit of a barney with him about politics or something. All in good spirit, though.' He hesitated, then said, 'Look Daisy, I don't know what you heard . . . about me and Rose, I mean. I wanted to marry her and take her back to Australia.'

'She thought you was married already.'

'It was all a misunderstanding. We wrote to each other and cleared it up in the end.'

'She's kept your photo. It's in a drawer in our room.'

He was wondering whether he should ask whether Rose ever brought it out still, when a footfall sounded and Mr. Hudson came in. He frowned for a moment, trying to place the soldier's face. Gregory helped him. 'Gregory Wilmot, Mr. Hudson. Rose's old friend.'

Daisy saw the surprise on the butler's face and tried to help. 'He's come to see Rose, Mr. Hudson. For old time's sake.'

Mr. Hudson regarded the Australian warily, recalling Rose's elation so soon to be followed by anguish, the general upset the brief encounter had caused both below and above stairs, his own instinctive disapproval of the man and the match. Now, though, there was some different aura about the soldier he faced, a man who, no doubt through the experience of war, seemed to have aged a good deal more than the two years since they had last met. He said at last, 'I'm afraid Rose is not here at the moment . . . Sergeant Wilmot. And I must say frankly I am surprised you should wish to see her again.'

'I don't bear her any grudge, Mr. Hudson,' Gregory said earnestly; and the butler had to admit to himself that it had been Rose who had let Gregory down, and not the reverse. 'I was asking too much of her, to uproot herself to an unknown country and leave all of you. I know she looked on you as her family.'

Mr. Hudson couldn't suppress a pleased twitch of a smile. 'That's very magnanimous of you, Sergeant.'

Daisy broke in eagerly: 'He was never married, Mr. Hudson. He's got nothing to blame himself for.'

'Thank you Daisy, Rose did confide in me later.' The smile

became an unreserved one. 'Well, water under the bridge. I see that's an Anzac badge you're wearing, Sergeant Wilmot. Naturally, though. I've read about the exploits of our Dominion forces in the newspapers. You appear to have done well in difficult conditions.'

'Well, they certainly weren't too pleasant . . . Look, Mr. Hudson, Daisy was telling me Rose gets home about six. Do you think I could . . .?'

The smile was replaced by a slight pursing of the lips and a slow shaking of the head. 'I'm afraid it would not be convenient for you to see her then. She has her household duties, you understand?'

'Doesn't she ever get any time off?'

'She has a half day on Saturdays. Unfortunately, time is something we're all rather short of these days. I must get back to my own work. Goodbye, Sergeant Wilmot.'

'Nice to see you again, Mr. Hudson,' Gregory said. When the butler left the hall he turned finally to Daisy, with a wistful, 'Well . . .'

Her animosity towards Rose forgotten under the spell of romance, she half-whispered to him, 'If you want to find her now, she'll be on a No. 25 omnibus – Victoria to Ilford.'

He let three omnibuses pass the No. 25 stop at which he stood. One of their conductorettes had been a real beaut – but she wasn't Rose. Then at last he saw her. Being by now first in the queue he was up the stairs before anyone else had so much as set foot on the platform. Rose, busy below, had not seen him get on. There were few people on the exposed upper deck. After what seemed like ages Gregory heard her intoning 'Fares, please', and the ping of her ticket machine. Then at last she was beside him.

'Fare, please.'

'All the way.' He handed her money without revealing his face. Automatically, she reeled off his ticket and rummaged in her leather pouch for change. As her hand advanced it to him he looked up slowly.

'Rose?'

She could only stare down at him, speechless.

'I'll see you at the terminus, shall I?'

She just managed to nod.

Still mentally numbed and feeling physically half-paralysed, Rose led him to a corner table of the London General Omnibus Company's Ilford depot canteen. She carried two cups of tea; he, two appropriately heavy rock buns. Not entirely on account of the buns he said, 'Can't I take you somewhere else? Proper teashop?'

She sat down and pulled out a chair for him. 'Haven't got enough time. Cor, why didn't you warn me? Nearly give me a heart attack on the bus.'

'Sorry, Rose. I had to wait quite a bit. You must have been going the other way.'

'Yeh. Well, how long leave you got, then?'

'Till next Monday. Then I'm off to a reinforcement holding unit in Gloucestershire.'

'Not fighting?'

'Not . . . for a bit. It's good to see you, Rose. I took a week wondering if I should come looking for you.'

'You wasted a whole week?'

'Didn't know what welcome I'd get.'

Rose said quickly, defensively, 'I did write and try to explain . . .'

'Yeh, Rose. It was a good letter. I accepted your decision. But now it's all over we can be friends, can't we?'

She nodded, searching his face, noting the tell-tale signs of what he must have experienced so far.

'You . . . had a bad time?' she ventured.

Gregory shrugged, and she noticed him wince slightly and half put his hand to one shoulder. 'Not as bad as some. Still in one piece, anyway.'

She took a sip of tea before nerving herself to ask the more difficult questions.

'You still got your farm?'

'Yeh. I've got people looking after it.'

'I suppose . . . women have to look after farms, and that, when the men go off to fight.'

86

He answered seriously, 'I'm not married, Rose, if that's what you mean.'

Embarrassed, too, he essayed a bite at his bun, and instantly regretted it. 'God! Nearly broke me blessed teeth!'

They laughed together. Then she said, 'How did you know what bus I was on?'

'Daisy told me.'

'Oh! You been to Eaton Place, then?'

'I saw Mr. Hudson, too. Seemed quite friendly. Praised "our Dominion forces" in Gallipoli. Huh! All I can remember of the place is I jumped out the boat in the dark, walked five yards, got a bullet in me arm, and found myself back in bloody Alexandria almost before I knew I left it.'

Rose's eyes widened. 'Your poor arm.'

'Just the fleshy bit up here.' He tapped it lightly. 'More painful than serious. Just the odd twinge left, now and again.'

Rose said, musingly, 'If I'd . . . gone with you, I'd be stuck out there on that farm now, wondering when you was going to be killed.' She sighed, and roused herself. 'Where you staying?'

'Potters Bar. With Dorothy and Hamish. You met them, remember?'

Rose remembered all too well the loud-mouthed husband and the predatory Dorothy, with her eye all too set on Gregory.

'Dorothy looking after you all right?' she asked, with an edge to her tone.

'They're putting me up in their front parlour,' he answered innocently. 'Look, Rose, I could take you to visit them again, if you like. Only, Mr. Hudson said . . .'

She smiled again. 'Don't take any notice of him. Proper spoil-sport, these days.'

A white-coated driver materialised at their table side, big leather gloves in hand. 'Come on, Rosey,' he said easily, in fruity Cockney. 'Back to work.'

'This is Charlie, my driver,' Rose explained. 'Gregory Wilmot, friend of mine from Australia.'

'Wotcha, Gregory.'

'He's been fighting in Gallipoli, and he got wounded.'

'Oh, yeh? Fightin' Fritz, was yer?'

'No. Johnny Turk.'

'Aw, the Bashi-bazouks. Heard about 'em. Come on, sweetheart. Don't she look loverly in uniform?'

She shook off the mock embrace, finding herself glancing guiltily at Gregory and pleased to see a glint of annoyance in his eyes.

'I get off at six,' she said hastily. 'At Victoria. Will you meet me then?'

Flustered by the suddenness of their parting after so long, and by the unexpected invitation, Gregory could only nod and murmur a promise. It was not until she and Charlie had gone out of the canteen door that he realised he had let her out of his sight again. Drivers, conductors and canteen workers stared with mild amazement at the spectacle of the dashing soldier who, miraculously avoiding collision en route, just managed to get out of the building in time to join Rose on the platform of her bus as it moved away.

Dorothy Matthews stubbed out her cigarette and washed its last smoke down her throat with the remaining contents of her whisky glass. She stood back and surveyed the table in a corner of the Potters Bar living room. It was colourfully and plentifully arrayed with fruit, meats, bread, cheese, bottles of red wine, and, at the forefront, a large baked ham, its golden fat scored into dozens of squares. Some of the highest hostesses in the land would have been pleased to contemplate so prodigal a buffet at that moment of the war.

'There,' Dorothy said aloud to herself. 'That's it. Specially for the little housemaid.'

'Now none of that talk, Dotty,' said her husband, overhearing her as he came in with an extra chair from the conservatory. 'She's Gregory's guest. We want to give them a nice evening.'

Dorothy flourished a fresh cigarette at him, an unspoken command that he should light it for her, which he hastened to do.

'Of course we will. What do you think all this is for? I just hope the little lady doesn't get any ideas above her station, like last time.'

Hamish uttered his ready laugh. 'It was Gregory who had the ideas. You can't blame her.'

Her only answer was to hold out her empty glass towards him. 'Pour me another drink, will you, dear?'

'You've had a couple already.'

'Pour me a drink please, Hamish.'

He obeyed.

As soon as Rose set eyes on them, after two years, she felt the return of the dislike she had felt before. She had hoped things might have seemed better this time. Last time, she had felt her humble status as a servant too keenly, had let Dorothy dominate her and cause the mischief that had led to misunderstanding and her break with Gregory. This time there was no uncertainty left, no unease; she felt only contempt.

In her years of service, both at Eaton Square and on visits to other big houses, Rose had learned to judge the genuine human article from the fake. Gregory had been her one major mistake, and that had been deliberately engineered. As to Hamish and Dorothy Matthews, she had no hesitation. From the vulgarity of the prominent food display, like a shop-keeper's window in pre-war days, to the yellow upholstered furniture clashing with the curtains and carpet, all very new-looking, the Benares brass tray over the mantelpiece, and finally the look of smug appraisal on the face of the woman who came to greet her with a cigarette in one hand and a glass of whisky in the other, while her husband from behind raked Rose's figure up and down with beady eyes, she could recognise a classic pair of wartime shirkers and slackers.

On the way over, Rose had asked Gregory what Hamish's war work was, and been told that, as a schoolmaster, he was exempt from military service, while a gammy leg, of a cause unknown to Gregory, ruled out any notion of volunteering for anything likely to call for exertion. Tell me another, she'd thought to herself, and had come to their house determined not to be put down again.

Gregory was the one who showed his nerves this time.

'Here she is,' he declared, over-exuberantly. 'Captured off a 25 omnibus.'

'Hullo, dear,' Dorothy greeted Rose. 'A bus conductorette. Not a very pleasant job, I should imagine? But then, you're used to unpleasant jobs, aren't you?'

'What are you talking about?' her husband asked sharply, embarrassed. 'Come and have a drink, Rose. Drop of whisky?'

He flourished a decanter. Rose hesitated. 'Go on,' Gregory urged.

'Well, just a very small drop.'

Dorothy was pleased to see her gazing fascinatedly at the array of food and drink, the like of which she had never seen in Belgravia for ages.

'Of course,' Dorothy said, 'it must be different for you, down in Belgravia. You obviously get all sorts of things we can't get up here. It's a real struggle to keep alive, out here in the wilds.'

'Doesn't look like it,' Rose murmured.

'Oh, thank you, dear. Just a little special effort, you know – for dear Gregory and his "guest".'

Gregory had brought Rose her glass of whisky. Dorothy reached up and stroked his cheek. He grinned. 'You've started a bit early, haven't you, Dotty?'

'She had one for her neuritis,' Hamish explained dutifully, taking his cue from a certain look in his wife's eyes. 'Cheers!'

They all drank; though Rose only sipped.

Dorothy gesticulated towards the table. 'Terrible times, though. I mean, that loaf of bread. Elevenpence!'

Forgetting himself, Hamish murmured, 'The price of a loaf of bread in the Napoleonic War rose to one shilling and elevenpence. That was the peak, when an artisan or labourer . . .'

'Always the schoolmaster,' Dorothy explained to Rose. 'Of course, he would have been fighting, like Gregory, but for this awful gammy leg. They've never been able to say what it is, have they dear?'

He shook his head, contriving a deeply wistful expression.

'Rose doesn't want to hear about Hamish's leg,' Gregory said, more at ease now.

'No, of course she doesn't,' Hamish agreed, brightening, effortlessly. 'Tell us about life on the omnibuses.'

'Yeh, tell them about her ladyship, Rose — the one who'd never been on a bus before.'

'Always had her chauffeur, I suppose,' said Dorothy.

'That's right,' Rose nodded. 'Hadn't got any money with her.'

'Did you boot her off?'

'I couldn't. She was a lady.'

'Oh. Would you have booted me off your bus, if you hadn't known me?'

'I don't . . . boot anyone, Dorothy.'

'But you'd have asked me to leave, politely. Because I'm not one of your smart ladies in Belgravia.'

'It's different,' Rose protested, knowing she had risen to the bait, but unable to restrain herself. 'You know about buses, and fares, and things. I'd think you was trying to swindle me. But this lady . . .'

She was annoyed to hear Gregory laugh and say, 'Even in wartime, one rule for the rich, one for the poor. Good old England!'

'What you come here for, then?' she retorted. 'If you don't think much of this country.'

He flashed back, with the anger of sincerity. 'I love this country, Rose. I'm risking my neck for it, aren't I?'

Dorothy had viewed the little fracas she had provoked with satisfaction, and it irritated her to hear her husband deliberately break it up with a suggestion that they dance to their newly acquired gramophone. As soon as the needle had been placed on the spinning record Dorothy took possession of Gregory and began propelling him around the room. Hamish turned from the machine to offer his arm to Rose. 'That seems to leave us,' he grinned. Rose noticed that for one with a leg so defective as to baffle medical science he moved remarkably nimbly.

'Last time we danced,' Dorothy remarked to them all, as

she and Gregory followed the lively tune, 'we were with neighbours, Bob and Patty Walters.'

'That's right,' Hamish laughed. 'There was an air raid whistle. We all ended up in a cupboard under the stairs.' Dorothy's eyes were on Gregory as she added, 'Might happen again tonight.'

Rose had had enough. 'What about your gammy leg?' she reminded her partner.

'Oh, ah – ah . . .'

Gregory seized the opportunity to detach himself from Dorothy and Rose from Hamish.

'That's right,' Gregory agreed, feigning concern. 'You should go easy on it, Hamish. Fill up the glasses instead, eh? Come on Rose – see the potted plants of Potters Bar.'

He whirled her unresisting through into the conservatory. A collision with a plant, which he had to save quickly from falling, halted their progress and separated them. When he went to take her hand and waist again Gregory was surprised to be seized, pulled towards her and kissed fiercely, passionately.

He was only too willing to respond.

Daisy was in bed when Rose came quietly into their room. The light was out but she was not asleep. An air raid whistle had woken her and she had been unable to go off again, but had lain indulging the self-pity into which her resentment of Rose had changed.

'Have a nice time, Rose?' she asked. 'All right for some.'

'Hello, Daisy,' Rose said, and switched on the light. 'I thought you was asleep.'

'Where was you?'

'With some friends of Gregory's, out at Potters Bar.' She had opened a drawer and brought out a small box. She took a ring out of it, and slipped it slowly, thoughtfully, on to the third finger of her left hand. Daisy sat up, wide-eyed.

'What's that?'

'He gave it to me a long time ago,' Rose answered, twisting the ring meditatively. 'When we was engaged.'

'But you broke it off.'

'He never asked for it back.'

'You going to start wearing it again?'

Rose replied, 'You get so many rough types taking liberties, I thought it might put 'em off.'

'What does Gregory think about it?'

'He don't know. And it's Sergeant Wilmot to you.'

'All right, Rose. Don't bite my head off.' Daisy fingered the ring on her own hand, and enjoyed the little satisfaction of its being a wedding ring, placed there by her man, not by herself. The thought mellowed her feelings towards Rose. Not unkindly she said, 'A man ought to be told . . . if you're wearing his ring.'

After a moment Rose answered, glumly, 'P'raps you're right.' She started to remove the ring.

Daisy said, 'You can wear it in here, though. At night.' Rose looked up, to see her smiling. 'I shan't tell a soul,' Daisy promised.

Happy again, Rose pushed the ring firmly back on to the finger.

As he entered the servants' hall next morning, carrying a basket laden with bottles of red wine, Mr. Hudson was not entirely surprised to find Gregory hovering just inside the area door, having once more failed to make anyone hear his knocking.

'Ah, hello, Sergeant Wilmot. If you're looking for Rose, I'm afraid . . .'

The soldier's expression was serious, though, and Mr. Hudson could detect an uncharacteristic nervousness.

'She's out at her work, I know,' Gregory said. 'It was . . . you I wanted a word with, Mr. Hudson – if you can spare a minute.'

Hudson put down his burden and motioned Gregory to a chair, taking another himself.

'I've just heard this morning, I'm on forty-eight hours standby to go to France,' Gregory began.

'Oh, I see. Well, I wish you God speed and . . .'

'Thanks. But it's not that I'm worrying about at the moment. It's Rose, Mr. Hudson.'

'Rose?'

'How am I going to put this? You see, when I came back here it was really in the . . . well, the spirit of friendship, towards all of you. Old times' sake. Honestly, I didn't mean to start anything up with Rose . . . spark her off, you know? But that's what I think I've done. It's not that I haven't great respect and . . . and affection for her, Mr. Hudson. But I just feel I can't offer her the sort of life I had worked out for us before.'

'I see. Your sheep farm in Australia – it's in financial trouble?'

'Not a bit. I suppose the trouble's in me. I'm the sort who likes to have everything tied up neat and tidy, and no loose ends. If things were different . . . this war . . . What worries me is, she's going to expect me to say something, make some sort of proposal. I don't feel I can.'

Mr. Hudson returned his appealing look with one of paternal approval and benevolence.

'I'm glad you've come to me. No one knows Rose better than I do. Most young men would have selfishly enjoyed the girl's company and left her with all kinds of wild dreams and half promises. But I like the way you've tackled this problem, and I'd like to help you. My suggestion, for what it's worth of course, is that you write her a letter, here and now . . .'

But saying what? I can't tell her what I've just told you without looking a fool.'

'No, no. Saying, in kindly terms, that you're not going to see her again.'

Gregory was plainly appalled. 'Not even to say goodbye? It'd kill her!'

Mr. Hudson held up a hand. 'With all due respect to your personal qualities, there are other pebbles on the beach, as the saying goes. She meets a great many people on the omnibuses. She's open to the possibility of romance as never before. Now, it may seem a little harsh, but while your feelings are as they are . . .'

He got up and indicated his pantry door. 'I have pen and paper. Come away in, and we'll compose the letter together, shall we?'

The task proved a long one, with many false starts, objections and changes of phraseology. By the time a fair copy was achieved Mr. Hudson noted with alarm that Rose might be back at any moment. He shook hands with Gregory, then almost bustled him off the premises, insisting, though, that a 'gallant Anzac' should leave by the front door, rather than the area.

He read the letter quickly through for the last time, sealed it in the envelope on which he had got Gregory to write Rose's name, and went looking for Daisy.

'Ah, Daisy – this letter is for Rose. Give it to her when she comes in.' Hearing the unmistakeable sounds of Rose returning, he half whispered the rest: 'Be extra kind to her these next few days.'

Utterly mystified by this cryptic command, Daisy handed the letter to Rose as soon as she had flopped into a chair. She wondered whether it would be diplomatic to offer to help Rose off with her boots, but out of the corner of her eye saw Hudson furtively beckoning her through the hatch to come through into the kitchen, where Mrs. Ganton was now beginning preparations for the evening meal.

Left alone, Rose ripped open the envelope eagerly and unfolded the letter. It needed only a few words of what she read to wipe the smile from her face, which had turned deathly pale. Scarcely able to believe her eyes, she forced herself to finish the letter, then read it through again. Her mind raced and whirled. She lowered the letter to her lap, and looked slowly up – to see Mr. Hudson watching her through the hatch.

To play the deceiver, except from the best-conceived motives, was beyond the uttermost bounds of Angus Hudson's character. To wish to witness another human being's inevitable distress was an equal impossibility in him. So unsubtle was he in the matter of cunning that it had not occurred to him that Rose might draw any conclusion from finding him watching her. He went on to compound the blunder by calling through, 'Is everything all right, Rose?'

She regarded him steadily and asked calmly, 'Did he come here, Mr. Hudson? Deliver it in person?'

Reluctantly, he allowed himself to respond less than truthfully. 'I, er, believe he did, Rose.'

'Did you see him?'

It was no use; he was too honest a man to lie, or even go on half-lying, to her. He came round into the servants' hall and stood before her.

'Rose . . .'

'Did he *talk* to you about me, Mr. Hudson?'

'Well, briefly . . . er . . .'

She flourished the letter at him, all restraint gone. 'You know about this, don't you? You know what it says. You put him up to it!'

'No, Rose, no . . . !'

'You don't want my happiness. You don't want me to leave this place.'

He tried to retrieve his dignity. 'Don't be absurd, girl . . .' But her fury was relentless.

'You don't — or you wouldn't have made him write this. No, you can't deny it. They're your words in it. I can hear your voice saying 'em.'

'He'd already decided, Rose. He came to me for help, and I merely gave him it.'

'Yes, you helped him, all right. Glad to! You've always had it in for me. You tried to stop me going with him last time. It was listening to you made me *didn't* want to go. You'll always stop me, won't you? I'll never leave this house. I'll grow old and rot.'

Her tears were flowing freely now. Daisy was standing in the doorway, listening alarmed. Even Mrs. Ganton had paused, out of sight, on her side of the hatch. Hudson stood helplessly before his distraught accuser.

'Why can't you let me have a life of my own?' were her last, shouted words as she stumbled out of the room, almost knocking Daisy aside, and ran weeping up to their attic, heedless whether any of the upstairs folk might see her.

Was it coincidence that one of the passengers on Rose's bus that next, wet morning was Hamish Matthews? The look he got from Rose should have turned him away to wait for the next one, but he determinedly took a cold seat on top and waited for her approach.

'You put him up to it,' she accused, having first done her duty to the omnibus company by taking his fare. He denied it, but she shook her head fiercely, as she hissed, 'You and Dorothy. Otherwise, why aren't you asking me *what* he's done?'

'Listen, Rosey,' he insisted, glancing round at the other passengers, impervious behind their newspapers; 'listen, when he told me I went straight at him. I told him he was the luckiest fellow in the world having you, and the biggest fool in the world to let you go.'

She regarded him suspiciously. 'What did Dorothy say?'

'Oh, well – you know Dotty.'

'Yeh. I know Dotty.'

'But she's got a husband,' he laughed, thumbing his chest. 'She can't have two. So you come and tell her – tell them both. We'll tell them together, if you like. Eh?'

But it was Gregory alone Rose told that evening. Hamish proved man enough for once to drag his wife away, even refusing to let her linger outside the conservatory door to listen.

'I didn't think you'd want to see me, Rose,' Gregory said nervously. 'I mean, I thought I'd said everything.'

'*You'd* said!' she flared instantly. 'What about me? Suppose I'm not allowed to say anything!'

'I expected you'd probably write.'

'What – an insulting letter like yours?'

'Oh, now, it wasn't insulting . . .'

'Wasn't it? When the whole staff knew about it? Knew you'd been there all afternoon, composing your littry masterpiece, and then waiting for me to open it, to see if I'd start crying or not? Well, d'you know what I did? I went straight up to my room and I ripped your photo into tiny little pieces. What d'you think of that?'

He tried to interrupt with some understanding comment, but she was inexorable.

'Couldn't even write it yourself. Had to have Mr. Hudson help you. Didn't they teach you to write at school, Mister Big Sheepfarmer?'

In her passion she was tearing the ring from her finger and throwing it at him. 'Well, I got some pride. You can find someone else for your hot, dirty farm. I just hope you don't treat her like you treated me, that's all. Good *bye!*'

She ran out of the room. This time it was Dorothy who nearly got knocked over by her precipitate dash.

'Little madam!' Dorothy exclaimed to Hamish after the front door had slammed and Gregory had come dazedly out to join them. 'Don't you worry, Gregory. You let her go. You're well rid of her.'

She went to take his arm, but he shook her off and ran after Rose. He was too late to find her.

He got to her next day, in the omnibus company's canteen at Ilford. At the cost of a few sips of the disgusting tea he was rewarded after a long wait by seeing her and Charlie come in together and collect their tea. They sat down without seeing him. Gregory promptly rose and went to their table. Rose looked up, and her face tautened.

'Rose, I want to talk to you — alone.' He turned to the driver. 'You mind leaving us?'

Charlie scowled. 'Hold on, Digger . . .' But he took the hint, and went away. Gregory sat down in his place.

'What are you doing here?' she demanded. 'What d'you want?'

'I want you to see my point of view.'

'Oh, not again!'

'Listen — ' He was almost shouting.

'People are staring — and you're spilling my tea.'

'I don't give a damn. Listen to me, Rose. I admit that letter was probably a mistake. I meant it sincerely, for the best — for both of us.'

'Huh!' But she was listening.

'You see, Rose, I'm going to France in the morning, and I don't know what . . . what you want from me.'

'I want a bit of honesty — about our feelings for each other.'

'I've given you that, in the letter.'

'Pardon me, but in the letter you said you was going to

France and you wasn't good enough for me, and you've nothing to offer me. You think that's being honest? What do you think I want, Gregory — Buckingham Palace? I know I'm not all that big a catch. Nobody come along and snapped me up since we was last together, did they?'

'Nobody snapped me up, either,' he said. 'Look, Rosey, we've had a good time together these last few days, but you know as well as I do it wasn't, well, really like it was before, was it? Now *you* be honest.'

She would not plead, and there was no more point in anger. Honesty was what was needed.

'All right, Gregory,' she said. 'I will. You're right, it wasn't like it was before, because you've changed. You used to have such . . . marvellous ideas. About life in Australia and . . . things. You was so . . . positive. It's what I loved about you, just hearing you talk. I've waited to hear it again this time, but it's gone, and I don't know where.'

He had known it himself, and had worried about it, and tried to explain it to himself, but in vain. Now it came to him clearly, and he found it possible to express it for the benefit of them both.

'It's true what you say, Rose. But you got to understand what it's like, being out in a place like Gallipoli. I don't mean getting hurt. I mean . . . I mean the stink of death in your nostrils, month after month. The flies swarming over dead flesh. I trod on something once . . . squelched under my boot . . . green and black, like a rotten mango. It was a human face, Rosey.'

As she registered her horror she automatically took his hand. He didn't notice, oblivious to everything except what his mind was saying to him and unconsciously translating it into words.

'Rose, he'd once been a person. Like you and me. You realise that and you start thinking about the whole human race. Not big new thoughts that are going to change anything. Just private thoughts; your own way of dealing with life. You find all the time you're switching — one minute high, full of warmth and love for everything, even your enemy. And next minute you hate and despise even the smallest thing. You don't know where you are. All the things you used to be sure about — your work, your future, the woman you love . . . It all suddenly becomes so meaningless, so God-forsaken, so bloody pointless.'

At last he returned to consciousness of his surroundings, and of her hand in his. She was saying, 'But you got to get those feelings back, Gregory, what you had before. Otherwise you got nothing to stay alive for.'

He held her hand more tightly. 'But it's better . . . if it's going to happen anyway . . . better to have nobody—'

'It isn't going to happen . . . necessarily. Doesn't to everyone. You got to have faith.'

'What in? You trying to give me religion?'

'Not that.'

'What do we do then, Rose? You tell me.'

Rose smiled at last. 'Dunno. Have a sort of . . . understanding, perhaps? Wait and see.'

The smile faded as he shook his head. 'No, Rose.'

'Why? It's all I want.'

'It's no good. Just a vague sort of promise. It's not fair to you and it's not my way of doing things. No, Rose, there's only one way — and that's a proper offer of marriage, which I put to you here and now.'

It was Gregory's turn to smile, at her look of astonishment. She began to stammer: 'But . . . but . . . just a . . . a minute ago . . .'

'Never mind that. You've helped me make up my mind, and you can't go back on it now.'

'Think I want to!'

'We'll get married — end of the war.'

'First day. Very first day. Promise, Gregory?'

'All right. I must get that ring back for you. I'll get Hamish to drop it round to Eaton Place. And mind you wear it — and show it to all those bus drivers.'

'Course I will. I will. Oh, Gregory . . . !'

Almost delirious in happiness now, she clutched his arm. 'Right,' he said, equally happy and relieved. 'Train leaves very early tomorrow, Rose. See me off?'

'Try and stop me. But first we've got to go and see Mr. Hudson.'

Gregory's face fell momentarily. 'Oh, no.'

'We must. He'll never believe me, otherwise. Think I'm making it up.'

'Well, he's just getting five minutes, that's all. Our time is precious.'

Their news produced in Mr. Hudson both perplexity and worry. While Rose and a now-delighted Daisy bustled into the kitchen to make some tea for them all, he asked Gregory urgently, 'Are you sure you want this, Sergeant Wilmot? Why, not two days ago, you . . .'

'I know, Mr. Hudson, and I'm sorry I bothered you. But, well, Rose is very determined. I reckon I was at a low ebb, and she helped pull me out of it.'

'So you're actually engaged to be married?'

'That's right. I hope to take her back to Australia when the war's over, just like we originally planned it. Well, she couldn't stay in domestic service for ever, could she?'

'Why not?'

'Because the war's changed people like Rose. If it's only done that it's been of some use. It's given them a taste for freedom.'

Mr. Hudson shook his head in bewilderment. 'But they owe everything to this way of life.'

'They owe their food and clothing to it, yes; but there's more to life than that.'

'You two talking politics again?' Rose asked, bringing in two cups of tea and seeing the set look on the butler's face. He ignored her and went on addressing himself to Gregory.

'I thought being an Anzac would put an end to your fanciful ideas. Aren't we all fighting for the survival of the English way of life which has been an example to the world for centuries? Isn't that what our young men – with admirable support from the Dominions – are dying for?'

'No, Mr. Hudson. We're fighting the Germans on the one hand. But on the other we're fighting for a change in our own lives. If you go to war just to hang on to some old belief, that's negative. You must be after something better at the same time.'

Mr. Hudson sighed and accepted his tea from Rose. 'Well,' he told her, 'I hope you can manage this kind of talk, Rose. I can't make head nor tail of it.'

'I'm learning, Mr. Hudson,' she smiled. She took Gregory's arm and squeezed it, as the unhappy butler wandered away to stare moodily and unseeing at his war map, hanging on the wall, and wonder what it was all going to come to.

CHAPTER SEVEN

DAISY was wearily cleaning the silver. Not for display in the dining-room, but so that it could be put away for the duration of the war in impeccable condition. Mr. Hudson handed her a jar of made-up plate powder, seeing that she had come to the end of hers.

'Thanks,' she said. 'I feel sad doing this. Makes me think of my Eddie. Wonder how many times he's cleaned this old jug? Oh, well . . . it's best put away till the war's over. I wonder when that'll be?'

Mr. Hudson was getting very tired of having sighing, discontented women about the house. He snapped at her, 'Instead of indulging in unrewarding speculation, Daisy, I suggest you unwrap the big teapot.'

'Whatever for?'

'We'll be needing it tomorrow. We are having a wounded officers' tea-party.'

Daisy looked aghast. 'Officers' tea! That means I'll have to clean it all over again. *Why* do we have to have officers to tea?'

'That's no concern of yours, Daisy. It is part of the war effort, Mrs. Bellamy being on Lady Prudence Fairfax's Committee, she has to take her turn at the wheel, so to speak, quite apart from the fact that Mr. Bellamy is a Minister of the Crown.'

Daisy was sulkily unwrapping the huge, ornate silver teapot, with its intricately-chased surface and strawberry-topped lid, a perfect beast to clean. 'Why does it have to be officers?' she muttered. 'They wouldn't have asked my Eddie to tea – not a common Tommy.'

'Common Tommies do not as a rule eat in the drawing-room.'

'The drawing-room's out of use,' Daisy flashed back. Mr. Hudson had an answer. 'We are reopening it for the occasion.'

'Oh no! Oh, it's too much. It'll take me all day to get the covers off and the place clean.'

'Rose will give you a hand, I expect.'

Rose, entering, heard him. 'Give Daisy a hand? What with?'

Mr. Hudson explained, and Rose's face, like Daisy's, registered mutiny. Since Daisy's outburst of fury at Rose's calm annexation of the advertisement for a conductorette their relationship had not been quite its old self. Although Georgina had tried to help by telling Daisy how noble it was to stay in her job and keep the home fires burning, Daisy still felt resentment that she had been left with the dirty jobs, more and more of them, while Rose went out in that flashy uniform meeting all kinds of people and getting paid good money; money that she and Eddie could have done with to set up house after the war. Rose, for her part, had lurking feelings of guilt towards Daisy. She lost no opportunity of 'making things up' to her. So now she said, 'Daisy's got quite enough to do. I'll do the drawing-room myself.'

Mr. Hudson sighed. 'I'll help you, then.'

'You're doing too much as it is, Mr. Hudson – up half the night on your patrols, and you're not getting any proper rest in the daytime.'

Mr. Hudson did indeed look tired, worried and old beyond his years. 'There's a war on, Daisy,' he said in his nearest approach to an appeal to her, an underling. But Daisy was beyond appeals. The general spirit of strain was as strong in her as in everyone else. She was missing Edward badly, she was desperately worried about him, and she had no more patience left.

'War or no war,' she threw back at the butler, 'I'm not going to open the drawing-room. I got the beds to do, the meals to serve, the whole house to keep clean, all the linen, and now the bloody silver to unwrap.'

'Daisy!' Mr. Hudson's face was a study in horror, Rose's scarcely less so. Daisy got up and stood with her arms akimbo in woman's time-honoured fighting stance. 'I need my head looking at, staying in this house, I really do. I should've gone off making munitions with Ruby. At least they've got rules against *slavery* in them places.' She stamped out, leaving Mr. Hudson pale with fury.

'That girl's becoming more impossible every day — giving cheek, insubordinate . . . In ordinary times I would have no hesitation but to see that she was put off without a reference.'

'I'll have a word with her, Mr. Hudson.' Rose got wearily to her feet, feet that were sore and aching from her stints of duty on the omnibuses. On the way out she turned back, hesitant. 'Mr. Hudson — about the drawing-room . . .'

'Yes, Rose.'

'Perhaps opening it up — you know, taking off the dust-sheets, cleaning it all up, washing the chandeliers — well, it is a bit too much at present.'

Mr. Hudson, within himself, agreed. He went up to see the mistress and to receive instructions for the tea-party, prepared to champion his staff.

'How many guests are you expecting, madam?' he enquired.

'Well,' Hazel said, 'it's very hard to tell until they arrive. Perhaps twenty, perhaps thirty.'

'Yes, madam. About the drawing-room . . .'

'I've been thinking, Hudson. I don't think we can possibly use it. There will be far too much preparation to get it ready in time. We shall just have to crowd into here. I'm sure the officers won't mind.'

Mr. Hudson was a shade taken aback to have the decision taken out of his hands, but it saved a great deal of trouble. 'Yes, madam.'

In fact, there was no crowding in the morning-room, for though Mrs. Bridges had provided mounds of cakes and sandwiches, and four ladies, including Hazel, were present to entertain the guests, only three wounded officers turned up. They were Lieutenant Bowman, a Canadian gunner, with injuries that kept him in a wheel-chair, Rupert Machin, a lively Royal Naval Lieutenant-Commander with an injured leg, and Jack Dyson, a young airman with his arm in a sling. Somehow he stood out in that assembly, Hazel thought, though he chose to place himself outside the circle round the table, as though something in him kept him apart from them in other ways. His face was boyishly handsome, though not too handsome, his eyes bright blue, and his long mouth had a humorous twist to it.

The morning-room was full of chatter. How delicious the cakes looked, just like Rumpelmeyers' before the war, so different from hospital food; how wonderfully the Empire, in the person of Lieutenant Bowman, had rallied round the Mother Country . . . Lady Prudence, Lady Berkhampstead and flighty little Mrs. Letty Vowles kept the wounded heroes in constant conversation. Rupert Machin gave them a frivolous and highy inaccurate account of the loss of his ship at Jutland, and Mrs. Vowles became extremely confused about the death of Lord Kitchener, having an impression that his lamented death by drowning was due to his having been in the navy.

Hazel had heard it all before, or something like it. Social chit-chat did not come easily to her. She drifted away to the one silent member of the tea-party, sitting quietly at the back.

'All by yourself, over here, like a mouse?' she said, and sat down beside him. He smiled. When he spoke it was with a strong Manchester accent, unlikely to appeal to the other ladies, but to Hazel warm-sounding and real. 'More like the owl that sat in the oak,' he said. 'The more he saw the less he spoke, The less he spoke the more he heard . . .'

'We all should copy this wise old bird,' Hazel finished, and they laughed. Something had already happened between them, a flash of the sympathy that binds like to like.

'I hope you're enjoying yourself,' she said, knowing that he had not been, up to that point.

'I'm not much of a dab hand at posh tea-parties. And butlers frighten me to death. But I'm billeted in an officers' hostel waiting for my board, and they came round asking for volunteers. You know – "You – you – and you".'

She had to laugh, though the joke was somewhat at her expense.

'You manage very well with your poor wounded arm,' she said.

'Oh, this is just camouflage, to get free bus-fares and sympathy – nothing much wrong with me. I smashed two machines in a week, so they sent me home because I was getting too expensive for the taxpayer.'

Hazel's unsophisticated mind was unaccustomed to taking in Jack's peculiarly Northern turn of wit. 'I – I expect you've seen all the shows . . .' she ventured.

'No. I'm not too familiar with London. Most days I pop down to Farnborough. They're building some ripping planes down there.'

Lady Prudence swanned over to them, bearing a plate of brandy-snaps, one of which Jack took with avidity. She gave him a gracious smile.

'We were just talking about the big new offensive in France – I wonder when it's going to start?' If she hoped to find out from Jack, she was mistaken. He gave her a blank, slightly uncomplimentary stare.

'I've no idea,' he said.

'Almost the whole army's involved – *everybody's* talking about it.'

'Well, that should be nice and helpful for the Germans,' observed Jack.

Lady Prudence gave him one of her looks, her eyebrows high-arched, and moved back into more civilised company. Hazel smiled. 'That's just what my husband would have said. He's in France.' She nodded towards a photograph of James.

'Oh.' Jack studied it without emotion. Near it stood one of Georgina.

'Is that your daughter?' he asked.

A pang shot through Hazel. That anyone – particularly this pleasant, interesting young man – should think she could have a daughter as old as Georgina. Her eyes registered her pain, and Jack was immediately contrite.

'I'm sorry. I'm afraid that was a floater.'

'Yes, it was. Georgina's twenty.'

'I meant sister, of course.'

He was very disarming. 'You can't get away with it,' Hazel said, smiling. 'She's a sort of cousin of my husband's.'

'I like the look of her,' he said, and a different pang attacked Hazel, who seemed to be particularly vulnerable that afternoon. But he went on, 'No time for pretty girls now.'

'I don't believe it.' But how she would like to.

'Gospel. Mind you, I don't say there wasn't a time when I had a look round the fair maidens of Wallasey. I always rather fancied red-heads myself. Coppernobs.' He looked pointedly at Hazel's russet crown, and she turned becomingly pink. There was a pause.

'And now it's aeroplanes,' she said. The subject of redheads was too dangerous.

'Always has been, ever since Louis Paulhan landed his Farman in our back yard to win the London-Manchester race. The day I started as an apprentice at Crossman's . . .' Mr. Hudson was pressing him to more tea.

'I don't mind if you do. Three lumps, please.' Suddenly he changed the subject. 'I don't suppose grand ladies like you ever go rowing?'

'*Rowing?*' She stared at him in amazement.

She had never been rowing; but she went with Jack. The boating-lake, in a little park in an unfashionable suburb, was a humble place, frequented by soldiers and their girls, mothers with children, and ducks. There was a nasty passage with a man who tried to race them to the last available boat; Hazel reaching the boat first, gave him a smart clout with a paddle, surprising him so much that Jack's few, crisp words sent him off without an attempt at resistance. Jack turned to Hazel, warm admiration in his eyes.

'You're priceless, you know. A grand lady like you seeing off a big lout like him.'

She said something she had never said to anybody else since her marriage. 'I'll let you into a secret. I'm not a grand lady at all. My father's a humble shipping clerk and my parents live in a seedy two up two down in Wimbledon.'

Jack stared at her. 'Well, I'll be . . . I don't understand. I don't believe it.'

'Don't, then. Why worry? It doesn't matter. We've both risen from the ranks.'

Jack burst into laughter. 'Priceless,' he said. 'Priceless.'

They took an oar each and began to row. Hazel was not very good at it, to say the least, and the performance entailed a great deal of laughter. She felt she could talk to him as she could to nobody else, and he, so silent at the party, opened up to her as though he had known her for years. He talked of his flying, of the right way to shoot down an enemy plane; of the time he attacked a Fokker, and saw, as the wounded plane swirled towards the earth, that the pilot had a little dog beside him in the cockpit. It was the only time he had ever felt like a murderer.

Hazel was very thoughtful. 'Supposing the same thing happened to you?'

'Nay, I'd never take up a dog.'

'I don't mean that.'

'It couldn't happen to me.'

'Why not?'

'I keep my revolver loaded ready,' he said laconically.

'Oh.' She changed the subject quickly.

He asked her to go to a show with him, and she went. Why not? James was away, and wouldn't care what she did or who took her out. Richard was at the House until all hours; she had sat at home alone long enough.

The show was *The Bing Boys are Here*. In the stalls at the Alhambra they sat very close to each other. Hazel felt the warmth of Jack's unwounded arm against hers, and wondered at herself for finding it pleasantly thrilling. She knew that whatever was between them would go farther; nothing could stop it.

Afterwards they went to a night club. It was in a small, dark, smokey cellar, the dance-floor crowded with officers and their girls, dancing to the music of *Baby Doll*, played by a jazz trio, and watched by those who preferred to sit with a drink at the little tables surrounding the floor. Hazel went to powder her nose. She had put on full war-paint for the occasion, a very rare thing for her to do. It transformed her from a pale, rather sad-faced woman in her thirties to someone ten years younger, the touch of rouge adding brightness to her eyes, the lipstick drawing attention to her mouth, and the pearly powder enhancing her fair skin. There was a diamond ornament in her hair, and her skirt was of rainbow colours, with a jagged hem like a gipsy's, and a black velvet top.

She saw the look in Jack's eyes as she approached the table where he sat. Joining him, she said, 'I did enjoy the show so much, Jack. Thank you for taking me.'

'It was very good of you to come out with me.' He had forgotten her revelation of her origins, made in the boat; he was feeling patronised.

'It's *not* very good of me. It's very bad of me.'

'Don't poke fun at me.'

'I'm not. I wouldn't, ever. It's not a wounded officers' tea-party any more. I'm not here for charity.'

'Charity? I don't understand.'

She began to flounder. 'Well, I don't make a habit of going out with — with people who haven't anything else to do.' He laughed. 'No, I didn't mean it quite like that. I mean, I'm enjoying every second so much, so please don't let's spoil it.'

He believed her. 'Oh, damn it, I wish . . .' he began. 'I wish things were a bit different.'

'It's no good thinking about it.'

'You're right. Why worry who we are, what we are, where we're going, where we've come from — doesn't matter any more. There's not much use in the past, and it's no good worrying about the future.'

'No. There's just . . . us.' With one of her rare flashes of fun, she quoted the hit-song from the show. ' "And nothing to mar our joy." '

'Hope not.' Jack spoke under his breath. Their eyes met and held.

The moment was interrupted by a waiter, bringing coffee. Hazel poured it out, sniffed it, and looked enquiringly at Jack. 'Doesn't look much like coffee to me.'

'Taste it.' His eyes twinkled. She took a sip. It was a generous measure of brandy. Hazel looked her surprise.

'Officers may drink no alcohol after ten o'clock.' He raised his cup and drank to her, silently. 'Have to go steady, though — I've got my board tomorrow. I don't know what the medics will think if I turn up with my eyes looking like a couple of poached eggs.'

'Do you think you'll pass?'

'Oh yes. No trouble.'

Hazel hardly dared to ask 'What then?'

'I'll fly the first tub that's ready over to France.'

'Then how long . . . before you come back?'

He answered with deliberate lightness, 'They say you last six months out there if you're lucky — three if you drink.'

'Be serious. Please.'

'I thought we weren't bothered with the future.'

'Tell them you're not fit — they'll always give you more leave.'

'That'd be breaking the rules.'

The brandy was skittling Hazel's inhibitions. 'Then *break* the silly rules, *I*'m breaking them. Married ladies with husbands at the Front should never dance with other gentlemen.'

'That's all right, I'm not a gentleman. And they aren't silly rules — and I'm breaking them already.'

'How?' She knew, more or less, what the answer would be.

'We're not allowed to have our hearts in two countries at once. That's what the skipper says, official.' Suddenly he rose and pulled her up and on to the dance-floor. Their steps fitted, as she had guessed they would. When the tune was finished Jack went over to the pianist and whispered something. The man nodded and smiled. He had been asked for that tune before.

Very slow and languorous, it began. Jack, holding Hazel very close, began to sing the words, very softly, in her ear.

> If you were the only girl in the world,
>   And I were the only boy,
> Nothing else would matter in this world today,
> We would go on loving in the same old way;
> A Garden of Eden, just made for two,
>   And no one to mar our joy,
> I would say such wonderful things to you,
> There would be such wonderful things to do,
> If you were the only girl in the world,
>   And I were the only boy.

He bent his head and kissed her gently. But she fended him off, pushing him from the room into a little pink-shaded anteroom where they were quite alone; and there she went into his arms and kissed him long and passionately, the kisses of a love-starved woman.

Mr. Hudson was rinsing out a decanter with small shot when Rose came into the kitchen, in her clippie's uniform. He called to her.

'Is the mistress in the house, Rose?'

'No, she's gone out to lunch, and she'll probably be out to dinner. I've told Mrs. B.'

Mr. Hudson snorted. 'Seems to be cavorting about all the time these days.' Rose stared. It was very unlike him to criticise the Family, and she resented it. Whatever next? 'I don't know what you mean by that, I really don't,' she snapped, 'except Mrs. Bellamy's very busy with her war-work.'

He sniffed. 'War-work? Coming back from my period of duty I happened to see her paying off a hackney-cab and opening the front door with her key.'

'What's so wrong about that?'

His reply was loaded with meaning. 'It was 5.30 in the morning.'

'Oh. Well. The canteens where she works on the stations are open all night.'

'Unusual to be serving in a canteen in an evening dress and fur coat, and jewels in her ears and *rouge* on her face.'

Rose approached him. 'I don't know what you're implying, Mr. Hudson, and I don't particularly want to. All I know is that there's no one in London works harder than Mrs. Bellamy to help us win the war, and no soldier's got a better wife either. And what's more, what goes on upstairs is none of our business — if I've heard you say that once, I've heard it a thousand times. You're doing too much, if I may say so. And you're worrying yourself into a frazzle over nothing.'

'If by "nothing" you mean the old moral order breaking up all around us, I would agree with you, Rose. I have the witness of my own eyes every night on my beat.'

'Don't you think *I* don't turn a blind eye to a few things that go on on top of my bus? There's thousands of boys going out to France every day from this country, most likely to get killed or maimed or wounded. Do you grudge them a happy memory of home to take with them?'

'Of course not, Rose. But that's not exactly the point.'

'You're prejudiced, Mr. Hudson.' Rose was angry enough to be cruel. 'You haven't got a loved one. You don't understand.'

She swept out, leaving him puzzled and a little sad. It was true, of course. Rose had her Gregory, Daisy her Edward, the mistress and Captain James each other (if that still meant anything); while he had nobody at all, for his long-standing friendship with Mrs. Bridges was hardly in the same category. He sighed, deeply, and returned to the cleaning of the decanter.

Hazel returned after lunch, changed into utilitarian clothes, and went off to her canteen. In spite of her early morning arrival home there were stars in her eyes and she looked a girl again. Rose watched her go. Whatever she had said to Hudson, she knew perfectly well that the mistress's bed had not been slept in the previous night, only rumpled to look as if it had been used. She wished her well.

Two hours later the bell rang. Daisy opened the door to a young officer in the Royal Flying Corps whom she recognised at once. When he spoke, asking if Mrs. Bellamy were in, she said cheekily, 'You came the other day, to the tea-party, didn't you.'

'That's right. Very good brandy-snaps, those were. Can I come in and wait for Mrs. Bellamy?'

' 'Course, sir.' She showed him into the morning-room. 'I'll bring you some tea.'

But Mr. Hudson, finding her preparing the tray, was not pleased. 'You shouldn't have let him in, girl. Goodness gracious, surely you know the rules by now?' Pulling on his tailcoat, he hurried upstairs to rout the visitor, who was looking at photographs.

'Good afternoon, sir. Was Mrs. Bellamy expecting you?'

'No, I don't think so.'

'Er ... Sir, I'm afraid Mrs. Bellamy is at her canteen and is not expected back for some hours.' It was a distortion of the truth, for Hazel had said she would be back about five, but Mr. Hudson had no intention of allowing strangers, even

113

in uniform, to lurk about the premises. Jack looked disappointed. 'Oh,' he said, 'that's a pity. I've got to fly an aeroplane over to France.'

'Might I take a message, sir?'

'No. No, thanks. I'll write a note. Oh — and no tea.'

'No, sir.' But Hudson remained firmly in place.

'It's all right — I won't pinch any of the silver.' Routed, Hudson went, and hovered in the hall. Jack sat down at the writing-table, picked up a pen — Hazel's pen — and began to write.

Lady Prudence, having supper with Hazel that evening, found her unusually abstracted, answering yes and no to the wrong questions, her attention far away, as far as the guns they could hear, rumbling and growling in France.

'The battle starts tomorrow at dawn, you know,' said Lady Prudence. 'It makes one feel almost part of it.'

'No,' said Hazel. 'Sorry, Prue, I meant yes, it does.'

Lady Prudence put down her coffee-cup with an air of resolution. 'Hazel, my dear. You know I'm a very old friend of the family — and I think we know each other well enough for me to be able to say something — well, quite frank — to you, without you minding.'

Hazel's air of vagueness left her. 'Yes, of course.'

'Agatha told me she'd seen you at the Alhambra the other night.'

'Oh did she? I didn't see her.'

'She said you were with a young Flying Corps officer.'

'Yes.' Hazel's tone was frank and unemotional. 'It was Jack Dyson, one of the three who came to our party. It was a very jolly evening. Poor boy, he was rather at a loss in London.'

'Yes, I expect he was. Er — I know nowadays all sorts of people are getting commissions, but he did seem rather — you know what I mean . . .'

'Common?'

This was a bit strong, considering what Lady Prudence was trying to say. 'Well — rough.'

'Not surprising, really. He was an engineering apprentice

in Manchester when the war broke out. I thought he was quite charming.'

'Yes. But we all have to be very careful, my dear – especially someone like yourself with your husband at the Front. You know what I mean. People *will* talk. Of course, if it had been one of James's friends or brother officers – I mean that's *quite* all right.'

Hazel looked her coolly in the eye. 'You needn't worry. Jack Dyson's back in France by now.'

Lady Prudence rose. 'Well, there we are. It was only just a tiny bit of advice from an old friend. I must rush now or I'll be late for my canteen. And Hazel, don't worry about your darling James – the Guards aren't going in for at least a month. Cocky Danby is at GHQ looking after the food or something, and he told Bulgy he'd heard Douglas Haig telling the King.'

When Lady Prudence had gone, Hazel opened the desk drawer and took out the note Jack had left for her.

> My lovely Hazel,
>> You are my only girl in the world.
>>> Cheerio,
>>>> Jack.

At the top of the note he had pinned his RFC pilot's wings.

Hazel pressed the paper to her cheek and held it there. The booming of the guns seemed louder.

CHAPTER EIGHT

SEPTEMBER had come. Summer prepared to retreat before autumn's advance; and on a ninety-mile front north of the River Somme in France the bloodiest battle in all history, begun back in July, still raged.

At No. 165 Eaton Place, Hazel remained as sole upstairs occupant, in Richard's prolonged absence on a tour of Naval establishments. Below stairs, Mrs. Bridges ruled the kitchen once more, but unhappily.

'Nothing but hashing, currying and making over, with no gentlemen to cook for,' she grumbled to the only male left in the household. 'Just look at this cold lamb she had last night for dinner. Why, it's hardly been touched. Pick, pick, pick!'

Mr. Hudson did not look up from the knife sharpener he was operating. 'Mrs. Bellamy has never been what I should describe as a hearty eater,' he observed.

'Not hearty, no. Only there's no pleasing her nowadays. I don't know, Mr. Hudson. This war's really beginning to get on my nerves, what with being short-handed in the house, tradesmen turning rude . . .'

Her colleague of so many years knew of old that a little gentle flattery was the best cure for her discontentment.

'If I may make a suggestion, Mrs. Bridges, why don't you send up some rissoles for Mrs. Bellamy this evening, with that delicious sauce? You have never failed with your rissoles.'

Her eyes brightened. 'Yes! Yes, I'll take your advice, thank you, Mr. Hudson. Mind you, in Lady Marjorie's day we'd never have served rissoles for dinner. Just imagine! Still, I have to use up the lamb. That reminds me, Daisy hasn't cleaned the mincer properly. I forgot to speak to her about it. Where is the girl?'

Her question was immediately answered by Daisy's approaching voice singing, 'All day long my telephone, keeps repeating hard, are you there, little Teddy Bear . . .'

The ditty was interrupted by a crash on the stairs and a

sharp yelp from Daisy, who appeared, limping, followed by Rose.

'Bedlam!' Mrs. Hudson cried unsympathetically. 'You ought to be ashamed of yourself, singing disgusting songs and crashing about.'

'She slipped on the stairs,' Rose explained, and was berated for her pains. 'Don't you start excusing her, Rose. That I won't stand for.'

'Hurry up, Daisy,' Mr. Hudson intervened. 'There's the servants' hall table to be laid, and it's nearly twelve.'

'And when you have time, my girl,' Mrs. Bridges added, 'perhaps you'd *care* to look at my mincer. One thing I'll say for Ruby, she may have been slow but she always cleaned things properly.'

'You see to the mincer, Daisy,' Rose said. 'I'll lay.'

'You ought to have more control over that girl, Rose,' Mrs. Bridges grumbled on, as the front door bell rang distantly and Mr. Hudson moved towards the stairs.

'I can't stop her slipping, Mrs. Bridges,' Rose protested. 'Mind, Mr. Hudson — there's wet on them stairs.'

But Mrs. Bridges was still not done with the subject of Daisy, who was by now out of earshot in the servants' hall, taking the mincer to pieces.

'Singing like that! I don't know where she picks it all up.'

Rose explained, 'She goes to the music halls with her friend Violet. To take her mind off Edward. And anyway, she's worked ever so hard, washing the paint in Mr. Bellamy's room.'

'I daresay. She still ought to get down here in time to help me . . .' Mrs. Bridges broke off to sniff. 'Oh, goodness me, my pie's catching!' She hurried to the oven. Rose went through to the hall.

'Whatever's the matter with Mrs. Bridges?' Daisy asked in a hushed tone. 'She's as cross as two sticks.'

'Got out of bed the wrong side, I expect. Never mind. Grin and bear it. You'll be getting a letter from Edward soon.'

'And you from Gregory.'

'Yeh. I meant to tell you, Daisy, I dreamed about him last night. And, d'you know what, he took me to the Crystal

Palace — and that's funny, 'cos I've never been there.'

'How do you know what it's like, then?'

'I've seen pictures. It was huge — all glistening in the sun. But when we got near it we could see all the glass was melting, like ice. Yeh, and I turned to him and asked him why it was like that, only I couldn't see him no more for the melting glass. But I heard him say, "We don't have palaces in Australia, Rose — but you'll always have me." And then he said . . . "darling". You know, Daisy, he's never called me that. It was so beautiful.'

She stared at the window, streaked with rain like the melting glass in her dream, savouring the memory of his words, not hearing Daisy reply, 'I don't never dream of Edward. Ooh, I'm ever so hungry, aren't you?'

Mr. Hudson appeared, carrying letters, as Mrs. Bridges came from the kitchen with the cottage pie. Hazel was lunching out, so the upstairs dining room needed no attendance.

'One for you, Rose,' Mr. Hudson smiled, handing it over.

'What did I tell you!' Daisy said, pleased for Rose, despite her own disappointment that there was clearly nothing for her.

'It's not his writing,' Rose said, opening her letter with a frown of curiosity.

'This journal appears to be for you, Mrs. Bridges,' the butler said. '*Occult*.' He raised an eyebrow.

'From my friend Mrs. Chambers,' she nodded. 'She gets in touch with her husband, on the Other Side.'

A cry from Daisy made them jerk their heads round simultaneously, in time to see Rose crumpling to the floor. 'She's fainted!' Mr. Hudson said. 'Water, Daisy. Quickly.'

He scooped up Rose and heaved her into one of the armchairs. Mrs. Bridges quickly loosened her uniform at the neck, then sprinkled her forehead with the water Daisy had brought. Rose was deathly pale. Her eyelids flickered and her lips moved.

'My . . . letter . . .'

'In your hand, Rose,' Mr. Hudson said. 'Take a wee sip of this water.'

She obeyed with difficulty, then roused herself a little to

say, wildly, 'The letter! Must . . . read it . . . Can't see too good.'

Mr. Hudson and Mrs. Bridges looked at one another. 'Shall I, Rose?' he asked gently. She nodded. He took the letter from her, and glanced at its foot first. 'From Sergeant Wilmot's company commander,' he said gravely, then commenced to read:

Dear Miss Buck,

I am very sorry to have to inform you that Sergeant Wilmot was killed in action this morning. He was returning from an early patrol when he was shot by a sniper. He was killed instantly and suffered no pain.

I want to tell you how very much we valued his cheerful and courageous nature, and what a great loss he will be to the Company in which he served. No officer could have had a better sergeant, or a more resourceful soldier. May I offer you my great sympathy for your most tragic loss?

Since no next of kin was recorded, all Sergeant Wilmot's letters from yourself, together with personal effects, will be forwarded to you in due course. I am so sorry to have to write this.

          Yours sincerely,
          PETER GRAHAM (Captain)

Rose's eyes were wide open now, staring unseeing. Mr. Hudson gently reiterated, 'He died instantly, Rose, and suffered no pain.' Automatically, she repeated, 'He died instantly, and suffered no pain.'

Then amidst a growing storm of shuddering sobs, she cried out, 'He can't be dead! He can't be! He's the only man I've ever loved! He can't be dead!'

She began to shake, her teeth chattering uncontrollably, tears pouring down her cheeks. None of them had imagined that Rose, their self-possessed Rose, could have collapsed so completely. The strongest tower falls heaviest, thought Mrs. Bridges, vainly trying to calm her; and Mr. Hudson, all dignity put aside, held her to him and called her 'My lamb.'

'Daisy, go and put the kettle on,' he ordered. 'Rose will be needing a hot-water bottle and some tea. She is in a state of shock.' He took one of Rose's hands between his, and it was ice-cold. 'Mrs. Bridges, have you anything to cover her?'

'I'll fetch a blanket for her and get me salts as well.'

Daisy, rushing for the kettle, looked back at Rose. Her cap was askew, her face like tallow. She was not aware of any of them, only of the terrible grief that had struck her down. Daisy herself began to cry, praying, as she filled the kettle 'Don't let Eddie die. Please God, don't let Eddie die!'

As Hazel waited for Hudson to answer the morning room bell that afternoon she stood looking into an opened drawer of the desk. In it lay a photograph of Jack Dyson and a pair of Royal Flying Corps pilot's wings. She closed the drawer as she heard the butler enter, his face unusually grave.

'You rang, madam?'

'I should like some tea, please.'

'Very good, madam.' He did not turn to go. 'Madam, I am afraid that Rose has had some very bad news.'

'What is it?'

'About her young man. Sergeant Wilmot has been killed in action.'

'Killed! Oh no! Poor Rose! I must go to her at once. Where is she?'

'If I may suggest it, madam, it might be better to leave her a wee while. Daisy has at long last got her to rest on her bed, and I believe she is sleeping. Mrs. Bridges administered a few drops of chloral.'

Hazel, who had halted on her way to the door, turned slowly away. 'I'm afraid she is considerably upset,' Hudson added.

'She really loved him. I know that. She's talked to me so much about him, these last weeks.'

'I imagine so, madam.'

'I'll wait until she wakes up, and then go and see her.'

'I will inform you, madam.'

The telephone rang. 'I'll answer it,' Hazel said. 'Perhaps you'd make up the fire, Hudson? It's so cold in here.'

He moved away to do so as she took up the receiver.

'Hello? Oh, Bunny! Where are you? Dover? Leave? Oh, I'm so glad for you. James? No, I haven't heard from him for about a fortnight. Three or four days! That's rather vague. *Really?*' Her changed tone made Hudson glance up momentarily. 'Oh, how wonderful! Yes, of course I'm proud, and so will Richard be. It's very kind of you to ring and tell me, Bunny. Enjoy your leave. Goodbye.'

She replaced the receiver and stood still for some moments, before turning to Hudson, who had attended to the fire but was waiting expectantly for some instructions or information relating to the telephone call.

'Major Bellamy is coming home on leave,' she said. 'Lord Newbury wasn't quite sure, but he thought in three or four days' time.'

'Then I will bring up the Major's favourite claret, madam,' Hudson beamed. 'And should I inform Mrs. Bridges? She will be most anxious to do her best for the Major's homecoming.'

'By all means. And, Hudson, you might like to tell the other servants that Major Bellamy has been awarded the Military Cross for his conduct in an action in the Somme battle.'

The butler's face lit up even more. 'The Military Cross! This is indeed a great honour.'

'Ye sit's good news. Poor Rose, though.'

'Yes, madam. May I say, though, how glad we shall all be downstairs that you will soon have a short respite from anxiety?' She seemed not to comprehend. He explained, 'Having the Major safe at home for a while.'

'Oh, yes. Thank you, Hudson.' She could not help her gaze drifting towards the drawer where Jack Dyson's photograph lay. 'I will bring the tea at once, madam,' she heard him say, and he left the room.

She went back to open the drawer and stare into it again.

'What I think,' David said, over the ironing, three days later, 'is, if the Major gets some leave, it's time Eddie had some. He's been fighting in the same battle.'

Mrs. Bridges glanced up warningly from her copy of

Occult, but Daisy was not looking in her direction, and it was too late for Rose to be spared.

'I mean to say, Mr. Hudson reckons it's the worst battle of the war. More people've been killed . . .'

A cry from Rose halted her.

'There!' Mrs. Bridges admonished Daisy. 'You ought to have more consideration for others, jabbering on about people dying in battles.'

Daisy pouted, but tried an apology. It was too late. Rose was in tears again, as she had been, on and off, ever since the news had come.

'Now see what you've done,' Mrs. Bridges snapped at Daisy. 'You can leave the ironing for now, and get off to your room. Leave poor Rose to me.'

As the younger girl went Mrs. Bridges beckoned Rose to her and cradled her like a child. 'There, my lamb, there. She didn't mean to upset you. She just don't know what she's saying. The worst thing that can happen to a respectable young woman is what you've had — but you'll get over it, believe me.'

Rose raised her tear-stained face. 'That's what Mrs. Bellamy said. But I can't believe it. I can't believe it's happened at all. Half the time I just feel numb. Then I have to tell myself he's dead, and it's like getting the letter all over again.'

'Listen, Rose,' Mrs. Bridges said carefully — she had been wondering ever since that first terrible day whether she should, and thought now that she should chance it — 'there are . . . certain people who can receive, well, messages from the Other Side. My friend Mrs. Chambers — she sends me this magazine — she knows one of them.'

Rose stared. 'Spiri . . .?'

'Spiritualists. That's right.'

'But Mr. Hudson says . . .'

'Oh, he's a man. They've different feelings from us women.'

'Yes, but . . .'

'Listen. I felt so dreadful, the day you got your . . . tragic news . . . While you was lying down I popped round to my friend Mrs. Chambers and asked her about this lady she knows. And bless me if there isn't a piece in this very paper about her. See? Madame Francini. Look, it says "Many titled ladies have received consolation for their tragic losses". There! Well, I asked Mrs. Chambers if she thought the lady might be able to help you, and she said it was her considered opinion she could.'

Rose, still on her knees, clasped Mrs. Bridges' hand with the tightness of fearful hope.

'Will . . . will I hear . . . his voice?'

'If you're lucky. Sometimes you have to go several times.'

'I bet it's expensive.'

Mrs. Bridges shook her head. 'Madame Francini never makes it more'n people can afford. You try it, Rose, that's my advice. But no word to Mr. Hudson, mind.'

Rose took the magazine from her and read the advertisement slowly, word by word – wondering.

Two days later she found herself in the darkened parlour of a small house in the Fulham Road. A grey-bearded old man, an elderly woman, a middle-aged woman and herself were the visitors. Their hostess was Madame Francini, an Italianate-looking woman with drawn-back dark hair and intense eyes. They sat round a plain table, the little fingers of their hands touching to form a continuous link. Madame Francini, eyes closed, was breathing deeply, seeming to be far away in spirit. Rose could not take her eyes off her. She was frightened, wishing she had never set foot in the place, despite the friendly reception and the ordinariness of the surroundings and furnishings.

A sharp rap, seemingly on the table's surface, made her jump and gasp. Madame Francini ordered, 'Everybody keep very quiet, and help Mrs. Speedwell to concentrate.' She turned her closed eyes towards the elderly woman. 'Look above my head, Mrs. Speedwell, and behind it.'

Rose looked, too, at the indeterminate landscape picture in a frame, high up on the wall behind the medium's head. To her astonishment, it seemed to glow faintly green, with a luminosity which intensified even as she watched.

'I feel a Presence forming,' the medium's monotonous voice droned. ' A handsome young man. He looks pale . . .'

123

'That's my Billy!' the elderly woman said promptly, eagerly.

'Have you a message for your mother, Billy?' the medium demanded. Another loud rap caused Rose to jump again.

'He's very tall, isn't he?' Madame Francini observed, rather matter-of-factly, Rose thought. She herself could see no young man, tall or otherwise.

'Well . . .' Mrs. Speedwell began, reservation in her tone.

'Tall, that is, compared to you,' the medium amended, rather quickly, and Rose noted a smile of relief on the older woman's face, as she nodded.

'Now Billy,' Madame Francini said, with what seemed to Rose to be unbecoming jocularity, 'Don't be shy. We know you're on the Other Side. We want to know whether you're happy.'

Rose, almost petrified, heard a high-pitched male voice answer from she knew not where: 'Very happy here.'

The light glowed even more greenly around the picture. A look of bliss had transformed the old lady's face, and she cried, yearningly, 'Oh, Billy, my darling, I can see you now. I can. I miss you so. Are you really all right, darling?'

'Quite all right,' the unearthly voice replied. 'All right, but tired. Very tired. Must go now. Must . . .'

Mrs. Speedwell almost leaped from her seat, and the light began at once to fade, as she begged, 'Oh, don't go, Billy! Don't leave me so soon. Please!'

But the light had faded altogether, and Madame Francini was assuring her, 'We mustn't try to stop them. I'm sure he will want to come again – on your *next visit*. Now,' she went on briskly, 'I think I have another message. Is it for the gentleman?'

Two raps rang out in reply.

'No? For another lady, then?'

A single rap, followed by a positive tattoo.

'Steady, dear,' Madame Francini admonished the spirit. 'We quite understand it's for a lady.' She spoke somewhat lower to the sitters: 'Everybody *must* remain very quiet, and concentrate.'

They did, Rose not least, hoping and yet fearing. She raised her eyes slowly in the gloom, and once again saw the greenness tinging the picture on the wall. Then, suddenly, a chilling thrill coursed through her, as a voice, high-pitched enough to have been a child's distinctly piped a fragment of a song:

> *And his ghost may be heard*
> *As you pass by that billabong,*
> *You'll come a-waltzing, Matilda, with me.*

Brief silence followed; then a succession of rapid raps. Madame Francini turned sightlessly towards Rose. 'That's an Australian song, isn't it, dear? Is it an Australian gentleman?'

The song was beginning again, the voice so grotesquely infantile, so unlike anything connected with Gregory's memory . . .

Rose fled from the room, the childish fluting dying behind her. She did not stop running until she reached No. 165, where she almost cannoned into Mr. Hudson as she dashed from the servants' quarters towards the staircase and her room. The butler, who had just taken in tea and the evening newspaper to Hazel, caught the distraught girl by the arm in the hall, urging her with a gesture to quieten the sobs which were now breaking from her.

'Not here, Rose!' he hissed. 'Control yourself, girl.'

She was not to be silenced. Her hysteria was too acute.

'This is no place for such a scene,' he urged helplessly, trying to pull her towards the stairs.

'Where would be the place for it, then? she half-screamed. 'Where? Tell me, 'cos I'd like to know.'

He resorted to the age-old remedy of slapping her face.

Within the morning room, Hazel heard the commotion. It was enough to make her put down the newspaper, at whose front page headline, AIR ACE KILLED, and the name Jack Dyson, she had been staring, and come to the door. Her butler mistook her paleness for anger, and stammered apologies.

'I . . . I'm afraid Rose is . . . is hysterical, madam. She had better go to . . . to her room – at once.'

'No,' Hazel ordered calmly. 'I think Rose had better come in here with me.'

She turned back into the room. Mr. Hudson looked dubiously at Rose, but the combination of his slap and their mistress's appearance had quietened her. Automatically putting up a hand to ensure that her hair was not altogether dishevelled, she followed Hazel into the room. Mr. Hudson closed the doors behind her and went wearily down to the servants' hall again. How much worse, he asked himself, were things going to become before they started to get better?

In the morning room Hazel made Rose sit on the settee. Beside her lay the newspaper which Hazel had had no more than a moment to glance at. Hazel's eyes lighted for a moment on it and its headline. With an effort of will she wrenched her mind away from it. There would be ample time to indulge her own sorrow afterwards; meanwhile, she was almost relieved to be able to blunt the shock by concentration upon another's problems.

'What is it, Rose? she inquired gently. 'Why were you so upset just now?'

Rose had pulled herself together to the extent of weeping no more.

'I went to see Madame Francini, madam. She's a very well known lady. She gets in touch with people on . . . the Other Side.'

'Oh, Rose!'

'She can get messages from them and to them, madam. Titled ladies go to her. I . . . I left before anything happened to me. After another lady had seen . . .'

'I don't want to hear about it, Rose,' Hazel stopped her almost sharply. You mustn't start playing about with such things. Now, promise me.'

Rose hung her head. 'Yes, madam.'

'You see, it only upset you. But, Rose, if there's anything else I can do to help you must never hesitate to speak to me. I know you've suffered a terrible blow, and I do feel so deeply for you. We all do.'

Rose said dully, 'I know Gregory's dead all the time now. Not in waves any more, with forgetting in between. It's come to be the only thing in my mind.'

126

'I do understand how dreadful it must be for you, Rose, but . . .'

'You can't! Excuse me, madam, but you can't have no idea. Since I was thirteen I've lived in other people's houses. I've never ever had a room to myself. I've never had any life of my own, really. I've been in service all my working life – I don't know anything else. Then at last I was going to live in another country, on a farm – be mistress of my own household, with children and a husband to look after. When I was old I'd have had them to look after me. Now I haven't got anything. When I get too old to work I'll have to find a room somewhere. I won't have been able to do more than scrape and pinch through to the end of my life. Before I met Gregory I didn't think about the whole of my life. I never thought I'd meet a man who would love me and ask me to marry him, and offer to look after me. But I did meet him, and that made me think about it, and now he's gone. I'm worse than back where I started now. You'll never be in that position, madam, whatever happens to you, so I can't see how you can understand.'

Hazel had let her talk it out uninterrupted. Now she said, 'Rose, we'd never let you end your days in the way you describe. We're all much too fond of you. I think we all owe you too much for it to be like that.'

'Oh, madam,' Rose said suddenly, 'I'm ever so sorry. I've said terrible things.'

Hazel took her hand. 'You haven't said terrible things – only true ones.' Her glance caught the newspaper yet again, and she looked away quickly. 'I . . . do understand – perhaps a little more than you might realise.' She ached to unburden herself, too. She knew she could do so with safety; Rose would never break a secret. But it wouldn't do. She was addressing herself as much as Rose when she said, 'The first weeks will be hardest, but you'll find that other threads of your life have some meaning. One doesn't forget, but one learns to live with the loss, until very gradually it becomes something that can be accepted.' She felt tears coming to her eyes and fought unsuccessfully to stem them.

'I'll think about what you said, madam,' Rose said, not noticing yet. 'Thank you for letting me talk.' She was getting up when she saw that Hazel was crying. 'Madam! Are you all right?'

'Yes, Rose. It's all right. You may go now. I'll ring when I want anything.'

Rose hovered uncertainly. 'Please,' Hazel urged. 'Will you go now?'

Rose obeyed. When the door had closed behind her Hazel picked up the newspaper. Once again, though, there was noise in the hall. There was no mistaking James's voice, greeting Hudson.

With a sigh, Hazel tossed the newspaper to lie inconspicuously on some others on a table, and quickly dried her eyes before the door opened and he came in.

Hazel was at the breakfast table next morning before James appeared. She had found him noticeably drawn when she had first looked into his face the previous afternoon. Now, though, he was positively haggard.

'You look exhausted, James,' she said, really concerned.

'I didn't sleep last night,' he answered, and the weariness was in his voice, too.

She had been already aware that if he had slept it had not been in their bedroom, for he had never come there. They had greeted one another on his arrival with genuine pleasure and more demonstration of affection than was customary to them; but with the news of Jack Dyson oppressing her she had found herself unable to face dinner and had been glad to go to bed early and remain alone.

Hudson served his breakfast, the principal feature of which was a cold partridge, roasted the previous evening by Mrs. Bridges as a special treat. James ordered his gratitude to be conveyed to her, but told the butler to leave the dish on the sideboard.

'Lady Prudence telephoned early, madam,' Hudson told Hazel. 'She wondered whether you had seen about Lieutenant Dyson in last evening's paper.'

Hazel did not dare look up from her plate as she answered, 'Yes, I did. Was that all?'

'Yes, madam.'

'Thank you, Hudson.'

When he had gone James asked, clearly without any real curiosity, 'Who is Lieutenant Dyson?'

Hazel managed a laconic reply. 'He was a wounded officer who came here to a tea-party Prudence talked us into organising. He is . . . was in the Royal Flying Corps. He's been killed, the paper said.'

He shrugged, as though to sum up the workings of fate.

'Shall you be going to your club?' she asked, glad to get off the topic.

'God, no. I can't face all those old chaps asking me about my medal, and wanting to be told a pack of lies about how the war's going. In fact, the thought of meeting anyone I know fills me with . . . with panic.'

'What do you mean?'

'It's the war. I don't believe in it any more.'

'Do you mean . . . that we aren't going to win?'

He left his chair, his breakfast almost untouched, and roamed restlessly to look out of the window.

'It's not a question of winning or losing. It's the appalling waste – the thousands and thousands of ordinary men who aren't really soldiers at all. Farmers, Post Office clerks, tradesmen – barely more than schoolboys, some of them – simply getting slaughtered like cattle. And for what – a few yards of mud. I remember, when I was at school, I played Fortinbras in *Hamlet*. Some soldiers were fighting for a bit of ground that they said wasn't any use anyway: it wasn't even big enough to bury their dead in. "We go to gain a little patch of ground that hath in it no profit but the name." There can't be any argument, any dispute, that's worth so many people's lives and so much blood. There's something monstrous, evil, mad about it all. It's all bolstered up by nobody here knowing what it's like. Almost some vast confidence trick.'

He turned to regard her. 'You see, even now I can't really tell you how awful it is. We perpetuate the lies. The letters I've written to the mothers and wives of some of my men: "He died like a man – instantly – no pain. His supreme sacrifice will not be in vain". I haven't written a single letter that didn't have one of those phrases in it. All the time, you see, it seems to me clearer and clearer that they've died for nothing.'

Hazel got up and went to where he stood, suddenly feeling an unusual protectiveness towards him. He made no move to touch her; just gesticulated hopelessly with one hand. 'I shouldn't be talking to you like this. It's against the rules. We're not supposed to demoralise the civilian population.'

'You *should* talk,' she insisted, shaking her head. 'You obviously need to tell someone.'

'I've told you hardly anything,' he answered. 'You couldn't stand the actual horrible details. So I spent all last night writing it down. What I feel.'

He took a bulky envelope out of a pocket and held it up. 'Here it is. I want you to keep it safe. If I'm killed, I want you to get it published, somewhere, somehow. Perhaps Geoffrey Dillon could arrange it. I know we . . . haven't understood each other . . . very well, Hazel; but will you promise me that one thing?'

She took the envelope without hesitation. 'I promise, James.'

Each seemed to be looking for something further to say, but nothing came. After some moments Hazel said, 'Now I'd better go and see poor Rose.'

'Rose? What's the matter with her?'

'Her fiancé was killed last week.'

'Not the Australian fellow?'

She nodded. 'She's dreadfully upset. I've tried to comfort her, but I don't seem to do much good.'

'Perhaps I'd better go and see her,' James offered.

'If you feel like it . . .'

'Yes. I shall go and speak to her — very frankly.'

He found her in the servants' hall, seated at the table. A small pile of things lay in front of her, which he guessed at once must be Gregory's effects, forwarded from his unit. She was holding a photograph in both hands, staring at it with a look of utter dejection.

'I'm so sorry, Rose,' he said, motioning her not to get up.

'I was trying to pull myself together,' she explained. 'Then his things arrived.'

He nodded understanding. 'I expect you had a letter from his Company Commander, didn't you?'

She was able to recite its gist by heart: 'It says how much they valued his cheerful and courageous nature, and what a great loss he will be to the Company in which he served. It says he was killed instantly and suffered no pain.'

James's expression gave away nothing of the feelings this too-familiar recital stirred in him. He only said, 'Then that's one mercy, isn't it, Rose?'

She turned to him. 'Yes, sir, I do know it is. But he's gone, you see, and I don't know what it's all for. I mean, if I could understand why he had to die and leave me . . .'

'You must always remember, Rose, that this is the war to end all wars. The greatest sacrifice any man can make is with his life. It places him among the heroes for all time.'

'Does it? Does it really, sir?'

'Yes, of course it does. When the war is over, people will raise memorials everywhere to our glorious dead, in thanksgiving and to honour them. He will be remembered for ever.'

She echoed wonderingly, 'Among the heroes of history.'

'And you, Rose – you've made your sacrifices, too. You've given the man you loved, to safeguard the future for others. It puts you in a very special position, among all the gallant women who have given and lost their nearest and dearest. You should be very proud, Rose, very proud.'

The dullness had left her eyes now: something shone in them in its place.

'Thank you ever so much, sir, for talking to me and explaining things. It's made all the difference. I *am* proud of him. I shall never forget that he's done something good and useful for everyone else – that he's died to make this country safe for everyone. That's what you said, wasn't it?'

'Something like that, Rose,' he nodded. 'Well, I must go upstairs and find Mrs. Bellamy.'

She rose respectfully as he nodded finally and went, swearing inwardly to himself all the way back to the morning room. He saw that Hazel was holding his envelope in one hand and its contents in the other.

'How is she?' she asked.

'Like all the other wretched women who've lost their men-folk. Needing to feel it was in a good cause.'

'James,' she said, 'I've read your paper. I hope you don't mind; but I'm very glad I did.'

'Not really stuff for a woman to read. But did you . . . see what I meant?'

Oh, yes. But it makes me feel . . . that I . . . that I hardly know you. You've changed.'

He nodded and took the papers from her, returning them to their envelope.

'How can you go back to fight now, James? Feeling as you do?'

'It's my duty. I haven't any choice. But I shall feel much better about it now that I've made some kind of gesture to posterity. Even if we have no children of our own, perhaps other people's children will read it one day, and understand.'

He opened the desk drawer to put the envelope away and paused momentarily, seeing the pilot's wings and the photograph. Then he dropped the envelope in and closed the drawer.

As he turned back to her he said, 'I was wondering . . . whether you might like to come out and have some lunch with me? We could go for a walk in the park afterwards.'

She looked up at him from the settee. 'Yes, James.' His hand came out to help her rise. 'Yes, I should like that very much.'

CHAPTER NINE

DAISY was absorbed in a letter from Edward. It was the first for three weeks, and she was reading it avidly, barely conscious of the others at the breakfast-table. Suddenly she gave a joyful cry. 'He's got leave — he's coming home! What's today?'

'December 27th,' said Rose.

' "Leave-boat sails early 31st . . ." New Year's Eve. That's Wednesday.'

'So he'll be here Wednesday night, eh?'

'With a bit of luck.' Daisy was almost weeping with joy.

'Ach, that's good news,' said Mr. Hudson. 'A fine start to the New Year for you, Daisy.'

Rose's face was sad. 'Perhaps 1917's going to be a bit luckier all round than 1916 was. Let's hope so, anyway.'

'Is Edward all right?' Mrs. Bridges asked.

'He says he's been in the thick of it, but he's all right, and hopes we're all in the pink. Poor Charlie, him that was best man at our wedding, he caught a packet but he come back last week fit for duty again.'

'Any more?' asked Rose.

'The rest's a bit private,' Daisy said, tucking the letter inside the elastic of her knickers.

When the morning-room bell rang later that day, Mr. Hudson answered it. Hazel looked up from her desk.

'Hudson, I gather from Daisy that Edward is coming home on leave.'

'That is so, madam.'

'I expect they'd like to have a little celebration in the servants' hall. It'll be New Year's Eve, won't it? I'm sure Captain James would have liked them to have some champagne or something.'

'That would be very much appreciated, madam.'

'Mr. Bellamy and I will be celebrating New Year's Eve very quietly. We'll dine early . . .'

She was interrupted by the ringing of the front door bell. Mr. Hudson answered it and returned with a visiting card. 'A Mrs. Hamilton to see you, madam. Are you at home?'

Hazel looked at it. 'Mrs. Hamilton? I don't know her, but you'd better show her in.'

Virginia Hamilton was petite, in her late thirties but looking younger, and very pretty, with a lively expression and a twinkle in her bright eyes. She looked as if it would take very little to make her laugh irrepressibly, and her manner was what Hazel's mother would have condemned as bohemian; in other words informal. She had barely greeted Hazel before she had dropped her gloves and was giggling as she sought round the floor for them. Hazel, amused, retrieved them, saying, 'Well. How do you do?'

'Oh, how do you do, I'm so sorry . . . I came down on the night train from Inverness and I'm not quite awake yet. It's so hard to sleep on a train, especially if one's berth is over a wheel, which mine was . . . anyway, I must explain why I wanted to call on you.'

'Won't you sit down?' The visitor was still standing, her eyes darting round the room with interested curiosity. She reminded Hazel of a squirrel.

'Oh, thank you. Well, it's your husband I really wanted to see. I need his help. In fact I've travelled from Scotland especially to see him.'

Hazel was puzzled. 'I'm afraid my husband's in France, in the trenches.'

Mrs. Hamilton registered astonishment. 'Oh. I didn't know that. I thought . . .'

'He's commanding a machine-gun company in the Front Line.' Mrs. Hamilton looked as though she had never heard of either.

'I expect,' Hazel said, 'the war seems rather remote and far away from Inverness.'

'Well, it is, a bit. We never see a Zeppelin up there or hear a gun — except on the grouse moors, of course.'

Hazel perceived that if she did not take a firm line they might be there all day, chatting about grouse. 'I don't think you've mentioned yet in what way you feel my husband can help you.'

'Oh. Yes. Well, I've heard he's a very kind man and it's a scheme I've become interested in. Actually we're a Committee of Navy Wives, and we're trying to raise money to start a Trust Fund for educating the children of naval officers killed in action at sea. It's to help pay their school-fees — so many naval officers leave so little money, you know, and . . .'

Hazel interrupted. '*My* husband's not particularly well-off, Mrs. Hamilton, and, as I told you, he *is* in the army. Much as I'm sure naval widows need money, I can't quite see why you've come to us. We do get quite a lot of demands for charity — we've had a family of Belgian refugees in the house, a bazaar for the Red Cross, but quite honestly . . .'

Mrs. Hamilton bounced up. 'Yes, I do see what you mean. I'm awfully sorry. It's just that I was under the impression that your husband was something to do with the Navy. I wonder if I've been given the wrong Mr. Bellamy. This is 165 Eaton Place, isn't it?'

Light broke in on Hazel's puzzled mind. 'Yes. And it suddenly occurs to me that it's my father-in-law you want to see, Richard Bellamy. I'm married to his son, Captain James Bellamy. My father-in-law is Civil Lord of the Admiralty.'

Mrs. Hamilton gasped, her pretty face pink with embarrassment. 'Oh dear! How awful you must think me. It was *my* dear old father-in-law who looked up the address for me. He's up at Aberdarrie near Inverness where I live with my children. So much for fathers-in-law. Well, not yours, of course. Oh, my goodness. I have got it all wrong, haven't I.'

Hazel smiled. 'Well, the address is correct and the name is correct. The only mistake was that my father-in-law lost his wife five years ago. She went down in the *Titanic*.'

'Oh dear. Oh, I'm so sorry. Do you think he'll be in soon?'

'It depends on his work. He's lunching in, so he should be here soon.'

The opening of the first door caused Mrs. Hamilton to jump nervously as Hazel said, 'I think I can hear him now.'

'Oh, good.' But she was very apprehensive. With justification, it proved, for Richard was in no good mood and far from pleased to find a visitor in the house.

'Ah, Richard,' Hazel said. 'May I introduce Mrs. Hamilton, who's called hoping to see you.'

Richard's greeting was curt. 'How do you do?'

She gave him a small warm hand. 'How do you do, Mr. Bellamy? I thought you were your son, wasn't it stupid of me?' Richard did not respond to her smile. 'Oh, indeed,' was all he said. Hazel came to the rescue. 'I've explained the family situation now, and Mrs. Hamilton has a request to make to you.'

'I see.' Richard looked at his watch. 'Have you offered Mrs. Hamilton some sherry, Hazel?'

'No. Do forgive me.' She brought sherry for them all, while Richard invited Mrs. Hamilton, who was still nervously standing, to sit down, and state her request. His tone implied, 'And get it over as quickly as you can.'

Mrs. Hamilton launched into her story, giving him the facts she had given Hazel. 'And being Chairman of the Committee I volunteered to come to London and ask the Admiralty to sponsor the scheme, sort of give us its blessing, and perhaps provide some money to "supplement the privately raised funds" as it were . . .' Her voice trailed off as she took in his lack of response.

'I see,' he said. 'Well, we have a department for dealing with such matters. I'll write the details down for you.' He went to the desk and scribbled a note, oblivious of Hazel's gentle attempt to back up the visitor. 'I think Mrs. Hamilton was hoping . . .' she began, but he had handed the note to Mrs. Hamilton. 'I suggest you put your request in writing to the Clerk concerned. That's the address to write to.'

'Oh. Thank you. How kind.' But she was deeply disappointed. 'I – I suppose there's nothing I could persuade *you* to do in the way of speeding things up?'

'I'm afraid we have many requests of this kind. We can't give priority to any one scheme.' He looked at his watch again.

'No. Well. Thank you.' She finished her sherry in one gulp. 'As soon as I get back to Scotland tomorrow night I'll write to Mr. — Price — and hope for the best. Thank you.'

'Not at all.' Mr. Hudson entered, fortuitously. 'Would you show Mrs. Hamilton out, please, Hudson.'

They all shook hands, Richard briefly and coolly, and Mrs. Hamilton followed Hudson out.

'You weren't particularly kind to that young woman,' Hazel said when the door had shut. 'It seems a long way to come — all the way from Inverness for a scrap of paper.'

Richard broke out irritably, 'I'm sick and tired of these wretched women endlessly pestering one with requests for favours . . . "Can you get my son posted to another ship, will you do something about the food at Dartmouth, can you this, can you that" . . . I suppose it's the price one pays for holding Ministerial Office.' He sat down and moodily looked through the paper.

'What's the matter, Richard? You're not well-tempered today.'

He flung the paper down. 'What in God's name do they think a criminal lawyer from Ulster can possibly know about naval affairs?'

'I believe Edward Carson is a more able man than Arthur Balfour. In wartime, surely an able First Lord is more important than an able Foreign Secretary?'

'I can't agree with you. He's not able. He's no idea how to deal with these German 'U' boats. Yet he won't support the convoy system, which every sailor I've spoken to believes in.' He had been going on in this way for some minutes before he noticed Hazel's downcast face. He broke off. 'You've got the blues too, haven't you?'

She nodded. 'Yes. However, pack up your troubles in your old kit-bag and smile, smile, smile . . .'

'Listen, I've got some tickets for a War Charity Concert tomorrow afternoon, at the Queen's Hall. Why don't we go, you and I?'

Her face lit up. 'Oh, Richard, could we?' She kissed him. 'What would I do without you?'

'I just want to see you smile.'

'It's funny. I've been so much more worried for James this time than ever before. You see — on his last leave, for all

137

sorts of reasons I can't really discuss, I — found a new respect for him, which makes me love him so much more than I used to . . .'

'I'm glad, Hazel. I just wish the news was better.'

'I know. You're not happy, are you? Is it just Carson?'

'Not really. I wanted office, very badly. Now that I'm Civil Lord I'm far from happy. It's being too close to things, I suppose.'

'With no one to share it with.' Richard did not reply.

Next morning, still out of spirits, he was finishing the paper after breakfast, while Hazel scanned a letter, when Mr. Hudson appeared.

'A letter for you, sir. By special messenger from 10 Downing Street.' Richard took it, and read it under the expectant gaze of his butler, whose intuition told him that he was, for once, the bearer of glad tidings. 'From the Prime Minister's Principal Private Secretary,' Richard said. 'Great Heavens.'

Hazel looked up. 'What is it?' Richard was a changed man, in an instant, hopeful and happy, years younger. Mr. Hudson held his breath.

'I've been offered a peerage. A Viscountcy in the New Year's Honours.'

She flew to hug and kiss him. 'Oh, Richard! Oh, how well deserved, how right. I'm so happy for you — oh, it's wonderful news!'

'I've Arthur Balfour to thank for this. And Bonar Law.'

Mr. Hudson could not contain himself any longer. 'Will there be an answer, sir?'

'Is the messenger waiting?'

'No, sir.'

'Then I shall be sending a note round by hand later on.'

Mr. Hudson almost gulped. 'I would be pleased to deliver your reply to Downing Street personally, sir, if you could spare me.'

'Certainly, Hudson. Oh, by the way. This news must remain confidential until New Year's Day.'

'Should I not inform the staff, sir?'

Richard turned to Hazel. 'What do you think?'

'I'm sure they can be trusted.'

Later that morning, during a visit from a congratulatory Sir Geoffrey Dillon, Richard received a telephone call from the First Lord's private secretary, summoning him to the First Lordly presence at three that afternoon.

'Not having you on the carpet, I hope?' asked Dillon.

'I've no idea. Damn it, I was taking Hazel to a concert this afternoon – she'll be bitterly disappointed.'

'I don't wish to depress you, Richard, but you know that a peerage is one way of getting rid of a Minister.'

'I know it is. I assumed Carson was telephoning to offer me his congratulations. Now I'm not so sure. I wonder why he didn't speak to me personally?'

'Well, you'll know this afternoon.'

'Yes, I will.'

It was half-past three when Hazel, who had declined to go to the Queen's Hall by herself, was astonished to be burst in on by Richard, crimson with fury. She looked up from her sewing, startled, as he slammed the door and strode up to the mantelpiece, glowering.

'Richard?'

'That damned woman – I'll strangle her!'

'Who? What?'

'That Scotswoman, who came here yesterday about some wretched education fund for naval officers' children.'

'Mrs. Hamilton.'

'Yes. I've just had a most unpleasant ten minutes with Carson. If you can believe such a thing possible, that woman met the First Lord dining somewhere last night, within a few hours of leaving this house, and told him she'd been to see me, that I'd been most unhelpful and offhand, then started going on about her schooling fund to him.'

'Then she was very sensible. You did nothing for her but give her the name of some Admiralty clerk.'

'I've got other, more important things to do, thank you very much, than listen to stupid, scheming, pushing women. And now Carson's asked me, ordered me, to take up the woman's case, have it gone into and make a report to him personally within a week.' He paused for breath. 'It's outrageous and immoral that such a matter should merit the full attention of a Minister in the middle of the war, with the seas infested by U-boats, merchant shipping going to the bottom every hour of the day and night . . . Who the hell does she think she is?'

'She must have appealed to him somehow.'

'Yes, well, I'll tell you who she is, if you're interested. It explains quite a lot. Steel told me, as I was leaving. Her father-in-law is a second cousin of Beatty's. And I object most strongly that any woman can go behind my back to the First Lord and accuse me of being unhelpful and offhand.'

'But Richard, you were,' she said gently.

He rounded on her. 'Are you taking her part? This — creature, who barges in here unasked and . . .'

The door opened. 'Yes, what is it, Hudson?' Richard barked.

'Mrs. Hamilton is here to see you, sir, if you are available.'

'No, I'm not,' Richard said.

'Yes, you are; you must be,' said Hazel. 'Be sensible.'

He shook his head like an angry bull. 'Very well then. Show her in, please, Hudson. By God, she's got a nerve.'

Virginia Hamilton sailed in, beaming and apparently unconscious that a warm welcome did not await her. 'Mr. Bellamy, please forgive me for coming back so soon, just when you thought you'd seen the last of me.'

Richard's 'Not at all' was icy enough to have put the fire out. Hazel made a hasty escape, under pretence of writing some letters. Richard invited the visitor to sit down rather as if he were suggesting that she kneel at the headsman's block.

'I've come to apologise,' she said. 'I was very distressed when I left your house yesterday, and rather angry, and I'm awfully sorry, but you see this education scheme is terribly important to me. Not for my own children so much — well, Michael, my eldest, is already serving as a midshipman in the navy, and my other two children's school fees are paid by their grandfather, but there are so many deserving cases—'

'I have been instructed by the First Lord to give you what assistance I can. Which I will do. But what I object to most

140

strongly is your choosing to go to Sir Edward Carson behind my back and tell him I've been "unhelpful and offhand." '

'That's what I've come to see you about. It was a wretched thing to do — an unfair way of getting help. I feel deeply ashamed, and I do ask you to forgive me. Please, Mr. Bellamy.'

Her blue gaze would have melted most men's hearts, but Richard's was still encased in hurt pride. 'There's nothing to forgive. I shall simply look into your scheme and make my report. As my Chief has directed.'

There was some desultory conversation about her committee, consisting of herself and a number of other war widows, before she sensed the interview had in fact been over for some time, and, collecting her gloves, got up to go. With relief Richard rang the bell. As she was leaving, he was faintly surprised to hear himself saying, 'When you're next in London, perhaps you'd care to telephone me at the Admiralty. I'd be glad to give you a report.'

Daisy tore down the kitchen stairs two at a time and flew into the arms of Edward, almost knocking him off his feet. As they clung together, Daisy laughing and crying at the same time, Mrs. Bridges tactfully carried the teapot through into the servants' hall, beckoning Rose and Mr. Hudson to follow her. At last Edward disengaged himself and held his wife at arms' length.

'You all right, then, Dais?'

'Yes, yes. Oh, Eddie. I can't hardly believe it.'

'Got a whole fortnight, I have. We'll go out and have some fun, eh?'

He looked happy enough, but there was a subtle change in him which Daisy was too excited to notice. The cheeky boy was a man, and a man who had seen and heard things that the boy could not even have imagined. He looked older, graver; even his voice had deepened. But he was determined that Daisy should know nothing of it. To her, and the rest of the household, he would be the same Edward as before.

'Been a good girl, have you?' She laughed up at him.

'What do you think?'

'I hear the master's been made a lord.'

'That's right. And we're having a celebration down here tonight for the New Year, and you being back on leave. Mrs. Bridges has baked a nice cake special, and there's Mrs. Hall's housemaid from next door, and Lady Newton's kitchen-maid and the odd man from number 169, Jack. So we'll have some laughs and a nice party, and Mr. Bellamy's letting us have a couple of bottles of champagne.'

'Sounds all right. Come on, let's go and have tea with the others.' They went into the servants' hall, entwined, Daisy's eyes adoringly fixed on her husband's face.

The New Year party was all Daisy had hoped. It was in full swing when Rose asked 'Here, what's the time?' Mr. Hudson compared his watch with the clock. 'Seven minutes to midnight.'

'Oh dear,' said Mrs. Bridges with a loud hiccup, 'pardon — we mustn't miss the New Year coming in, must we?'

'Almost 1917.' Rose poured more champagne, and Mr. Hudson raised his glass. 'To our returning hero — Edward.' They all followed his example, and Edward, looking rather dazed and embarrassed, continued to smile and to hold Daisy's hand.

Upstairs Hazel and Richard sat alone by the fire.

'Must be getting on for midnight,' Richard said.

'Yes.'

'What are you thinking about?' He silently cursed himself for asking, but she looked at him calmly.

'A poem . . . I read it the other day. It's called "To the Year 1916".'

'Can you remember it?' He watched her pensive face with mild surprise; it was not like Hazel to read poetry.

'A little.' She gazed into the fire:

> What hast thou brought us? We can see
> Only our hopes and dreams laid waste
> In blood and tears and agony—
> Yet we forbear to judge in haste.

Stunned by the tumult of the guns,
  The frenzied tumult, who can tell
What strange, deep undercurrent runs,
  Perchance, beneath the angry swell
Of the world's madness and distress?
  Not yet thy final fruits appear.
'Tis Time alone can curse or bless
  Thy memory, O dying year.

They were both silent. Then she said 'Richard. Would you think it very dull of me if I went up to bed?'

He glanced at the clock. 'Now? Aren't you going to see the New Year in? It's almost time.'

'I — find it rather sad. I think I'd rather go up, if you don't mind.'

He nodded, and getting up, she kissed him. 'Good night, Richard, and a happy New Year.'

'Good night, my dear.'

A few minutes after she had gone upstairs the clock began to chime midnight. All over London clocks echoed it. At the first boom from Big Ben a cheer went up from night-revellers, and a lesser but resounding cheer from the servants' hall, followed by laughter and happy shrieks and the chorussing of *Auld Lang Syne*, of which only Mr. Hudson sang the correct version. It gave way to the less dignified strains of *Mademoiselle from Armentieres*, accompanied by rhythmic clapping. Richard smiled. They were certainly making a lot of noise down there; it was pleasant to hear people enjoying themselves. He sat, lost in his thoughts, until he found himself cold and yawning. He lifted a still-burning coal to the side of the grate, for economy's sake, turned out the lamps, and set off upstairs.

From somewhere above him came a single loud sob, then another. He looked up. Edward was sitting crouched on a stair, his head in his hands. Richard, concerned, went up and touched his shoulder gently.

'Edward?'

Edward looked up. His eyes were bloodshot with weeping and his face twitched nervously. 'Sir?'

'Why aren't you downstairs with the others? What's the matter?'

Edward tried to control his voice. 'Sorry, sir. Found it . . . just a bit noisy, sir. They're all . . . singing and cheering and that, you see. And I . . . can't stand the *din* . . . got a bit of a headache . . . excuse me, sir . . .' He began to cry again. Richard took his arm and gently raised him and propelled him down the stairs. 'You come with me and sit quietly in the morning-room for a bit.'

Edward tried to pull away. 'Oh no, sir, I'm quite all right, sir, honest.'

'You're not all right. Come on.' In the morning-room he switched on a lamp and sat Edward down in Hazel's chair. 'There. Make yourself comfortable. Whisky?'

Edward nodded. 'Might help, sir. Thank you, sir.' He took the drink and downed it gratefully, while Richard poured one for himself and talked easily, calmingly. 'Mrs. Bellamy's gone up to bed. She doesn't care much for New Year celebrations. So we can have a quiet drink together, eh?'

'Thank you, sir.' Edward put his glass down. 'That's better.' Richard studied the boy's face, fallen into lines of stress, marked with dreadful experience. 'I expect it feels a bit strange, back in this house again, within a day or two of being in the firing line?'

'It does, sir. It's like . . . waking up from a nightmare. Like I was never there, just imagined it all. But I didn't, sir. It's real, all right.'

'You've been in some pretty fierce fighting?'

Edward began to talk, for the first time since he had entered the house. He talked compulsively, rapidly, needing to exorcise from his mind the memories that bedevilled him. 'All the time, sir,' he said. 'Specially October and November, on the Somme. We had over sixty of our lads hit in the first hour one day, going over the top to get back some trenches we'd been pushed out of by the Fritzes. They . . . chopped us up with their machine-guns. Corporal in my platoon had both legs off when we got him in. And Charlie Wallace, my pal, that was my best man . . . he'd only just got back to duty . . .' He stopped, choking. 'When a big heavy shell burst

144

right by him. He was trying to get close to the Boche wire to cut a gap in it . . . and when the smoke cleared we seen him laying there all tangled up in the wire, with his arm off. He had to stop out there all night . . . moaning . . . but we couldn't get out to him, they had the position covered. So he just lay out there all night. In the morning, at dawn, stand-to, we could still see his shape, like, outlined, hanging on the wire, but . . . he wasn't moaning any more . . . He was a wag, was Charlie, sir.'

Richard refilled Edward's glass. 'I expect you'd rather not talk about it, on your leave.'

'It's all right, sir. It helps a bit, to tell someone. I mean, I couldn't tell my family about Charlie, nor them down there. Spoil their fun, New Year's Eve. I'll have to go and see Charlie's family and tell 'em. I – feel a bit better now, sir. I ought to get back down, or Mr. Hudson'll wonder where I am, and Daisy . . .' He got up, staggeringly, but not with drink, and leaned heavily against the wall. 'Sorry, sir. Just come over a bit giddy. Thanks for the whisky, sir.' He smiled faintly. 'Oh, sir, I'm sorry. My lord.'

'Not until tomorrow morning, Edward. Of course it's that now, isn't it. Enjoy your party now – and a happy New Year.'

Edward went slowly back towards the servants' hall, from which song and laughter still rang out. At the door he paused, summoning all his will. Then he opened the door, and bounded in, a clown making an entrance.

'Now, now, now,' he shouted, 'too much noise in the barrack-room, I'll have you all in close arrest. Come on, Mrs. Bridges, give us a New Year kiss, eh?' Laughing, she obliged, and they all closed round him, nearer and nearer, shouting, singing, yelling, louder and louder, until their voices turned into the crash of exploding shells and the rattle and thunder of gunfire.

Edward began to scream.

The doctor, hastily sent for next morning, declared that Edward had had a complete breakdown, caused by shell-shock. Richard found himself in a slight quandary; on the

145

one hand, he realised only too well from his midnight talk with Edward that the boy was quite unfit to return to the Front Line, but would be the last to admit it. On the other, knowing that he, Richard, had the power to intervene, he hesitated. He had never abused his Ministerial power by pulling strings for personal reasons. Should he do so now? He remembered Edward's face as he told the story of Charlie Williams, and his scruples faded. It happened that Geoffrey Dillon was his first visitor on New Year's Day. Richard took him into his confidence.

'Geoffrey, I feel the time has come for me to invoke my Ministerial privilege for once.'

'And get your footman invalided out?'

'Or seconded to light duties. I want you to approach your friend General Nesfield at the War Office, and get Edward medically discharged.'

'I see. What's his name and regiment?'

It was so simple, just a word here and there, a few papers signed, an official form filled up, to save a man's life and sanity.

Geoffrey Dillon came to dine with Hazel and Richard that night. As Mr. Hudson was serving the sherry they were all startled by a great, far-off explosion. The house itself seemed to move, the windows rattled, and there was a flash like sheet-lightning across the sky, visible through the curtains.

'My God, what was that?' Richard exclaimed. He hurried to the window, switching off a lamp as he passed it. 'Put the other light out, Hudson.' He drew the curtains, and they saw the sky to the east illuminated by a fierce orange glow, fading as they watched.

'That's a big fire,' said Dillon, 'if it *is* a fire.'

'Could it be a thunderbolt?' Hazel suggested.

'Too cold for that, my dear. It's down river somewhere. A bomb? Well, whatever it was, we shall no doubt read about it tomorrow.'

Hazel was sleeping soundly that night when a touch and a light in her eyes startled her wide awake. Rose was standing by the bed, in her dressing-gown, her hair loose on her shoulders.

'Rose? What's the matter?'

'Oh, madam, I don't like to wake you — only — Ruby's here.'

'*Ruby*? Where?'

'Downstairs. In the kitchen. She's been in a terrible accident, an explosion, madam.'

Hazel struggled to clear her dream-clouded mind. 'What explosion? Where?'

'Out at Silvertown, where she was working — the munitions factory.'

'Is she hurt?'

'Only shocked, madam. But I think you ought to see her.'

'Of course. I'll come down.' Hazel got out of bed and into her slippers and wrapper.

Ruby, surrounded by her ex-colleagues, in various stages of undress, was a strange apparition. She still wore her coat and thick scarf, but her hat had gone. Her hair stood up on end like that of the newly-invented gollywog toy, but, unlike his, her face was bright yellow, streaked with dirt. She was sobbingly telling her tale to the others.

'I were on night-shift, along far end of t'building, when suddenly there were a great roaring noise and smoke, and something hit me in t'back, and I fell down. Must have fainted. When I come round there was people screaming and crying, and all smoke and broken glass. I could hear flames crackling and . . . there was dead bodies laying around . . . lots of the girls . . . and . . . the older women . . .' She broke down completely, Mrs. Bridges patting her shoulder. Mr. Hudson took up the tale.

'Ruby ran out of the factory across the street to her lodgings, madam, but there was nothing left of the house. We think she must have lost all her possessions.'

'Only her coat and purse, what she had with her,' said Rose.

Richard had appeared, roused by Mr. Hudson. 'That must have been the explosion we heard just after dinner.'

'Yes, m'lord, undoubtedly,' Mr. Hudson replied, reflecting

to himself that one might have expected any factory in which Ruby worked to blow up sooner or later.

Mrs. Bridges had soothed Ruby's sobs into mere snuffles. 'It'll be all right to keep her here now, won't it, madam? I mean, she's learnt her lesson.'

'What lesson?' Richard asked.

'Not to go monkeying about in factories and that.'

Ruby raised a swollen face. 'Never. Never again, sir. I'd sooner stop here.'

'That's right. Where you belong.' Mrs. Bridges put the kettle on.

Hazel and Richard glanced at each other, in silent agreement, as Mr. Hudson said, 'I think Mrs. Bridges hopes that, since Ruby has made her own small contribution to the war outside, she will now be allowed to resume her duties in this house, madam.'

'Of course she will – if she wishes to.'

'Oh, I do, madam. I've missed them all – dreadful. Being here and . . . and . . .'

Mrs. Bridges became her normal self towards Ruby. 'Right, up to your room, girl, and into bed with you. Rose'll bring you up some clean sheets, and scrub that muck off your face.'

'Yes, Mrs. Bridges,' said Ruby happily.

Rose had brought tea to Hazel and Richard in the morning-room, and they were drinking it before returning to their beds.

'Do you know, Richard,' Hazel said, 'When I first came into this house with my typewriter that day in 1912 I thought there was just one family living here – the Bellamy family – and that down below stairs was a collection of slaves; men and women, all working away, like people in factories and mills. But I was wrong. There are two families living here. There's us, the Bellamys. And there's the family downstairs, with Father Hudson and Mother Bridges and their son Edward, "in the army now and so proud of him, we are"; then there's the eldest daughter, Rose, who, alas, lost her young man at the Front – and the two youngest daughters.'

'No. One daughter-in-law, Daisy, Edward's wife, who lives with her in-laws.'

'That's right. And Ruby, the youngest child, rather simple. Perhaps one day, we'll all be one big family, not two.'

'I think we are now, in one sense,' said Richard. 'As for the future, I have my doubts. But then, tomorrow's still quite a long way off – isn't it?'

CHAPTER TEN

MR. HUDSON was not at all pleased when the doorbell rang. He had been looking forward to a peaceful morning catching up with some postponed tasks, such as inspecting the wine-cellar and consigning a quantity of silver and crockery to storage. It was unlikely that any large dinner-parties would be given until after the war. His lordship would no doubt entertain other Cabinet Ministers from time to time, but not on the scale to which 165 had been accustomed. The house-hold was very small now; particularly so at the moment, with Mrs. Bellamy away at Eastbourne, and only his lordship was in residence. It was a nuisance to be interrupted. On the way upstairs the dreadful thought struck him that a messenger with the dreaded telegram might be standing on the step. He opened the door with his heart in his boots.

But it was only Lady Prudence and a gentleman. Mr. Hudson's apprehension gave way to mere annoyance, for Lady Prudence's visits were usually the prelude to some tiresome interruption of routine, such as the tea-party for officers which had resulted in Mrs. Bellamy behaving so frivolously and suffering for it; the staff had not overlooked the news-paper headline announcing the death of the young air ace who had been so briefly her escort.

'Good morning, m'lady,' he said, and was happy to add, 'I'm afraid Mrs. Bellamy is not at home.' But Lady Prudence advanced undaunted, the gentleman behind her.

'Well, we'll just come in for a moment. I want to show Mr. Maitland the drawing-room.'

'The drawing-room, m'lady, is . . .'

'Sheeted. Yes I know. We just want to see the proportions.'

Her companion, a strikingly handsome man radiating charm, handed his hat and stick to Mr. Hudson with a dazzling smile which confirmed the butler's suspicion that he had seen him before, though in quite another setting. Lady Prudence sailing on ahead, they went into the drawing-

150

room. Mr. Hudson followed them, and was alarmed to hear Lady Prudence saying, 'It would suit you perfectly,' and the gentleman replying 'Ye-es. If one imagines all the furniture taken out.'

'Excuse me, m'lady,' he interrupted. 'Would you care for coffee?'

'Oh, yes, what a good idea. Gerald?'

'That would be too lovely.' Another flashing smile, as to an admirer at the Stage Door. Mr. Hudson disregarded it. 'I think you would be more comfortable in the morning-room, m'lady.'

'No, no,' she waved him away. 'We'll have it here, and then we can go on working and planning.'

Alarmed, he reported to Mrs. Bridges and Rose downstairs.

'He's not going to buy the house, is he?' Rose asked.

'I hope not!' said Mrs. Bridges. 'What's his name, Mr. Hudson?'

'I recognised him at once. He is Mr. Gerald Maitland, the actor-manager.'

'Goodness gracious! he's ever so famous,' said Rose.

'I daresay. But we still don't want him buying this house.'

However, Lady Prudence and Gerald Maitland were contemplating quite a different project as they wandered about the dust-sheeted room.

'We could build a little stage at this end,' she said. 'And if we moved all the furniture and got in some little gilt chairs – how many do you suppose we could seat in here? Fifty?'

'Oh, more than that, I should think.'

'At two guineas a head—'

'Or seat.'

'Gerald, really!'

'I wonder if we could get Ivor to play the piano.'

'Ivor who – Churchill?'

'No, Ivor Novello. The composer of *Keep the Home Fires Burning*. Such a talented young man, so beautiful. I do feel that talented people should be beautiful, don't you? That's why I find D. H. Lawrence so depressing. If we are going to do this thing at all it must be simply beautiful, something which people will remember long after the war is over.'

The door opened. Richard, slightly surprised, stood on the threshold.

'My dear Prudence, what on earth are you doing?'

'Oh, Richard.' She advanced and pecked his cheek. 'We're hatching a little plot, and we want your approval. This is Gerald Maitland. Gerald, I don't think you've met Lord Bellamy.'

Gerald made beautiful noises significant of joy and apology combined.

'We were going to have it in Wimborne House,' Lady Prudence said, 'but it was bombed in that dreadful raid, and so many other big houses have been hit — really, one would think the Germans had a map. We were in despair. And then I thought of you.'

'But what exactly . . .?'

'Tableaux, Richard. A matinee of historical tableaux, in aid of the Red Cross. We're getting them up among ourselves. The Duchess of Mitcham has written the words, and Connie and I are to be responsible for the rest of it.'

'I didn't think there *were* any words in tableaux.'

'Well, you know, a sort of accompaniment, in rhyming couplets. We shall sell seats at two guineas a head, and take up a collection as well, and we should make quite a nice little sum for the Red Cross.'

'Surely it would be simpler just to ask for donations?'

'Oh, I know that's Hazel's view — that no one should have any fun over raising money. But people will *always* come to see their friends making fools of themselves — not that we're going to do that, of course, because we have our dear Gerald to advise us, so it's all going to be a great success. Now, we *can* borrow the drawing-room, can't we?'

'But, Prudence, with Hazel away . . .'

'That's just the point. Hazel is away, and by the time she gets back we shall have given our little performance. There! That's settled, and now we can really get to work.'

Being Lady Prudence, this was no sooner said than done.

That afternoon a dressing-up box from somebody's attic was spilling its contents on to the Bellamys' drawing-room floor. Lady Prudence and Lady Constance Weir were trying on and rejecting certain items, to the accompaniment of hammering from an elderly and badtempered carpenter working on the stage area.

'Who's to be Florence Nightingale?' Connie Weir asked.

'Well, Dorothy promised, faithfully, but now she's been asked to play the Virgin Mary at the Gaiety, and she flatly refuses to do both.'

Connie thoughtfully tried on a picture hat. 'Inviting Dorothy to portray the Virgin Mary is like asking Henry the Eighth to play a celibate monk.'

'Perhaps that's why the idea appeals to her so much. Maud's to be Cleopatra.'

'*Maud?*'

'She's – very swarthy.'

'Yes. You'll have to shave off her moustache, or they'll think she's Antony.'

'I thought her husband could be Antony.'

'Is that the little man with a squint?'

'No, that's her cousin. I thought he could be Nelson. Well – he'll have a patch over one eye.'

'Yes, but which eye?' They dissolved into laughter, in the midst of which Richard entered.

'That's a very attractive hat, Connie.'

'Do you like it? Good. I thought I might wear it for Lady Hamilton. It's just like the one in the painting where she's sitting in a cave looking pensive.'

'Oh. I thought your programme was to be called *The Hero's Farewell*?'

'It is,' Prudence said. 'The hero's farewell to his wife or – or lady – love. Nelson and Lady Hamilton. Antony and Cleopatra. Christopher Columbus and Queen Isabella.' Richard's face was a study in puzzlement.

'To please the American generals,' Connie explained.

'We still haven't solved our main problem,' said Connie. 'Who's to be Florence Nightingale?'

At that very moment Mr. Hudson was opening the front

153

door to Georgina, a striking figure in Red Cross uniform and cape.

'Miss Georgina! What a pleasant surprise. You were not expected until next week.'

'Hello, Hudson. I had to change leaves with another nurse who was getting married, and there wasn't time to let you know.'

'Allow me to take your bag, miss. Did you by any chance encounter Captain James in France?'

Georgina's complexion betrayed her; her cheeks flushed a deep, wild-rose pink. 'Well, yes, actually I did.' She talked very quickly, conscious of her blush. 'He came to collect me at the hospital – it's a chateau, really – and we had supper together.'

'I hope he was well, miss?'

'Well? Oh yes, very. He sent love to everyone here.' She remembered that evening, the stars in the summer sky, the wine they had drunk in the little estaminet, their talk about Hazel, and James's marriage, and themselves, and the long kisses with which they had parted. The benevolent proprietor had enquired of James, in a whisper, whether they required a room for the night. She had often wished since that James had said yes, though of course that wasn't . . . She was recalled to the present by hearing Hudson say, 'Lady Prudence has – if I may so express it – struck again.'

'What? You mean all that hammering? Whatever is going on?'

'In the drawing-room, miss. Lady Prudence—'

'Don't tell me. I'll find out for myself.'

Entering the drawing-room she passed the carpenter, muttering to himself. He had just resigned. Prudence greeted her joyfully.

'Georgina, my dear! Just the very person we need. You can be Florence Nightingale.'

When Lady Prudence made her mind up there was very little to be done about it. That was why, two days later, Georgina found herself meekly helping to drape a large Union Jack

154

across the back of the improvised stage, while Rose and Daisy put up the curtain. The carpenter, after receipt of a large gratuity, had consented to come back to the job, and the stage machinery was now in reasonable working order.

Prudence surveyed a gilded cardboard breastplate. 'I suppose the Crusader will have to have this, but we really need it for Antony. Now if Antony wore this purple tunic, and had a sword . . . we really need a round shield.'

Rose turned on the ladder. 'When we were children we used to use saucepan lids. There's a big one downstairs.'

Lady Prudence recoiled. 'Antony saying farewell to Cleopatra, carrying a *saucepan-lid*?'

Daisy spoke up. 'You could use the copper-lid, m'lady.'

'Run and fetch them both, Rose,' said Georgina. 'Bring everything that looks like a shield.'

Rose collected all the likeliest lids from the kitchen, then suddenly caught sight of the clock. 'Oh no! I must go and change. I'll never get to the depot on time. Ruby, you'll have to take them up. And get the lid off the copper — take that up as well.' She vanished up the stairs.

Mrs. Bridges was scandalised. 'A kitchenmaid in the drawing-room! I never heard of such a thing.' But Mr. Hudson decided otherwise. Bashfully, Ruby went upstairs, clanking.

The Duchess of Mitcham, a bustling little lady who was in charge of the production side of the pageant, arrived in the drawing-room just as Lady Prudence was trying on a German helmet, with curious effect.

'What's this I hear about Celia Bedlington playing Belgium?' she asked. 'And who's this?'

Lady Prudence introduced Georgina, whom the Duchess surveyed without enthusiasm. '*She* won't do for Belgium, either.'

'No, she's playing Florence Nightingale.'

'Too young, but I suppose she'll do. But I absolutely refuse to allow Celia Bedlington to play Belgium. We need an innocent, open face. Celia looks like a ferret — all those Bedlingtons do. Belgium must be represented by a simple peasant girl. The whole point of the scene is the contrast between the gallant British Tommy with his tender, womanly wife, and the brutal Hun — who's playing the brutal Hun?'

'Er — Prudence is,' said Connie.

Prudence looked embarrassed. 'We're rather short of men.'

'Yes. Well, keep your back to the audience. Just an impression of jackboots and evil, and beneath your upraised hand, innocent and helpless, a simple country girl, her face full of terror and dismay.'

Right on cue, Ruby appeared at the door, her arms full of saucepan lids, which, as all eyes turned on her, she let fall with a fearful clangour. Her simple peasant face was full of terror and dismay.

The servants were working so hard on preparations for the tableaux that a little extra nourishment would not have come amiss at mealtimes. But unfortunately they were about to be exposed to yet another of the horrors of war. Mrs. Bridges had been to a War Cookery lecture, which had so fired her that she had produced a Win-the-War pie, a combination of things which would otherwise have been thrown away. The general feeling at the table was that they should have been. Even Mrs. Bridges, proud as she was of her economy, was not quite able to finish what was on her plate.

The day of the dress rehearsal saw a new offering to patriotism. Mr. Hudson eyed the dish set down in front of him with ill-disguised revulsion.

'*Faggots*, Mrs. Bridges?'

Mrs. Bridges bridled. 'Certainly not. We've never served faggots in *this* house. Them are meatless rissoles. Oatmeal, onions and yesterday's gravy.'

'I think I'd rather have faggots,' said Rose, wistfully picturing those objects despised at aristocratic tables as being made from 'offal', but in fact extremely tasty.

Mrs. Bridges snorted. 'I'm sure Mr. Hudson will approve, oatmeal being his national dish.'

Mr. Hudson smiled feebly. 'Yes, Mrs. Bridges, but not — er — customarily in rissoles.' He eyed hopefully the two vegetable dishes; at least they were getting vegetables, which in the Win-the-War pie had been nauseously combined with the other ingredients. Daisy lifted one lid and they were gratified to see a healthy, normal dish of cabbage. But beneath the lid of the other lurked a strange, greyish substance. Nobody said anything, until Mrs. Bridges volunteered 'Potato substitute.'

'How can you make potato substitute?' Rose asked.

'Ground rice, flaked maize and milk.'

'But a little while ago they was asking us to use potatoes instead of flour,' said Daisy.

'Yes, but now there's a shortage of potatoes, so they've asked the better-off householders to leave them for the poor.'

'I wish we was the poor, then,' Daisy muttered under her breath to Rose. Mr. Hudson bowed his head in his hand, as though in intercession to the Deity to make him truly thankful, however difficult it might be, for what he was about to receive.

The dress rehearsal was in full swing. People in costume and out of it were swirling about in the drawing-room, a Crusader in woollen chain-mail, his lady in a tall pointed hennin, looking, as the Duchess bitingly said, like a fox wearing a dunce's hat; Nelson with the wrong eye covered by a patch, a falsification necessary because of the actor's unfortunate squint, and Hardy having trouble with his hat, which kept coming down over his eyes. Gerald Maitland's temper was reaching its limits. Everything had gone wrong that could go wrong, even with a bunch of amateurs. The carpenter had been retained only by means of a series of bribes, and the curtain still didn't work smoothly, while the lighting was unpredictable. The scene in which Georgina, as Florence Nightingale, stood by the bedside of a wounded Crimean soldier, played by her officer friend Philip Manning, had been so repeatedly marred by outbursts of giggles on the part of nurse and patient that Gerald had stalked out in a monumental huff.

Lady Prudence was sad because Hudson had refused to wear the kilt. It would have made his appearance so much more interesting. But at least the servants were helping with arrangements, and Edward looked particularly appropriate in his blue hospital uniform. It was a pity that Ruby was so extremely dim, but at least she *looked* right. And Rose, Daisy, Mrs. Bridges, Mr. Hudson and Edward were obligingly providing a stand-in audience for the rehearsal. The room was shuttered, its floor-space full of small gilt chairs, the curtains were drawn across the stage, and the Duchess stood beside it, in the person of the British Muse, wearing a flowing white robe with a Union Jack on the bosom.

Gerald clapped his hands sharply. 'Now, come along, everyone. This is only a dress rehearsal, but let's pretend it's the real thing. And audience, I want applause after each tableau, please. Ready?'

Reluctantly and jerkily, the curtains parted, to reveal The Death of Nelson, who reclined stiffly in the arms of Hardy, now on reasonable terms with his hat. The Duchess declaimed sonorously.

> The Hero of Trafalgar sinks at last,
> Here in the *Victory*, all battles past . . .

She stopped and addressed Gerald. 'You see, that is a little pun on the word "Victory", because it refers to the ship *and* to the battle.'

Gerald drew a deep breath and said, with great self-control, 'Yes, Duchess. Go on, please.'

'Shall I start again at the beginning?'

'No. Just – *go on*.' She went on:

> Dying, one sight springs up before his eye . . .

Gerald called to his lighting assistant. 'Now, bring the light up *very* slowly.'

> His lovely Emma, waving him goodbye,

finished the Duchess, as a dazzling beam flared up like a Verey light, revealing Lady Connie, gracefully poised in the traditional attitude of Lady Hamilton seeing off the British Fleet. As the light hit her she gave a loud shriek and threw her arm over her eyes.

'Not like that!' cried Gerald. 'Gradually, gradually, for Heaven's sake. Hold your pose, Connie, please.'

'But my mascara's running.'

'Never mind. Now, let's see if we can get the curtains right this time.' Edward, in charge of the curtains, worked them closed and open, while faint applause cheered him on. Again and again the curtains were opened and closed, until Gerald was sufficiently satisfied to let the next tableau be staged. The Duchess rendered her Crimean epic.

> He breathes his last on Balaclava Height,
> Cheered at the end by one unfailing light;
> What though his eyes be dim, his forehead damp?
> Beside him stands the Lady of the Lamp.

And there was Georgina, touchingly pretty, gazing tenderly down at the young officer dying becomingly in a scarlet uniform, both, by a mighty effort of will, keeping straight faces.

'All right, on to the finale,' Gerald said.

'What's the finale?' Mrs. Bridges whispered to Mr. Hudson.

'I fancy it's Ruby,' he replied in tones of some apprehension.

Just at this point Richard appeared, and sat down beside Georgina and Philip. 'How's it going?' he asked.

'Awful. We feel such idiots.'

'You didn't look too bad.'

'Wait,' said Philip, 'till you see Lady Prudence as a German soldier.'

'Good gracious!'

'What are you going to say in your Introduction, sir?'

'My what? If Prudence thinks I'm going to . . . where is she?'

The curtains parted, and it was obvious where she was. Her back squarely turned to the audience, her slim form clad in field grey, the awesome German helmet on her head and her long legs in jackboots, she looked, as Rose muttered to Daisy, not half bad. She was menacing with a bayonet the kneeling form of Ruby, in gingham dress and peasant handkerchief, looking up at her with a sheepish smile, while a British Tommy, embracing his girl-wife, pointed to 'Belgium', and the Duchess spoke for him.

> The rape of Belgium by the evil Hun
> Brings to her aid each gallant British son.
> Forgive me, love, I must to her succour;
> I loved thee not, loved I not honour more!

Everybody found this impressive but the producer. He advanced upon the actors.

'Just a minute. Belgium, you're not supposed to be smiling.'

Ruby turned a face of limpid ignorance towards him. 'Beg pardon, sir?'

'I've told you before, you're supposed to look terrified.'

Ruby beamed gratefully. 'Oh, yes, sir.'

'Well, *look* it! You're about to be raped, girl. *Raped*!'

'Don't, Gerald, you're frightening her,' said the Brutal Hun.

'I'm *trying* to frighten her. Am I frightening you, Belgium?'

Ruby simpered. 'Oh, no, sir.'

Gerald's control slipped finally. 'God Almighty!' he shouted. 'Will *nothing* make you look startled, horrified, alarmed?'

As though on cue, there was a tremendous, shattering explosion. The noise of splintering wood and shattering glass filled the air, the great chandelier in its linen bag rocked wildly from side to side, and a cloud of dust came showering down from the cracking ceiling. Amid shouts and screams, Mrs. Bridges clutched Mr. Hudson's arm. 'Oh, whatever is it?'

He pulled her to her feet. 'It is an air-raid, Mrs. Bridges. Quick, all of you, towards the doors.'

Ruby, her face now the very image of startlement, horror and alarm, began to shriek like a fog-siren.

Somehow, amid the noise and the dust and confusion, Mr. Hudson got everybody shepherded downstairs. Mrs. Bridges put a sharp stop to Ruby's automatic screams, kettles were boiled, and the great anodyne of tea soothed everybody's nerves.

Everybody's, that is, until the boom of the anti-aircraft guns started up outside, and Edward, his hand poised to light an oil-lamp, began to shake uncontrollably. 'Oh my God! Oh my God!' he was saying, over and over, when Daisy came into the kitchen to find him. Quietly she took the lamp and the matches from him, carried them into the motley assembly hob-nobbing in the servants' hall, and, returning, led him into the little glory-hole cupboard under the stairs. He tried to resist her. 'I'm all right, Dais, really I am.'

'But I'm frightened of the bombs,' said his wily wife.

'Not bombs. Guns.'

'Yeh, well, whatever they are, I'm frightened of 'em. Let's get in here. Now, you put your arms round me, and I'll be all right.'

The most incongruous sight in the servants' hall, outdoing Antony and Cleopatra, the Crusader and his foxy lady, and the now normally squinting Nelson, was Lady Prudence still in her German uniform.

'Really,' said Lady Connie, 'with all those devils raining bombs down on us it's too bad of you to sit there wearing their uniform.'

'I can't very well take it off,' returned Lady Prudence with reason.

'At least you could take the helmet off.'

'I expect Prudence thinks it might give some protection,' said Richard laughing.

'Exactly,' said Lady Prudence. 'But if you insist—' She had just removed it when another crash from the guns rattled the ornaments and sent the pictures askew. Hastily she resumed it, to the accompaniment of a roar of laughter. War had drawn them all closer together; even the Duchess, who had probably never seen the inside of a servants' hall in her life, was chatting affably to Mrs. Bridges, who, however, observed with alarm Mr. Hudson putting on his Special's greatcoat.

'You're never going out in this?' she cried.

'It is my duty, Mrs. Bridges. I must report to the nearest police station. I shall be perfectly all right. Don't allow any of the guests to leave before the All Clear.' And he went out into the darkness and the thunder of the guns. She watched him with a face heavy with misgiving.

Rose was having tea with Gerald Maitland, which was not many rungs of the ladder away from dancing with the Prince of Wales. He had nobody else on whom to exercise his charm at that moment, and she had been one of the only people to give him no trouble during the entire tiresome exercise. He treated her to one of the smiles which had caused so many swooning vapours among the young females of England, and she capitulated utterly.

'Are you frightened?' he asked tenderly.

'Oh no, sir. Perhaps I should be, but I'm not.'

'There. You see, I said you were a heroine when I saw you in that very fetching uniform.'

She was thrilled. 'Oh, not me, sir. But I've been out in a few raids on my omnibus, and . . . well, I reckon either you get it or you don't.'

He eyed her, feature by feature. 'You're very brave. And very pretty.'

She looked down.

'Hasn't anyone ever told you you're pretty?'

'Well . . .'

'I'm sure there's some gallant soldier who's looking forward to coming home to you when the war's over.'

Her eyes met his. 'I was engaged to be married, but – he was killed.'

'Oh no. I'm so sorry. How you must have hated our silly charade.'

'No, sir. I thought it was beautiful.'

'I don't know how to put it. I think sometimes it helps people to see something that isn't . . . too real.'

He shrugged and smiled. It was the perfect justification for the non-serving actor in wartime.

Outside a policeman was shouting 'All clear! All clear!' In the servants' hall people began to move, to drift upstairs guided by Rose with a lamp, still in their tableaux costumes, for it would be impossible to sort out their own clothes in the bombed drawing-room. Lady Prudence, aware of the impression she might produce on passers-by, thankfully borrowed Richard's overcoat. Soon they were all gone, in search of taxis, into the blackout.

Edward and Daisy emerged from the glory-hole. He looked sheepish. 'I'm really ashamed of myself, Dais, it was hearing the guns. It took me right back.'

She squeezed his arm. 'I'm glad. Everything that happened

162

to you out there — I couldn't share it. But this — we was in it together.'

He kissed her, and she responded eagerly. 'Dais, you're the best little wife a man ever had.'

Daisy giggled. 'It's just as well Mr. Hudson didn't see us, cuddled up in there.'

'Mr. Hudson? What does he know about it? He's not even in the army.'

When Mr. Hudson arrived home he looked tired, and seemed disinclined to talk. 'Was there much damage?' Mrs. Bridges asked as she made his cup of tea. He looked at her blankly. 'Damage? Another bomb fell at Hyde Park Corner. Quite a number of people were killed and injured.'

'Oh, dear.'

'They'd left the shelter before the All Clear, and that was just when the bomb fell.'

Daisy, coming into the kitchen as the lights went on again, found him sitting slumped in his chair, his eyes shut, pale-faced. She shouted for Edward, when he failed to respond to her calling him, and Edward, beginning to lift him up, found blood on his hand.

'He's been hit, Daisy! Quick, tell his lordship!'

Fortunately the hospital pronounced the wound was not serious. A graze from a piece of shrapnel had caused Mr. Hudson to lose a lot of blood, but he was perfectly fit to return to his duties next morning provided he kept his arm in a sling. Richard, meeting him in the hall, told him not to worry about the battered condition of the house. 'I'm sure Mrs. Bellamy won't care about that, once she knows that *we* are all safe. But if you're really fit for it I wonder if you'd come and look at the damage upstairs, so that we can decide what's best to be done.'

'Certainly, m'lord.' They were on their way up the stair-case when the bell rang. Rose, who was nearest, answered the door.

'Mr. Hudson! Telegram. For the mistress.'

Richard came downstairs. 'All right, Rose. I'll open it.'

Georgina, in her morning wrapper, appeared behind him as he slit the envelope. There was no need to ask what was in the telegram. Richard's face was enough.

'James!' Her hand went to her throat.

Richard spoke flatly. 'Missing. Believed killed.'

CHAPTER ELEVEN

JAMES had been missing for over a week. Day after day the household waited for news. Mr. Hudson was away on a police course, and Edward, now something like his old self, and back in khaki, was acting as voluntary second-in-command to him. Nobody had much heart for anything, even an unexpected bonus of bacon; and Hazel hardly ate or slept. A letter had arrived from Georgina, who was nursing in the Passchendaele sector, reporting that she had seen no sign of James, who would almost certainly have been brought to her hospital. 'So that's good news of a kind, isn't it?' Richard said to Hazel, affecting a cheerfulness he didn't feel; the news had a distinctly bad side when one remembered shell-holes and the numerous ways in which a body could disappear. Hazel shook her head, then said, 'Have you spoken to the War Office this morning?'

'No. I don't want to pester them too much.' He saw with pity her heavy eyes and pale face. 'Didn't you sleep, my dear? I slept quite well, for some reason. I don't believe it's all over. Do you *have* to go to your canteen today?' He glanced out at the bright frosty winter morning, the bare trees glittering in early sunshine. 'It's a beautiful day. Why don't you go for a walk in the Park?'

'If I'm alone I think of *all* the possibilities, and I can't get comfort from any of them. It's better for me to be at the canteen. I – read through all his letters last night. I wanted to feel him alive, but . . . they were all so formal, so military. I felt, for the first time, positively, that we'd never see him again.' As Richard began to reason with her the telephone rang. She turned away sharply as Richard answered.

'Yes, Edward. Yes, put him through, please.' To Hazel he said, 'It's the Regimental Adjutant.' After a few words on the telephone he said to her, 'Will you be here at four o'clock this afternoon?'

'Yes, I can be.'

He thanked his caller and put down the instrument, carefully assuming his calm cheerful expression. 'James's servant is back on leave – Trooper Norton. Philip thought he should come and see us.'

Trooper Norton was tall, handsome and silent. As he stood in the servants' hall beside the big suitcase which had belonged to James ('had'?) nobody quite knew what to say to him. 'Well,' Edward ventured, 'leave it there and I'll take it upstairs and unpack.'

'I'd like to do that myself,' Norton replied. 'Get it unpacked.'

Edward accompanied him and watched nostalgically as Norton impassively extracted one after another familiar object from the suitcase. His proprietary instincts made him want to take the uniform and the shirts from the Trooper, put them in their accustomed places. It seemed all wrong that someone else should be doing it. 'I used to valet for Major Bellamy,' he said, into the silence. 'Country house weekends. Before the war. It's been terrible here this week. Not knowin'. 'Course I was able to tell 'em what it's like – goin' over the top. I was at the Somme. Middlesex Regiment. 12th Battalion. 18th Division, Corporal Barnes. You must have bin there as well.'

'Yeh, I was.' He went on grimly unpacking. It was a relief when Hazel entered and greeted Norton, who said, 'I took the opportunity of bringing back some of the Major's personal belongings, madam.'

'Yes, I see.' Dully she stared at a packet of letters in her own handwriting.

'The Post Corporal asked me to bring them, madam.'

It seemed like the last shovel-full of earth on James's coffin; except that he wouldn't have one, she thought, and one of the dreadful images that haunted her flashed into her mind. 'You seem to have given him up, then. Please come down and see Lord Bellamy.'

Before Richard, Norton told his story without emotion. 'We'd come up to the line that morning, m'lord. In a right downpour. We was near Poelcapelle or Passchendaele, I think. Anyway, there was woods in front of us, and Fritz was in 'em. Some of our guns had bin knocked out, but Major Bellamy told us we had to get to this objective, this ridge. So over we went — and it was all havoc broke loose. We couldn't move fast because of the mud. And before we'd bin goin' a few minutes, there was a great explosion . . .'

Richard was listening intently, anxious for the least clue. 'You were quite near Major Bellamy, just before this?'

'Yes, m'lord, about twenty paces away.'

'And after the explosion?'

'I couldn't see him. There was a lot of smoke.'

'And it was late afternoon? Dusk?'

'No. Just after lunch, m'lord, and raining hard — pelting down, something rotten.'

'And you didn't actually see him hit. Did anyone?' Hazel asked.

'Not actually, madam, but . . . well, Corporal of Horse Willis thought he saw him fall into a shell-hole — crater — and I heard somebody shout "The Major's bin hit". Corporal of Horse Willis went to try to get him, but just then we gets the order to withdraw. The Boche was comin' for us. We scrambles back behind the line, and Corporal-Major Baker says it's hopeless goin' to get him now, we'd have to wait till dark.'

Hazel sighed. It was an ordeal having to ask and listen, but it had to be done. 'What happened that night?'

'Nothing, madam. We was joined by some Lancashire Territorials, and it wasn't till the next afternoon we got back again. We searched for our old position, but the rain had messed everything up and the trees were all splintered by the gunfire. We couldn't find any trace of him.'

'But if you couldn't find him,' she said eagerly, 'and you didn't find his body, then he could have been taken prisoner!'

'That's what we was all hopin', madam, but . . . Trooper Apthorpe said he'd heard from a sergeant in the Irish Guards they'd seen a German officer goin' round shootin' all the wounded that day. There was a grudge on and no prisoners were taken.'

Richard and Hazel did not look at each other. Then Richard snapped, 'We don't have to believe Trooper Apthorpe's gossip. It's quite possible to survive four or five days in a shell hole, even in bad weather and with very little food. We're hearing stories of it every day. If he'd merely been wounded, he could have been picked up by French, Australian, Canadian forces . . .'

'But General Nesfield has been checking all that, Richard. And there's nothing. Nothing.'

'I still refuse, without any proper evidence, to believe James is dead.'

Hazel turned to Norton. Her eyes and voice were bleak. 'But you believe he is, don't you, Norton? And his Regiment believes he is, because they've sent all his belongings back.' Norton said nothing, only looked at his feet.

'Well, Norton.' Richard was finding determined optimism more and more difficult. 'If you've nothing further to tell us, perhaps you'd better return to your barracks.' Norton rose and stood to attention.

'I'd just like to say one more thing, m'lord. Major Bellamy was admired and respected by all who served under him. He was certainly the best officer I've had the privilege to serve under, and there was no shortage of volunteers to go back and look for him, when . . .' A very slight crack in his voice was the first sign of emotion he had shown.

'Thank you, Norton,' said Richard, meaning it. He knew sincerity when he heard it. When Norton had left, Hazel began to cry, and Richard put his arms round her.

It was easier for Georgina to wait for the news which might never come, one way or the other. The field hospital which had once been a graceful chateau was in a constant state of violent activity. Every few minutes a new wounded case was brought in and lined up for attention or prepared for the operating theatre. Nurses dashed to and fro, dealing with the demands for help, soothing men who cried out continually with pain, taking them water, adjusting bandages; too often covering the face of one who was beyond aid. Georgina was very tired. About to go off duty, she went into the staff room where Surgeon-Major Rice, a middle-aged man who had perfected the art of concealing his own stresses beneath a faintly facetious professional manner, was checking Sister Menzies' list of operations to be done that night.

'Nine in a day. It'll be an all-time record.' Sister Menzies, Scottish, stern of aspect and ultra-efficient, poured him tea, containing the condensed milk at which he made a routine face. 'Using tea as a stimulant is not healthy.' But he drank it gratefully, glancing back at the list. 'I don't know who's more unfit for this next operation, the surgeon or the patient.' He departed for the operating theatre, as Georgina's friend Jenny came on duty, casting her a flirtatious smile as they passed, and receiving a hero-worshipping smile in return.

Taking off her rain-soaked cloak, Jenny said, 'You won't need the extra candles tonight, Sister. We can keep the lights on – there'll be no air-raids in this weather. It's coming down in torrents.'

'Don't shake that cloak in here, please, nurse,' Sister replied. 'You're not a spaniel. And quickly to your duties. You're late.' She bustled out. 'How's it been?' Jenny asked Georgina.

'Awful. I'm exhausted. Private Nicholls has gone. And the young French officer at the far end.'

'Go and get some sleep.'

'I can't wait to.' She trailed out, and Jenny went into the ward to start her spell of duty, seeing as she did so the only vacant bed being claimed; two orderlies were carrying a wounded man towards it.

'Get that one ready first,' Sister snapped, and Jenny started towards him. He was in a dreadful state, filthy and soaked, his uniform in rags, blood everywhere from a cruel wound in the thigh. The first thing to do was to give him a tetanus injection. Then Jenny began to get him out of the soaking clothing. From the torn jacket pocket fell some limp papers. Picking them up, she stopped in her work, staring, and suddenly left his side and began to run down the corridor, oblivious to Sister's cries of 'Nurse! Where are you going? Come back.'

But Jenny was running and shouting, 'Georgina, Georgina!'

until she caught up with her at the end of the long passage. Then they were both hurrying back, and Georgina was bending over the bed, wiping the mud and blood from the face of the very sick man who lay there, oblivious, in a raging fever.

'Jumbo?' she whispered. 'Oh, Jumbo.'

The news came to Hazel by telegram. 'James alive. Very ill. But in good hands. Hopeful. Love Georgina.' Richard confirmed it by a telephone call at the Admiralty from Nesfield. They were almost incoherent with joy. The staff were equally speechless, and frustrated by knowing no details. They stared at a photograph of him in the morning paper.

'Nice picture of him,' said Daisy.

'What are his wounds?' Ruby asked ghoulishly.

'Doesn't say.' This was Edward.

'Probably doesn't like to.' Ruby ruminated. 'Probably lost an arm or leg.' Mrs. Bridges pushed her chair back with a sharp scraping sound. 'You keep quiet about that, Ruby. Come with me, my girl.' It made a difference, Mr. Hudson not being there to preserve decorum and keep the discussion on a dignified level. Rose stared across the table at Edward. 'You've seen what happens to 'em, haven't you,' she said.

Edward looked uncomfortable. 'The wounds, you mean. Yeh, I have.'

'I don't think I could bear it if he lost an arm or leg.'

Daisy looked at her in surprise. 'We'd all have to get used to it.'

'Better to be killed outright. Got to die sometime. Better to have a memory of somebody whole, than see 'em livin' only half a person.' It was a sort of consolation to keep thinking that. She dared not admit that Gregory alive though maimed would have been better than Gregory dead.

Richard, who had just put the telephone down, cast a speculative eye on Hazel. 'What on earth did you say to Geoffrey Dillon the other day?'

Hazel looked innocent. 'You mean when I went to see him — about James's affairs, in case . . . well, I told him the happy news, of course.'

170

'I know that. But did you say anything about the possibility of going out and bringing James back?'

'Well . . . I may have mentioned it. Yes. I did.'

'Mentioned it. Yes. Well, Geoffrey "mentioned" it to my dear mother-in-law, and *she* mentioned it in a very prompt letter to Lord Derby, and the result is we have a private ambulance with our own driver and a trained nurse ready to take us across to France this coming Thursday morning; and there's nothing we can do about it.'

Hazel's face was alight with joy. 'But that's wonderful news!'

'Hazel – you don't seem to understand my position. A member of the Government, a peer, is seen to be pulling every known string to get his son back from a field hospital, while the sons of thousands of ordinary families up and down the country have to wait their turn into the hospital ships . . .'

If Hazel had not been so happy and so completely determined to accept whatever gifts the gods might hand out in return for the black days of waiting she would have felt real exasperation. Men! Politicians! Idiotic creatures who put public opinion and what-the-P.M.-will-think and all that sort of nonsense before the life or death of their own flesh and blood. It was all too silly, and she felt sometimes that since Richard had been made a peer he had become just the least bit pompous.

She smiled sweetly at him. 'You owe it to James to do everything in your power. We must have the best doctors money can buy. After all, you pulled strings for Edward.'

'We didn't send out a private ambulance to a field hospital to bring back Edward!'

'Well, then – can't it be made plain that Lady Southwold has requested it?'

'The whim of an aristocratic old lady? They'll see it as a flagrant abuse of privilege.'

'Lady Berkhamstead sent one to get back her nephew.'

'I am not interested in Lady Berkhamstead. She is nothing to do with the Government.'

Hazel's fine eyes flashed back the message 'And I'm not interested in the Government – only in my husband!' Aloud

171

she said coolly 'All right. I'll go alone and fetch him back. I'll carry the burden of guilt for you.'

On Thursday morning Richard was meekly waiting for her by the converted Rolls-Royce as she emerged, warmly furred for travel. It had become clear to him that it is never the slightest use arguing with women, and he earnestly hoped it would be a long time before they got into ministerial office.

They stared, horrified, at the sights and sounds of the field hospital. Hazel had seen plenty of casualties before, but none so new, or so near the scene of action. Legless, armless, blinded, or supine on stretchers, they were all around, as though humanity itself were reduced to this. It was a relief to see the starched figure of Sister Menzies approaching them down the corridor. 'I'm pleased to meet you, my lord,' she said in a tone which conveyed quite the opposite. 'I'm Sister Menzies. Mrs. Bellamy.' She led them towards the Staff Room. 'Major Rice, the surgeon who operated on your son, wishes to speak to you. He's just finishing another operation.'

'Could I see my husband?' Hazel said eagerly.

'Well . . . Yes, you can. But only one of you at a time, and for a short while.'

James was lying very still, wax-pale, his head bandaged, his eyes closed. She sat down by the bed and spoke to him softly. 'James? Darling? It's me, Hazel.' He made no sign of hearing her; she took his hand and held it. From the other side of the ward Georgina saw the scene, out of the corner of her eye. There was a fractional pause before she crossed over and kissed Hazel lightly. 'Hello. I heard you were coming.'

'How is he? He looks awful. Is he conscious?'

'He was in pain last night – he's been given quite a lot of morphine. I'd rather we didn't wake him at the moment.'

Hazel, who had risen to greet Georgina, saw her slip neatly into the vacated chair and wipe James's brow professionally. The action said more clearly than words 'This is my place, not yours.' Hazel, with a backward look, returned to the Staff Room.

Surgeon-Major Rice greeted her, finished washing his

hands, and got out James's notes. 'Now then, your son, Lord Bellamy. Shell-wound in right thigh, gangrenous. But we've managed to stop the infection spreading, and the leg should be spared, unless there's any late change. A piece of shell grazed his forehead, just above the left eye. Superficial – clearing up all right. Our main concern about him was shock, exposure. He'd been wandering about all over the place, it seems. He's got some temporary paralysis, and he's had a high fever. But I'd say he's probably over the worst. Just needs to lie still.'

Richard, feeling happier after this cool summary, went to look at James, and returned with Georgina, who accompanied them out of the chateau afterwards. 'Can you dine with us?' he asked her.

'Love to – but I'm on duty. Perhaps tomorrow night. Things are fairly quiet at the moment.'

'We still don't know what happened to James, do we,' Hazel said.

'I know a little. He came round for a few minutes last night, and said something about being in a shell-hole, and a German officer – and then being taken prisoner, and escaping.'

'How amazed he must have been to find you looking after him.'

'Yes,' added Richard, 'probably thought he was dreaming.'

Georgina only said 'Yes,' and avoided Hazel's eye. By the splendid ambulance they stopped. 'I do hope you'll be comfortable at the village inn,' she said politely. They embraced, and Hazel asked, 'Will we see you tomorrow morning?'

'Afternoon. I come back on duty at four.' She was looking at the transformed Rolls. 'I love this ambulance – if that's what it is. Did someone give you a ride from Boulogne?'

Hazel looked surprised. 'It's ours.'

'Or to be more accurate,' said Richard, 'Granny Southwold's. She hired it specially for James.'

'For *James*? I don't understand.'

Hazel was just a little pleased to enlighten her. 'To take him back to London.' And Richard, seeing Georgina's puzzled face, said 'My dear, didn't you realise? That's what we're here for.'

'Take him *back*? When?'

Hazel spoke quickly. 'As soon as possible. Tomorrow or the next day. As soon as the doctors allow it.'

'Have you asked them?'

'Not yet.'

Georgina ceased to be a relative and became a nurse, crisp and disapproving. 'I'm afraid there's no chance of him leaving. He's still very dangerously ill. He must have complete rest – he mustn't be moved for several weeks yet.' Suddenly she turned on her heel and walked swiftly away.

The decision, of course, was in the hands of Major Rice.

'Well, the leg wound's clean. No more treatment needed, apart from the normal dressings. But the body needs its own time to mend, and I can't predict how long that will take, nor what effect a journey will have.'

'We have a trained nurse accompanying us,' Richard said, and Hazel added, 'And another one waiting at home.' Major Rice debated with himself.

'If he were my son . . . well, let me just say, if you want to risk it, that's up to you. But don't blame me if he doesn't survive the journey.'

'I accept the responsibility, naturally,' Richard said.

Georgina, coming on duty, saw that the ambulance had been reversed and was now backed up to the main entrance, where a nurse and the driver were preparing a stretcher under Richard's eye. Horrified, she rushed past them and into the ward. Jenny was encasing the drug-hazy James in blankets, and Hazel, standing by the bed, was smiling down at him. 'Darling.'

His eyes flickered open. 'Hazel?'

'It's all right. You're not dreaming. We're taking you home.'

Georgina, furious and frantic, had swept up to her. 'You *can't* take him. He mustn't be moved. You'll kill him if you move him!'

Hazel surveyed her coolly. 'We've spoken to Dr. Rice. It's all right.'

'Dr. Rice doesn't have to nurse him. Look at him. Can't you see how ill he is?'

'We have our own nurse. He'll get the best care, I promise you.'

Georgina could barely speak for angry distress. 'The roads are – mud-heaps . . . treacherous. Even if he gets to Boulogne he'll never survive a sea-journey. Oh, can't you realise?' (Can't you realise he needs me, I'm the only one for him, sick or well, I love him and I want him and I've saved his life? Get back to England and leave us alone!) Hazel understood the unspoken words perfectly. Sister Menzies interrupted the altercation. 'What's the matter here? Nurse, is the patient ready?' Georgina turned to her. 'Sister, tell her, please, that he mustn't go. He'll die if they take him.'

'It's already been decided,' the Sister said. She was the final Court of Appeal. Georgina pulled herself together.

'I see. He'll need another blanket.' She watched the orderlies wrap him in it, settle him on the stretcher, and carry him away towards the door. Then she followed, and walked by his side to the ambulance. On the way she passed Hazel, ignoring her completely. Outside, the inert figure was placed in the ambulance, the nurse entered it, and the doors were shut. Richard kissed Georgina. 'Goodbye, my dear. And thank you for all you've done for James.' But Hazel said nothing, only gave Georgina's cheek a token peck before getting into the passenger-seat.

The ambulance moved lumberingly away down the bumpy drive.

Mrs. Bridges was in her element. She had opened her special recipe book at the 'Invalid Diet' section, and was busy making a selection of draughts and dishes for the nourishment of James. She looked up as Nurse Wilkins, an efficient woman with a firm, pleasant manner, came down the stairs.

'Oh, nurse. Can you spare a minute? I just wanted your opinion on the matter of diet.'

'We shall have to see how the Major is when he arrives, shan't we. But in any case, plenty of liquids.'

'That's what I thought. Well, I've got a nice chicken broth for his first supper, and then of course there's beef-tea — I always swear by that . . .'

Nurse Wilkins smiled. 'Yes, of course, an excellent pick-me-up, but we must remember that it is a strong stimulant, and must be alternated with other foods, not given continuously.'

Mrs. Bridges nodded, running her pencil down the page. 'Well, there's my German Egg Soup, that's very nice, and Barley Broth, and I've sent Ruby round to Mr. Goslin's to see if he can let me have some calves' feet for jelly. When the Major gets a bit stronger I can do him milk-stewed fish, or a Veal Panada, and pigeons is very strengthening . . .'

'Well, let's wait and see.' The door-bell rang and Mrs. Bridges jumped up in a flurry. 'Oh my goodness, that'll be them already. Go on, Edward, hurry.' Followed at a more sedate pace by Nurse Wilkins, Edward sped upstairs and opened the front door, near to which a wheel-chair was waiting in readiness. Richard and Hazel stood outside.

'Oh, Edward,' Richard said. 'Major James is in the ambulance, on a stretcher. Will you help the driver bring him in?'

'Of course, m'lord.' Hazel, in the hall, greeted Nurse Wilkins, thankful to see such a capable-looking being. 'How was the journey?' enquired the nurse, though Hazel's tired drawn face told its own story.

'Rather an ordeal, I'm afraid. I only hope . . .' she looked apprehensively towards the door, through which Edward and the ambulance-driver were carrying a still form on a stretcher. Rose appeared from upstairs.

'The room's all ready, madam.' Her gaze was fixed on the stretcher. Mrs. Bridges and Ruby had appeared in the hall, and were hovering by the pass-door to catch a glimpse of the sick man. Their eyes rounded with horror at what they saw.

'Up to his room and straight to bed,' Richard was saying.

Downstairs again, they were all shocked and despondent.

'I've never seen anybody looking so ill in all my born days,' said Mrs. Bridges, mechanically stirring the chicken broth, and cutting two fine slices of white bread to accompany it.

'Death's door.' Ruby enjoyed a drama, but she was deeply

affected. The Silvertown explosion had taught her what pain and mutilation were like.

'Ah well,' said Mrs. Bridges, 'his supper's ready. Who's going to take it up?'

'I will.' Daisy stepped forward, but Rose's hands were already on the tray. In fact neither was to have the honour, for Nurse Wilkins was approaching briskly. At the sight of the tray she shook her head. 'He won't want any of that, I'm afraid. Mrs. Bridges, could I have some boiling water, please?'

Boiling water? The servants exchanged fearful glances. That usually meant some kind of medical emergency. Sighing, Rose put the tray down again, and plucked up courage to ask, 'Is he going to be all right, nurse?'

Nurse Wilkins took the covered jug Mrs. Bridges had just filled. 'Oh yes,' she answered brightly, 'with a lot of rest and care.'

They breathed a unanimous sigh of relief.

James was awake. Only his eyes moved, roving round the bedroom, taking in the familiar surroundings. Hazel came in, and sitting down by the bed took his hand. He pulled it fretfully away, and pointed towards a vase of great golden chrysanthemums. 'Flowers,' he said weakly.

'Yes, aren't they beautiful. Rose says the florist told her . . .'

He tried to shake his head. 'Scent . . . reminds me . . . smell of gas. Sorry.'

'Of course — how stupid of me.' She got up and put the flowers outside the door. In fact, she had no idea what the poison-fumes smelt like; how should she? Something in her mind gave a small wince of pain at James's rejection of the very first thing with which she'd tried to please him since his return; but she smiled and gave no sign. James pointed to the dressing-room. 'You . . . sleeping in there?'

'Yes. I thought you'd rather be alone. If you need anything, there's a little bell here for you to ring.'

He nodded. 'Poor darling. Nurse. Not wife.'

'Oh yes! Nursing you back to health is part of a wife's duty, a happy part.'

His eyes clouded dreamily. 'Georgina?'

'She stayed at the hospital in France,' Hazel said shortly. He looked quite different when he spoke of Georgina. 'They . . . were all in love with her . . . in the ward . . . all wanted to marry her,' he said.

And you? asked the voice in Hazel's mind. Were *you* in love with her? Did you think how much you would have wanted to marry her, if I hadn't been in the way? Or didn't you let that stop you? There had been something, some hint in what the landlord at the inn near the chateau had told them, how Mademoiselle Worsley and her cousin made such a handsome pair, when they dined at his hotel, how he had taken them for fiancés, sweethearts, had even (here he roared with Gallic mirth) ventured to whisper to the Major that a room would be available for them if required. And when Hazel had somewhat coldly identified James as her husband, M. Bully had become suddenly quiet and gone hastily away to his kitchen.

She laid her head down on James's arm. 'I love you,' she said.

It was not long before James recovered sufficiently to be thoroughly cantankerous. The furious ringing of his bell brought Hazel and Nurse Wilkins in, to be told that he was hungry, the plaster-of-paris on his leg was itching, and the jug on the chest of drawers was so ugly that it must be removed at once. Mrs. Bridges' pleasure, when Hazel told her in the kitchen that the Major wanted something solid to eat, was touching. Hazel, cutting bread for a ham sandwich, turned to her.

'One forgets — so concerned for oneself, it's awful — how marvellous you've all been, and I've scarcely given you a thought. As soon as possible, I want you all to have an outing of some sort, as a mark of my gratitude. Would you like to go to the theatre? The music-hall? There's *Zig-Zag* on at the Hippodrome, with George Robey.'

Mrs. Bridges beamed. 'That'd be very nice, madam. I'm sure the others would appreciate it, too.'

'Then I'll make it my special treat.'

Hazel opened the letter from Georgina with some trepidation, but it was a very innocuous one, expressing pleasure that James was getting on so well, admitting that she had been wrong about letting him make the journey, love to all, and so forth. James seemed uninterested. He was, to Hazel's alarm, getting himself slowly and painfully out of bed.

'What on earth are you doing?' she asked.

'Getting up. Is Edward around? I need some help getting downstairs.'

'James, you can't.'

'Yes, I can. I want to surprise Father – it's his birthday. I've been planning it all night. Want to be downstairs, with champagne, when he gets home. Come on, give me a hand and get Edward up here.'

Somehow they got him downstairs, and brought up the champagne, and gave him a glass of it to refresh him after his efforts. He was in a good humour, having got his own way and caused a great deal of anxiety to other people in the process. He raised his glass to Hazel.

'You're my medicine. And this, being home, surrounded by good care and attention. Thank you, Edward.' Edward retired.

'And my love,' James added, putting his arm round Hazel's waist. They kissed. Then he said, 'Will you do something for me? When Father comes in, will you leave us alone together? It's so long since I've had a talk with him.'

'Yes, of course I will.'

The servants had gone off to the Hippodrome and the house was quiet when Richard returned. Hazel, hearing his key in the door, had left James in the morning-room and gone up to her own room. Richard was utterly taken aback to see James not only downstairs, but cheerful-looking and slightly flushed from the champagne.

'Hullo, Father. Happy birthday.'

'My dear boy – what a wonderful surprise. I was going to ignore my birthday, but this is the best present I could have wished for. Are you really feeling better, or are you playing truant with the doctors?'

James was, in fact, feeling very weak, and heavily overshadowed by the cloud of black depression which had followed him from France. But he laughed it off. They talked of the Rolls-Royce ambulance, and James settled Richard's fears that he might have resented the special treatment he had been given. 'Don't feel too badly about it. Mother would have insisted on it. Anyway, why shouldn't I be borne in splendour? It damn nearly killed me, anyway.'

'Georgina thought it was going to.'

James looked thoughtful. Bits of the scene in the chateau had registered with him, in a dream-like way, as had the look on Hazel's face when he had first mentioned Georgina after coming home. 'Oh yes. There was some sort of — well, scrap — between her and Hazel, wasn't there?'

'Nothing serious. They were both concerned for you in their different ways, that's all.'

'Nice to know someone was.'

Richard repressed his annoyance at such unwarranted bitterness. 'My dear boy, if you knew how many people were asking after you daily . . .'

'Yes. One forgets the other side of it. You must have had a frightful time of it here. How long was I missing?'

'At least a week. Can you remember what happened to you?'

James poured himself another glass of champagne. 'I remember a few things very clearly, but the rest is confusion. I remember the shell-hole, and the mud, waist-deep . . . and hours of waiting. There was a German staff officer, when I was in the shell-hole. He was working his way through the trees, after the attack, killing off our wounded with his automatic. He was coming towards me, nearer. I tried to get my Webley out of its holster, but I'd no strength to my fingers. He saw me. He was standing just a few paces away — it was him or me. He raised his pistol, took careful aim, and I was fumbling with the damned trigger. I was done for — I knew it.'

Richard's hand, holding his glass, was shaking.

'We stared at each other, and then — inexplicably — he dropped his arm. He stood there, watching me, while I finally got a grip on the trigger and fired. I blew the top of his head

180

off. Why didn't he kill me? I can only think he was killing the worst of our wounded humanely, to spare them suffering, and he saw me, and I didn't look so bad. Is that why? I felt we were brothers, or even the same person, and it didn't matter who killed whom. It wasn't important.'

There was a silence. 'And then,' Richard said, 'you were taken prisoner and you escaped.'

'Was I? Yes. A Boche patrol took me to one of their dressing-stations. I got up, and walked out into smoke and chaos. Nobody stopped me. Kept walking, God knows where.'

'You walked mercifully straight into the path of a Canadian unit. They took you to a dressing-station, and later to Georgina's hospital.'

'Yes. That's all. And what happens now doesn't matter. It has no meaning.'

'You mustn't say that. You've been spared. You have so much to contribute, when the peace comes . . .'

'The peace is for grandfathers – and grandsons.'

'And survivors.'

'Don't count on them to put the world to rights.'

Richard put a hand on his shoulder. 'Between us, James, we can do it. Grandfathers, grandsons, survivors, all helping each other. You owe it to us to try.'

James was shivering and the champagne flush had faded. 'Well,' he said, 'at least we're talking, Father. That's a start. But I'm afraid . . . this fizz isn't going down very well, after all. I think . . .' He was shaking badly now. 'I think I must – go back to bed. Can you help me?'

Richard caught him as he slumped forward. 'My dear boy! I'll ring for Edward.'

'No. They're all out. The servants have gone to a music-hall, Hazel's buying your present, Nurse Wilkins is off duty. Just you and me.'

'Come along then.' James got into the wheel-chair and Richard said: 'You know – when I was in that shell-hole . . . I could feel Mother's presence – more strongly than anything else. I didn't know whether she was protecting me or whether she'd come to claim me. It didn't matter. She was there.'

'She was here too,' Richard said softly. He wheeled the chair into the hall, got James out of it, and then, taking the full weight, his arm beneath James's shoulders, he helped his son up the stairs.

CHAPTER TWELVE

ON 23 April 1918 – St. George's Day – a Royal Naval and Marine Force succeeded in the audacious task of blocking the entrance to the Belgian harbour of Zeebrugge, one of Germany's principal U-boat bases for operations in the English Channel. A simultaneous operation at Ostend failed; but the news of the Zeebrugge success, involving stirring deeds of individual heroism and implying a sharp curtailment of German naval activity in those waters, raised morale in Britain markedly.

It was a much needed tonic. On land the Germans were advancing inexorably towards Paris. Retreating Allied forces left behind them hundreds of guns and thousands of dead and wounded to add to the already horrifying tally exacted by getting on for four years of war.

Field Marshal Earl Haig found it necessary to address a special order to the army: 'There is no course open to us but to fight it out. There must be no retirement. With our backs to the wall and believing in the justice of our cause each one of us must fight on to the end. The safety of our homes and the freedom of mankind depend alike upon the conduct of each one of us at this critical moment.'

It sounded uncomfortably like some sort of preparation for an admission that it had all been in vain.

Mr. Hudson, thoroughly *au fait* with the situation from his close study of events but nevertheless maintaining his best efforts to bolster up morale below stairs, scanned Richard's face anxiously as he took his coat and hat. He would not have presumed to ask how the prospects for defeat or salvation were viewed at Whitehall, but he constantly hoped, or feared, that he might read something in His Lordship's countenance that would tell him more than any newspaper headline.

He never had, and did not on this occasion. Lord Bellamy's face bore no marked expression, until the butler told him, 'There is a visitor in the morning room, my lord.'

An enquiring eyebrow was raised. 'Oh? Who?'

'I believe she is an acquaintance of Mrs. Bellamy, m'lord. A Mrs. Hamilton.'

Frowning with the effort of trying to place the half-remembered name, Richard was just turning towards the morning-room doors when Hazel greeted him from the stairs as she descended.

'How's James?' he asked. 'Shall I go up, or . . .?'

'Not now. He's asleep. He had another go of the horrors this morning. Dr. Foley came and gave him an injection.'

He grimaced unhappily, but she took his arm reassuringly. 'Anyway Virginia Hamilton's here.'

'Virginia . . . Hamilton?'

'You remember. The widow from Scotland, about the naval charity.'

'Oh, no! Not again!'

Hazel's expression was grave. 'It's nothing like that this time. Richard, she's in terrible trouble. We must help her. She came off the Dover train in a state of near-collapse and came into my canteen. I insisted she came back here.'

'Why? What's the matter?'

'Her son — the one in the navy. He's going to be court martialled.'

Richard passed a hand across his face. 'Hazel, my dear,' he almost pleaded, 'I am Civil Lord of the Admiralty . . . the very last person who can interfere in any way with a naval court martial.'

'I'm not asking you to interfere,' she told him. 'Only to help.'

In the morning-room Mrs. Hamilton looked up from her teacup beside the fire and began to rise at Richard's entry. He waved her down, forcing warmth into his tone. 'Mrs. Hamilton — how nice to see you again.'

He had, indeed, forgotten how nice she was to see, with her trim little figure, melting blue eyes and bonny Scottish complexion. But her return smile was only fleeting, and as she sank down again her whole bearing reflected deep despondency. Hazel took her the aspirins she had been upstairs to fetch, and Mrs. Hamilton took them thankfully, washing them down with tea.

'I'll be quite all right now, thank you,' she murmured. 'I really must be going. I've done nothing but make a nuisance of myself to you twice.'

'Nonsense,' Richard told her, as Hazel gave him his tea. 'Mrs. Bellamy tells me there's some trouble over your son. A Midshipman, wasn't he?'

She nodded. 'Promoted acting Sub-Lieutenant last month – above all his term. It was pathetic how pleased he was, poor Michael. Since he was tiny he's never had any thought in his head except to join the navy and follow the family tradition.'

Richard seated himself beside her. 'Then?'

'A couple of days ago I had a telegram to say he was under arrest at Dover.'

'On what charge?'

The single word had to be forced out. 'Cowardice.'

Richard recognised at once how carefully he must tread. Through the years of the war there had grown mounting disquiet about the interpretation of supposedly cowardly behaviour, with allegations of injustice and counter-demands for more rigorous application of military law for exemplary purposes. It was a highly delicate area of debate; yet he felt himself impelled at least to hear what this distressed woman, whose former behaviour had irked him so much, had to tell.

'Do you know why?' he asked.

'Not exactly. Michael was on a coastal motor boat in some action against Ostend . . .'

The failed action on the night of Zeebrugge, Richard told himself. It had not been stated publicly, but everything pointed to the enemy's having been forewarned.

She went on, 'Something happened to Michael, but . . . It sounds so silly, I know, but I couldn't find out the details. No one down there could talk about it. Even some of my late husband's old friends. They were very kind but . . .'

'The matter's *sub judice*. Understandable. Mrs. Hamilton, have you a good lawyer?'

'In Edinburgh – though he's rather an old fuddy duddy.'

Richard had reached a decision before she finished speaking. 'Edinburgh's rather a long way away, and my advice — *not* as Civil Lord of the Admiralty, you understand? — my advice is that you see a good lawyer quickly. If you would like me to recommend one . . .'

'Oh, but it would be troubling you.'

'. . . Sir Geoffrey Dillon is both a very good lawyer and a personal friend. I'll telephone him with pleasure.'

He read her thanks in her look, and went over to the telephone, turning as he raised the instrument. 'Just to begin with,' he said, with half a smile, 'you may think he's a bit of an old fuddy duddy, too.'

'You know,' Sir Geoffrey remarked with satisfaction as they returned to the morning-room for coffee after dinner that evening, 'I thought that sweet was delicious. Such a change to eat things not swamped in cream and sugary sauces.'

He was the only one of that opinion. Faced with orders for dinner for two unexpected guests, and not enough of the meat ration left, Mrs Bridges had deliberately got out her war recipe book and given them cabbage leaf soup, Victory oatmeal rissoles with potato substitute, followed by the sugarless rhubarb tart. And she had let a thrilled Ruby do all the cooking. Mr. Hudson had taken it upon himself to convey Mrs. Bridges' apologies for the 'somewhat patriotic nature of the dinner'. No one had commented. All except Sir Geoffrey were too preoccupied to care.

No discussion of the matter troubling them had taken place over the table. Now, however, with his coffee and brandy beside him, Sir Geoffrey at once opened his black case and produced a slim bound volume. He looked over his spectacles at Virginia Hamilton.

'Mrs. Hamilton, I have found out what I could in the short time available to me. The proceedings come under the Naval Discipline Act, Part One: Articles of War, paragraph two. "Misconduct in the Presence of the Enemy." I managed to have a word with the Judge Advocate, and I have the precise charge. Shall I read it?'

Virginia nodded.

' "For that he, Acting Sub-Lieutenant Michael Drury

Hamilton, then being the Officer commanding His Majesty's Vessel Coastal Motor Boat 47B . . ." '

'Commanding?' Richard queried.

Sir Geoffrey looked at him balefully: 'I believe the Commanding Officer had been killed.' He read on, ' ". . . and being a person subject to the Naval Discipline Act, on the twenty-third day of April nineteen hundred and eighteen, from cowardice, did not during the action between His Majesty's Fleet and the Fleet of the German Empire in his own person and according to his rank encourage his inferior officers and men to fight courageously." ' He lowered the book, and looked directly at the unhappy woman.

'Mrs. Hamilton, I was able to arrange for your son to come here this evening – under escort, of course. He is due quite soon. In the meantime, however, I should be grateful if you would tell me how you see him – as a person.'

His tone was kindly, encouraging. She thought for a moment, then answered, 'Rather shy . . . if you don't know him. But, underneath, very brave. To me, he's thoughtful, unselfish . . . funny: my other children adore him.'

'When you saw him at Dover, what did he say to you?'

'Not much, I'm afraid. He didn't seem able to talk about anything, except how terribly sorry he was that he'd let . . . his father down.'

Sir Geoffrey almost tossed the volume into his case, and said emphatically, 'Clearly, the less he has to do with his own defence, the better.'

'Whom do you suggest, Geoffrey?' Richard interposed. His old friend assumed an uncharacteristically coy expression. 'Well, the regulations demand no specific qualifications. You may have heard the old adage that in every solicitor there's a barrister pleading to get out. I, er, confess I would be interested to see how the Royal Navy conducts its legal affairs – that is if I were acceptable to you, Mrs. Hamilton.'

'Oh, of course, Sir Geoffrey. How kind . . .'

She was interrupted by the opening of the door by Mr. Hudson, his expression a mixture of bewilderment and concern.

'Sub-Lieutenant Michael Hamilton . . . and . . . er . . . escort,' he announced.

After introductions, Richard and Hazel bore Virginia Hamilton off to another part of the house. The escorting officer, a trim young man in uniform, with the formal addition of a sword, was accommodated with brandy and coffee on a chair outside the morning-room doors. Within, Sir Geoffrey and Michael Hamilton talked alone.

'I was lying on the deck,' the seventeen-year-old boy was explaining haltingly, as the lawyer took notes. 'I was . . . sort of . . . shivering. I was very frightened.'

'What were you thinking?'

'I was hoping no one would notice, and trying to pull myself together. But Chief Webb came and knelt beside me. I think he thought I'd been wounded. He told me the skipper had been killed. That meant I was in command.'

Sir Geoffrey nodded and waited. The pale, good-looking boy went on: 'I knew perfectly well it was my duty to go to the bridge and take over . . . but I . . . I couldn't move. My body . . . it just wouldn't move, somehow.'

'So what happened?'

'I managed to say something and Webb went away. He didn't say anything. He's a ripping sort of fellow — was my navigation instructor when I was a Middy — but he knew I was funking, as well as I did. Well, when the firing had stopped I felt all right again. That's the worst part, in a way. It's no good shirking the truth, sir. I behaved like a rotten coward, and I shall simply have to say so.'

Sir Geoffrey slowly put his propelling pencil away. 'It seems to me you have said a great deal already. Are you willing to have me to defend you?'

'Of course, sir, thank you. But what can I say, if I know I'm guilty?'

'You will plead "Not Guilty". You will not be required to speak in your own defence. I shall do the talking. The officers of the court will be senior naval officers, and frankly much better able to judge your behaviour than you can yourself.'

'I . . . see, sir.'

'From now on, keep your mouth shut, except to me. And now I want you to write down every single thing you can remember about that night. Every single thing.'

'Very well, sir.'

He began the task, while Sir Geoffrey quietly watched. Outside, in the hall, the escorting officer yawned comfortably and winked at Daisy, who had crept wide-eyed up the stairs from the servants' hall to goggle at his sword. She retreated at once.

The telephone shrilled in the butler's pantry soon after breakfast next morning. Mr. Hudson answered it and almost recoiled.

'Edward! What on earth are you doing speaking on the telephone?'

'Please, Mr. Hudson,' he heard the anxious voice at the other end, 'it's urgent. Can I . . . speak to Daisy, please? Just for a mo'?'

Struck by the effrontery, Mr. Hudson could only reel away to find Daisy in the kitchen, and shoo her away in the direction of the telephone.

'Edward,' he told Mrs. Bridges. 'Telephoning!'

'What! Well, I never did!'

When Daisy reappeared a few moments later Hudson addressed her in his severest tone: 'I would like to make it clear to you, and you make it clear to Edward, that never again under any circumstances may he telephone this house. That instrument was not installed for us. It is for the use of those upstairs, and no one else.'

'He said he was sorry, Mr. Hudson, but it was a . . . emergency.'

'What sort of emergency?' Mrs. Bridges demanded.

Daisy looked at the floor. 'He . . . won't be able to get down here today.'

'I don't call that an emergency.'

'He wants me to get a bus and go up there to him . . . if I could have the afternoon off, please, Mr. Hudson.'

'Well, of all the . . .! No, Daisy, with Rose away on her holiday that can hardly be . . .'

'I can manage,' the timid voice of Ruby managed from the background.

He turned to tell her to mind her own business, but restrained himself. He had read the worst of the war news in the morning newspaper already. Although there seemed little likelihood of Edward's ever being sent back into the fighting, Mr. Hudson had read that any soldier remotely fit enough to take the place of a more active man at a behind-the-lines job would be getting posted to France again before long. His temporary anger against Edward driven away by sympathy, he nodded to Ruby and addressed Daisy simultaneously: 'All right, girl. All right. But not till upstairs luncheon is cleared, mind.'

'Oh, no, Mr. Hudson. Thank you, Mr. Hudson.'

'And mind what I said about the telephone,' he added, as the stern last word.

The court sat in a stone-walled room in Dover's great castle, standing high above the town whose Admiralty Harbour was the base of the Dover Patrol, the force which had striven so hard and successfully to keep Britain's supply lines open against all that the enemy could do with his mines, U-boats and surface craft. The St. George's day raids on Zeebrugge and Ostend had been planned to bottle up these two vital bases of attack once and for all. Zeebrugge had proved a glorious, though bloody, success. Ostend had been a disaster: and one of its survivors now sat facing a long table behind which were seated five officers – a Captain in the centre, three Commanders, and a senior Lieutenant, all frock-coated, bemedalled and hatless.

On the table before them lay lengthwise Michael Hamilton's sword, in its scabbard. Another sword, drawn, was in the hand of the escorting officer standing slightly behind Michael, whose own seat was at a corner of a table occupied by Sir Geoffrey Dillon. At another table, to the left of the long one, sat the Judge Advocate, a qualified lawyer, there to ensure the legality of all stages of the proceedings, and a W.R.N.S. writer, busy with her pencil and shorthand pad.

The prosecuting officer's table was across the room from Sir Geoffrey's, close to the door where the Officer of the Court, a Lieutenant, stood on guard. At the back of the room, furthest removed from the members of the court, were public benches, sparsely occupied. Virginia Hamilton and Hazel Bellamy were the only women on them, amongst a scattering of naval officers.

Standing in the very centre of the room at this moment was Chief Petty Officer 'Beatty' Webb, a hard, seasoned, fine figure of a man, about forty years of age and sea-experienced to his fingertips. He occupied the small witness stand, and was about to be questioned by the prosecutor, Michael Hamilton's flotilla commander, a cool Lieutenant wearing the ribbon of the D.S.O. His name was Lightfoot.

'Chief Petty Officer Webb,' Lightfoot addressed him, 'during the operations against Zeebrugge and Ostend known as Z.O. you were coxwain of Coastal Motor Boat 47B?'

'Yessir.'

'Will you describe to the court what happened to your boat after she departed from Stroombank Buoy?'

'We proceeded inshore towards Ostend harbour on a course set for the Bell Buoy, which was our start point for laying smoke. As we turned to starboard and began to lay smoke the enemy opened up on us from the shore. It was as if they'd been waiting . . .'

The President of the Court interrupted, 'Please confine your evidence to what actually happened.'

'Sir. Well, the boat was exposed to very heavy gunfire . . . machine guns at close range. The wind being unfortunately off shore we were shown up against our own smoke. I've never experienced fire like it. It was . . . like the sea was boiling all round us. The boat was hit by three or four shells and raked by machine gun fire. I observed two of the foredeck Lewis guns with their crews blown into the sea. It was like hell . . . Beg pardon, sir.'

'Carry on,' Lightfoot said, intent.

'It was a miracle anyone stayed alive up there. The skipper – Lieutenant Twiss, I should say – was hit by a shell splinter and killed instantly. I put over the helm and turned back into our own smoke, and the firing decreased and became inaccurate.'

'What then?'

'I proceeded to the foredeck to find Acting Sub-Lieutenant Hamilton, who was in command of the Lewis guns. I came upon him lying inert on the deck. At first I thought he was dead, but he was breathing and his eyes were open. I knelt beside him and asked if he was all right. He did not reply.'

The witness stopped and waited, as though hoping not to have to continue. The prosecutor told him to do so, and he did, hesitantly.

'I informed Acting Sub-Lieutenant Hamilton of the death of Lieutenant Twiss. He did not reply. I asked again if he was wounded. He replied, "No."'

'Did he say anything else?'

'Yes, sir. He said, "You carry on, Chief." I returned to the bridge and put the boat back on course. When we had laid all the smoke I was joined by Acting Sub-Lieutenant Hamilton and on his order we proceeded back to the rendezvous.'

'Did you discuss what had happened?'

'There was too much to do, sir. The dead and wounded to see to, and the boat near to sinking.'

'When Acting Sub-Lieutenant Hamilton told you that he was not wounded, and yet made no move to get up, did you conclude that he was incapable of doing so through fear?'

Sir Geoffrey Dillon was on his feet immediately. 'I object. The prosecuting officer is putting words in the mouth of the witness.'

The President looked across towards the Judge Advocate, who made a dismissive gesture. The Captain nodded at the witness. 'You may carry on.'

C.P.O. Webb, whose heart had leaped with relief at the possibility of not having to answer, mumbled, 'I wouldn't like to hazard an opinion, sir.'

It seemed as though the prosecutor would press him for a more positive answer. Instead, after a moment's hesitation, he merely said, 'Thank you. That is all.' The chairman ordered

Webb to stand down, which he did with a smart salute and marched from the room.

Lieutenant Lightfoot addressed the court. 'CMB 47B rejoined the flotilla at the rendezvous at 02.47 hours. Owing to her poor condition I took her in tow and took her crew on board my own boat. By the orders of the force commander I then proceeded to port. On the passage Acting Sub-Lieutenant Hamilton was ordered to my cabin to give an account of the operation. He said to me . . .' Lightfoot read from a slip of paper '. . . "Don't ask me what happened, sir. I funked it and let you all down. If you want to know what happened, ask Webb. He saved the day. He ought to get a medal." '

Lightfoot lowered the paper and faced the court again. 'I asked him to explain himself, but he became incoherent and, er, broke down. On return to port I put Acting Sub-Lieutenant Hamilton under arrest and charged him with his present offence.'

The prosecutor sat down. A grim silence of some moments was broken by the Judge Advocate inviting Sir Geoffrey Dillon to speak in defence. In emotionless, measured tones he proceeded to do so.

'Acting Sub-Lieutenant Hamilton has not yet attained his eighteenth birthday. He is a young man whose record in the Royal Navy up to this point has been unimpeachable: he would hardly have been selected for promotion at this tender age if that had not been so. He was chosen to take part in this possibly difficult and dangerous operation for that reason. No one was to know that within a few minutes of his going into action against the enemy he was to undergo an ordeal of shot and shell few sailors are ever called to endure in their whole career. "The sea was boiling all around." The foredeck which was Acting Sub-Lieutenant Hamilton's command was "like hell". "It was a miracle anyone stayed alive." These are the statements of the prosecution witness, an experienced sailor and a man not given, I would imagine, to statements of a wild or exaggerated nature. Yet one man on that foredeck did survive that living hell: Acting Sub-Lieutenant Hamilton. Is it surprising that as a result of the shocking explosions all around him his brain and body suffered a temporary paralysis, in spite of which he was able to summon up enough commonsense to order Chief Petty Officer Webb to carry on, knowing that he himself was temporarily incapable? I would not myself call that failing to encourage his men to fight courageously. I would not call that the act of a coward. I can see that you gentlemen have some considerable experience of gallantry in action against the enemy. How would you have fared if at the tender age of seventeen you had been called upon to endure the same terrible ordeal?'

He paused for a moment, to let the thought register, then said, 'I call as witness Lieutenant Lightfoot.'

The President looked across to the Judge Advocate, who frowned, and reminded Sir Geoffrey, 'Lieutenant Lightfoot is prosecuting officer.'

Sir Geoffrey nodded. 'He is also the accused's commanding officer and a vital witness in the case. May I refer you to the Naval Discipline Act, section 685, paragraph two: "The Prosecutor is a competent witness and is not necessarily disqualified."?'

The Judge Advocate nodded in turn. 'Please carry on.'

Lightfoot arose and walked smartly to the witness stand. He was a self-possessed regular officer who had no intention of allowing a civilian to browbeat him, even if that civilian were an eminent lawyer.

Sir Geoffrey's tone was still mild and matter-of-fact. 'Lieutenant Lightfoot, if Acting Sub-Lieutenant Hamilton had not confessed to you his supposed failure, do you think he would be here now?'

Lightfoot stared back impassively. 'That is a hypothetical question which I am unable to answer.'

'You told us he made incoherent statements and broke down. Did you not consider he was in a state of shock?'

'I think everyone is in a state of shock, to some extent, after an action.'

'Didn't it occur to you that he was ill and ought to see a doctor?'

'He didn't request it; and, as it happened, the one doctor

194

then available had twenty-three wounded men to attend to, some of them dying.'

Sir Geoffrey coughed and tried again. 'You quoted the accused as saying, "Don't ask me what happened, sir. I funked it and let you all down. If you want to know what happened, ask Webb. He saved the day. He ought to get a medal." Is that all Hamilton said to you?'

'I believe so . . .'

'I do not think so. Your report is in your hand. Pray consult it.'

With obvious ill grace, Lightfoot obeyed, then answered. 'He did make one other remark. "I'm terribly sorry, sir. It won't happen again. I'll know what to expect next time."'

Sir Geoffrey at last allowed himself a smirk of satisfaction, glancing significantly at the court before finally telling Lightfoot, 'I want to ask you one more question. Don't you think that instead of arresting Acting Sub-Lieutenant Hamilton you would have been wiser to have told him to pull himself together and forget the whole thing?'

Lightfoot, impassive again, answered without hesitation, 'I believe I did my duty.'

Sir Geoffrey sighed audibly and asked the witness to stand down. Then he addressed the court.

'Every man is entitled to his own opinion, but I don't think fair-minded and experienced officers such as yourselves, gentlemen, can have any doubt that when this young man blamed himself to his commanding officer, so that his Chief Petty Officer should receive the recognition that was undoubtedly his due, he realised that he was risking his whole career. What, therefore, could be more honest, more unselfish, more honourable . . .? I would say that in judging this young man we should talk of courage, rather than cowardice. I ask you to acquit Acting Sub-Lieutenant Hamilton, give him that honourable discharge he so justly deserves, let him prove to you by his future conduct that your trust in him has not been misplaced, and that the steel of his courage has been tempered by his first and terrible ordeal.'

He sat down abruptly. It had been one of the rare occasions when his habitually dry tone of voice had become in some small degree emotional and urgent. It was obvious from the way the members of the court were exchanging glances that his speech had had its effect.

The Judge Advocate was saying to Lightfoot, 'It is for the prosecuting officer to sum up.'

Lightfoot stood up behind his table, to tell the court dispassionately, yet firmly, 'This country is facing one of the greatest crises in her history. The whole service is awaiting your verdict with great interest. Any weakness in your judgment might give the backsliders an opportunity to let their country down in battle. Let your verdict on Acting Sub-Lieutenant Hamilton be an example to them all.'

He sat down, and the Judge Advocate ordered the court to be cleared.

Michael Hamilton managed to give his mother a brief smile of reassurance before he was marched away by the officer with the drawn sword.

When everyone was called to reassemble, little over half an hour later, no room for doubt as to the verdict was left them: Michael Hamilton's own sword now lay drawn on the long table – and it was pointing directly at his place.

Deadly pale, and looking very, very young, Michael stood to attention to listen to the presiding Captain read out from a paper: 'The Court finds that Acting Sub-Lieutenant Michael Drury Hamilton, through cowardice, did not during the Action between His Majesty's Fleet and the Fleet of the German Empire, in his own person and according to his rank, encourage his inferior officers and his men to fight courageously, and is guilty of the Act charged against him.

'The Court sentences the aforesaid Acting Sub-Lieutenant Michael Drury Hamilton to be reprimanded.'

The only immediate sound came from the public benches, where Virginia and Hazel simultaneously gasped with relief. No one paid any attention to them. The slight glint of satisfaction which had been in Lieutenant Lightfoot's eyes since he had returned to the room to see the accusing sword conveying the verdict in advance died away; but Sir Geoffrey

Dillon's hitherto grave countenance now bore a smile combining pleasure, relief, and not a little self-satisfaction.

That evening, in the morning-room of 165 Eaton Place, Richard was fulsome in his congratulations to Virginia. From being escorted himself, Michael had taken over an escort's role, bringing his mother and Hazel back to London. Hazel had insisted that they stay the night, and that Virginia should remain on for a day or two after Michael's return to duty next morning.

'It could hardly have been a better verdict, in the circumstances,' Richard said to Virginia. 'Old Geoffrey's a tower of strength when it comes to a crisis. He pretends to be a dry old dragon, but he really has a heart of gold.'

Virginia was still looking apprehensive, though. 'I just hope everyone – Michael, too, for that matter – won't think I played the interfering mother, using influence to get him off lightly.'

Richard shook his head decisively. 'When my son was wounded at Passchendaele last year I was easily persuaded against all my principles to go out in a private ambulance and bring him back. We're only human. My advice, for what it's worth, is to stop thinking about it.'

'Yes,' she answered, though still doubtfully. 'I wish I could persuade Michael to do that.'

'He will. He's got a fresh start. That verdict won't damage his career in the long run.'

'I wonder,' she persisted. 'I know the navy so well. It's such a small family, really. In the future, whenever Michael's name comes up for a job, or even in a conversation, they'll think, Michael Hamilton, Charles's boy who got court-martialled for that business at Ostend.'

Richard could see the truth of what she said. He could only nod sympathetically. At that moment Michael came in, smart and smiling.

'Good evening, sir,' he said. 'Excuse me, Mother; we ought to go.'

'Michael's taking me to supper,' Virginia explained, getting up. 'Then we're going on to a show.'

'*Chu Chin Chow*,' Michael added. 'For the third time.'

His mother went out to get her things. A small awkward

silence fell between Richard and Michael, until the latter said, 'Thank you very much, sir — for your help.'

Richard patted him reassuringly on the shoulder. 'All's well that ends well. Put it down to experience. You'll be all right next time, I'm sure.'

'I think I will . . . but I don't expect there'll be a next time for me. So many other chaps wanting to have a go. But I just would like the chance to show them all I was . . . all right. For Mother's sake, as much as mine.'

His mother's reappearance brought the conversation to an end. Having ascertained that Hudson had got a taxi for them, Richard watched them leave, the handsome, tall young son and the small, pretty woman who looked too young to be his mother. His expression was thoughtful as he returned back into the morning-room.

In the servants' hall Ruby was seated at the table, concentrating on the innocent occupation of cutting out coloured pictures of soldiers for her scrapbook. She appeared to be at ease, but was in reality deeply worried.

One of her causes for concern promptly came to a head, as Mrs. Bridges bore down on her from the kitchen, flourishing a large saucepan.

'Ruby!' cried that obviously angry woman. 'What's happened to all my meat scraps? They've gone. That steak the Major couldn't eat last night . . .'

Ruby answered a little too promptly, 'Must be the mice again . . .'

'Mice indeed! I'd like to see the mouse that can climb up the side of this saucepan, lift the lid and put it back on again. Human mouse if you ask me. But it's you I'm asking, Ruby. Have you been stealing my scraps?'

'Oh, no, honest, Mrs. Bridges,' Ruby faltered, blushing deeply.

'Hm! Then I shall have to ask Daisy.'

'Oh, she's feeling a bit poorly, Mrs. Bridges. She's gone to lie down.'

Mrs. Bridges regarded her long and hard, and made up her mind to bring the matter to Mr. Hudson's attention when he'd finished talking in his pantry with that sergeant who'd called unexpectedly a few minutes before. At that moment the area door opened and Daisy came in, in her street clothes.

'Well!' Mrs. Bridges exploded at Ruby. 'Lying down poorly, is she? One lie after another. Just you wait, my girl, till Mr. Hudson's free.'

'I just popped out for a bit of air,' Daisy tried. 'I do feel a bit better for it.'

Before Mrs. Bridges could expostulate further, Ruby had interrupted, 'Oh, Daisy! There's a sergeant . . . there with Mr. Hudson. He's got M.P. on his arm. Isn't that . . . Military Police?'

Mrs. Bridges looked from one to the other of them. Each girl looked equally frightened. She was about to demand an explanation when the pantry door opened and Mr. Hudson, serious-faced, ushered out a middle-aged sergeant and escorted him to the door. Having seen him off the premises, Mr. Hudson closed the door and came to them.

'Daisy,' he said, and his voice was quiet, 'that was the provost sergeant from the Middlesex Regiment's depot at Mill Hill. He wanted to know the whereabouts of Edward . . . who is absent without leave.'

'Oh, my Lord!' Mrs. Bridges cried. 'I hope he hasn't been took ill again.'

'Daisy should know,' Mr. Hudson answered, his eyes not leaving the parlourmaid's face. 'She was the last to see him. Was he ill, Daisy? Was that why he had the effrontery to telephone here?'

She looked down without replying. Mr. Hudson's voice was harder when he spoke again.

'Did he tell you he is one of the draft due to leave for France tomorrow?'

It was Mrs. Bridges again who reacted. 'Oh, Mr. Hudson, surely they can't. It isn't right.'

'No it isn't right,' Ruby said, with surprising warmth. 'Not Edward.'

Daisy looked up at last and said, 'You all know as well as I do, if Edward has to go through another barrage of shelling like before he'll be stark staring mad for the rest of his life.'

'Daisy,' Hudson insisted, his expression one of concern rather than annoyance, 'where is Edward?'

'How should I know?'

'You know, and you're not leaving this room until you tell me. You, too, Ruby. I think you know.'

Daisy gave Ruby a sharp warning look, and retorted, 'What business is it of yours?'

Mr. Hudson flushed. 'It is my business because as long as I am butler here I shall not stand aside and see disgrace, scandal or worse brought on this house. He is a former employee, with his wife still working here . . . Besides which I . . . I am very fond of the boy.'

'Huh! You're so fond of him, you'd send him to a loony bin for life.'

'And you're his wife. Are you prepared to ruin his life and yours for ever?'

'How do you mean? A week or two in the glasshouse is better than France for him. Where's the ruin in that?'

A new urgency entered his tone. 'Daisy, you evidently do not realise that deliberately missing a draft for France is considered as much desertion as running away from the enemy in action. Worse, perhaps, especially when the crime is committed by a seasoned soldier with a stripe on his arm. It is a terrible example to the young men in his regiment, and there is a terrible punishment for it.'

The three women stared back at him awestruck. The dreaded picture of a firing-squad at dawn was in all their minds without his having to tell them in words. Daisy's voice was almost a whisper when she spoke again. 'I . . . I don't believe you. That Mrs. Hamilton's son was court martialled for being a coward. He got away with nothing more than a telling off.'

'It's different,' Mr. Hudson told her desperately. 'Can't you understand, there are different degrees, different . . .' He broke off, unable to explain those differences in any way that would convince her. He looked appealingly at Mrs. Bridges. She nodded, and said gently, 'Daisy. Mr. Hudson's right. Tell us. For pity's sake.'

It was Ruby who burst out, 'Mr. Hudson, Edward's in . . .'

Daisy silenced her. 'I'll tell him. Edward's in his father's house at Walthamstow. It's been bombed and it's all boarded up. He couldn't go, Mr. Hudson, he just couldn't.'

Hudson thought for only a moment before ordering Ruby, 'Fetch me the money-box – our holiday money. Quickly, girl. Daisy, you will find a taximeter. Drive to Walthamstow, collect Edward and take him immediately to the depot at Mill Hill.'

'No! I can't! I won't!'

'You must and you will. I will telephone the guard room at Mill Hill and explain that Edward has been suffering from temporary loss of memory, but is now better. And don't worry, Daisy. The sergeant assured me that men in Edward's state are only to be employed releasing fit men for the trenches.'

'You . . . promise, Mr. Hudson?'

'I promise, Daisy. Now, are you clear what to do?'

'Yes, Mr. Hudson.'

He had the box from Ruby now, and gave the whole of its contents to Daisy. He added a pound from his own pocket. 'The taximeter will be expensive for such a way. Now be off with you – and wish Edward the best from us all.'

Mrs. Bridges and Ruby chorused their agreement, and Daisy, able only to nod acknowledgement, ran out of the door.

'Well,' said Mrs. Bridges, 'whatever next?' Her eye fell on Ruby, and her expression changed as understanding dawned. 'So that's where the scraps were for, eh?' But she was smiling as she concluded, 'One of these days that tongue of yours is going to frizzle up and stick to the roof of your mouth. Now, what about them vegetables?'

As the relieved girl hurried off to the kitchen Mrs. Bridges turned to Mr. Hudson and delivered her final verdict: 'The wickedness there is in this age!'

Two days later Richard Bellamy let himself in through his own front door, and met Mr. Hudson in the hall, holding Virginia Hamilton's two suitcases. The butler stared to see his lordship back at so unprecedented an hour as eleven o'clock in the morning.

'Ah, Hudson,' Richard addressed him unsmiling. 'Would you find Mrs. Bellamy and Mrs. Hamilton and tell them I should be very obliged if they would come to the morning-room immediately?'

Hudson set down the cases. 'M'lord, I think Mrs. Hamilton is already a wee bit late for the train to Scot . . .'

'Just do as I say,' Richard interrupted, and went into the morning-room.

He was joined a few minutes later by the two women, who greeted him cheerfully.

'Back so soon?' said Hazel.

'I thought we'd said our goodbyes,' Virginia smiled.

Richard's expression was still grave. 'Virginia, my dear,' he said, addressing her by her Christian name for the first time, 'please sit down.' She obeyed, puzzled now. 'You know . . . how fond we've become of you . . .' he began again, then had to stop. 'It's no use. Virginia, I have to tell you Michael was killed in action at Ostend last night.'

Virginia, though seated, reeled. Hazel flew to her side, and Richard hurriedly poured a glass of brandy. She shook her head at it, holding Hazel's hand with a fierce grip. 'Please tell me everything you know . . . Richard,' she asked, keeping her voice under all the control she could muster.

'The evening you went to the theatre, Michael and I had a little chat,' he said. 'The next day I happened to bump into Roger Keyes in the Admiralty. He commands the Dover Patrol. He knew about Michael, of course. I think even before I mentioned it he'd decided to give him another chance immediately. There was this new Ostend affair just being prepared.'

'Keyes is . . . was . . . Michael's great hero,' Virginia said softly. 'Do you know . . . what happened?'

'I have a report,' he said, drawing it from his dispatch case. 'It was dictated to my secretary on the telephone from Dover this morning. I'll leave it here for you to read.'

'No – please . . . Read it to me.'

He glanced at Hazel. She nodded. 'I should explain,' he told Virginia, 'Michael was on the Coastal Motor Boat ordered to lead and escort the blockship *Vindictive* up the channel to the lock gates at Ostend, and to place a phosphate light buoy in position to guide her into position.' He raised the report and began to read: ' "As the port torpedo was discharged at the lock gates the boat came under heavy and accurate enfilade fire from the western and eastern piers. Commanding the foredeck, Acting Sub-Lieutenant Michael Hamilton continued to return the enemy fire with his Lewis guns, in spite of the fact that he was badly wounded. When the signal came he somehow managed to launch the marker buoy single-handed and light the fuse, before dying at his post. There is no doubt that the success of the whole operation was ensured by the consummate bravery and the complete disregard for his own safety shown by this very gallant young officer." '

Richard laid the report aside and went to Virginia. 'Please forgive me, Virginia . . . for my part.'

Her answer was almost fierce. 'Don't apologise, Richard. It is exactly what Michael would have wished if his father had been alive to hear of it. And he would have known just how I would feel, too. Please excuse me.'

She got up and walked steadily from the room. With a glance back at him Hazel followed, to escort her back upstairs.

Richard stood still, looking at the doorway. So recently it had been the mother and son; now it was the mother alone. And he found himself experiencing feelings that had nothing to do with pity or respect, but reminded him of the first time he had been introduced to dear Marjorie, at that reception in the Paris Embassy, so many years ago.

CHAPTER THIRTEEN

MR. HUDSON'S mood was as gloomy as the dark October day. It was almost a year since Major James had come home from France. The wound in his leg was healed, but the wound in his mind still festered, and the atmosphere of discontent radiated throughout the household. Mr. Hudson was frequently shocked by the way the Major shouted at Nurse Wilkins. She had left once, but had been persuaded to return, for the invalid's demands were too much for Hazel's strength, called into his room as she was, night after night, to reassure him after a nightmare or bring him a hot drink, not to mention all the hours of trying to keep him entertained. Mr. Hudson was even more shocked by the Major's behaviour to his wife, surly, irritable and silent in turns; he had seen her face after she had come downstairs from the room where her husband spent most of his time.

Mrs. Bridges, too, was getting towards the end of her patience, fond as she was of James, when dish after dish, so thoughtfully prepared for him, was sent downstairs untouched or merely tasted. 'Can't do no right for him these days,' she grumbled. 'Never get strong if he doesn't eat.'

Mr. Hudson was agreeably surprised, therefore, as he was laying out the afternoon post in the hall, to see Rose burst through the pass door with a radiant face.

'Oh, there you are, Mr. Hudson. Oh, Mr. Hudson, I've had a letter from Australia and you'll never guess . . .' She stopped, breathless. 'Anyone in the morning-room?'

'No, you may speak normally, Rose.'

'Well, just read that letter, and tell me if I'm not seeing things. Just you read it, and tell me it's not someone playing a joke.' Mr. Hudson put on his glasses. As he read his face changed to astonishment and pleasure. Rose went on, 'I mean I knew he had some property out there, and not that many relatives, but I never dreamed . . . that he'd remember me

. . . and all that much . . . my Gregory.' She was on the verge of tears.

Mr. Hudson, impressed, handed back the letter. 'Twelve hundred pounds is a great deal of money, Rose. But then, he was your intended — you were to have been his wife.'

She sniffed. 'Yes, I know. I suppose that's it.'

'It will make a difference to your life, Rose. It will bring you a certain independence.'

'Yes, I suppose it will. Funny, how a letter can come in the post like that — and suddenly change your whole life.'

'Aye.' He looked round, from habit, to see that none of the Family was about. 'There's a letter here for his Lordship, bearing an Inverness postmark, which could well alter the course of *his* life, if I'm not too much mistaken.'

Rose's eyes widened. 'Inverness?'

'One could hardly fail to notice the recent exchange of almost daily correspondence between the master and Mrs. Hamilton, leading one to certain inevitable conclusions. Now you can put out of your head what I have just said, Rose, and rejoice in your own windfall.'

'Oh, I'll rejoice all right, Mr. Hudson. I'm going up to tell Mrs. Bridges. Of course, I'll buy you all something nice with it, that goes without saying.'

As Mr. Hudson looked after her benevolently there was the slam of a taxi door outside. A moment later Georgina stood in the doorway, in her nurse's uniform with a large suitcase. He hastened to take it from her. 'Miss Georgina! What a pleasant surprise. Mrs. Bellamy didn't mention . . .' She began to take off her cape.

'I know. There wasn't time to send a telegram or anything, I only just got to Boulogne in time to catch a leave boat. They've sent me home to rest — isn't it ridiculous?' Mr. Hudson, noting her strained look and the lines round her eyes and mouth thought it was not at all ridiculous. 'The Matron said I'd been overworking,' she went on. 'We've had more casualties through our hospital than we could really manage. None of us had a wink of sleep for weeks until yesterday — up all night, you see, because the orderlies kept bringing in more and more bad cases . . . Well, I fainted twice in the ward from exhaustion, so they said I was to go and get some rest, so here I am.'

'You're certainly looking a wee bit tired, Miss. Shall I get you some tea?'

'No tea, thank you. Just early bed tonight and a good sleep. Where is everybody?'

'His lordship is out, I'm afraid, and Mrs. Bellamy at her canteen work, miss. Er – the Major is upstairs in his room.'

'How is he?'

'Going on as well as can be expected, miss.'

'Good. I'll go up and see him at once.'

James's room was almost dark when she tapped on the door. As she entered, he was by the window, staring out at the yellow street lamps.

'Come in. Who is it?' he asked without interest.

'It's me. And I'm not a ghost.'

He turned sharply. 'Georgie! Good God. You're back, then.'

'They've sent me home, just for a bit. They say I'm overtired.'

'So I should think.' He gave her a cousinly kiss on the brow. 'Sit down and talk to me. I'm so bored and lonely up here.'

They talked about James's leg, and the trials put upon him by Nurse Wilkins, and sundry other things; how Georgina had gone to Paris for her last leave with a young officer called Martin Adams, who had come back with her on the leave boat, and how the nurse who had taken Georgina's place in France had said that St. Thomas's Hospital had five wards filled with victims of Spanish 'flu. It was, altogether, a slightly stiff, uncomfortable situation, and Georgina was relieved to end it on the excuse that she heard Hazel coming in.

Hazel was, in fact, in the hall at that moment. She greeted Georgina warmly. Suddenly they found themselves talking freely, as James and Georgina had not. It was Georgina who came out with the subject which all of them had on their minds. 'Hazel, if I behaved stupidly over James leaving in the ambulance, I do hope you'll understand and forgive me. You see, I was so afraid for him – the bumpy roads and going on to the boat and . . . well, perhaps I felt – after nursing him through the worst part . . .'

Hazel took Georgina in her arms, something she had not done since the early days, when the girl had first become part of the household. 'My dearest child,' she said. 'If I didn't understand exactly how you felt I wouldn't be much of a person. I know that James has been very important to you, always. I think he touched your heart, as a good-looking, charming man can always touch a young girl's heart. After all, he touched mine.'

Georgina, who was crying gently, nodded.

'Naturally,' said Hazel, 'I've known how fond of him you've been and still are. And he of you. You're young and pretty and so full of life. I'm afraid I've been rather a disappointment to him. I'm still dreadfully shy, you know. I feel only part of this family – I suppose it's something to do with the circumstances of our marriage, our different homes. I think James was looking for someone to take the place of his mother. I've tried so hard to make him happy and to be a good wife to him, but . . . well, for one thing we've never been able to have children.'

'Oh, but you will, Hazel. I so want you to.'

'Perhaps we shall, now, God willing. It's all been quite different since he came back on his last leave after the Somme. We found an understanding, almost a new kind of love, we'd never experienced before . . . At least he's safe now and finished with the war – so we can plan our future. And now you must go straight up to bed and rest. I'll come up and tuck you in.'

But as they were making their way upstairs Richard appeared, looking, Georgina thought, a different man from the one she had last seen in France. His face was whipped to a healthy colour by the cold air outside, and he looked younger, more vigorous. He was pleased to see Georgina, but there was a slightly preoccupied air about his greeting, as though the unopened letter in his hand, at which he kept glancing, was more important than her arrival. At last, unable to wait any longer, he opened and read it, swiftly, then put it in his pocket. 'What's the time?' he asked Hazel.

'Getting on for six.'

'Good heavens. Then I must go. I'm sorry, but I've got to go out at once.'

'But you've only just come in.'

'I know I have. Change of plan. Sorry, my dear, you'll have to tell Hudson I'm dining out after all. I've got to meet a train at King's Cross.'

Hazel couldn't restrain her curiosity. 'This person you're meeting – is it the First Lord?'

Richard hesitated fractionally before saying, 'No, it is not the First Lord or the Prime Minister. It's someone a damn sight more important than either of them. Sorry to have to rush off – take care of yourselves.'

And he was gone, as if borne away by a whirlwind. Mr Hudson, who had emerged into the hall, nodded his head sagely to himself. There were more changes coming. He broke the news to Mrs. Bridges that there would be only 'trays' that evening, no proper dinner. She was not pleased.

'This house is getting like a hotel. Had another letter, has he?'

'Aye. Postmark, Inverness. Hurried off to King's Cross to meet a train – you can guess where from.'

'Not staying here again, is she?'

'Not this time. At least I've had no orders to that effect. Going to a hotel, I expect.'

'There's two younger children, isn't there?'

'There are indeed.'

'Poor woman, losing a husband and a son in the war . . . How did she strike you, Mr. Hudson?'

Mr. Hudson did not need time to deliberate. 'I have formed, so far, quite a favourable impression of the lady. She strikes me as being a woman of breeding and good looks, much character and a good deal of dignity. Not to be easily – shall we say "pushed around" – but kindly, and with courage and a sense of her position. And a cheerful soul to boot.'

Some half an hour later the lady to whom he had paid this tribute was looking particularly cheerful at a small restaurant table. The black she wore became her fair colouring excellently. She looked up from the menu.

'I'd like to order some roast chicken and spinach, please, and perhaps a little fruit salad. I'm afraid long train journeys always make me ravenously hungry.'

Richard could barely take his eyes off her long enough to address the waiter who stood patiently by. 'I'll take the same, please,' he said, as he would have done if she had ordered cats' meat. 'And a bottle of hock — whatever the wine-waiter recommends.'

Virginia smiled at him across the table. 'You're being so kind, really spoiling me. I didn't tell you our arrival time meaning you to meet us — it was just by way of information.'

'How could I leave you standing on a draughty platform with two young children and a senile Nanny?'

'Oh, there are always porters. And to come here first and make sure our rooms were ready *and* order flowers — it was so kind and thoughtful.'

'The flowers were to welcome you to London, with the compliments of the Hyde Park Hotel.'

'That's not true. Because when I telephoned down to the manager's office to thank him for them he knew nothing about it. I'm afraid you're just a very kind and chivalrous man. And now to invite me to dinner in my own hotel . . .'

'Well,' said Richard reasonably, 'the children are in bed and Nanny MacIndoe's having her supper, so what is there left for you to do but join me in a leisurely dinner so that . . .'

'So that what, Richard?'

'So that we can discuss the future.' His voice shook a little from nervousness, as it had never done yet in the House.

'Whose future?' she asked.

'Ours.'

In the silence, he was sharply aware of the little orchestra playing *Roses of Picardy* very badly. Virginia was arranging two forks in different patterns on the table-cloth, studying them intently. Then she looked up.

'Did you really mean what you said in your last letter?'

'Every word of it.'

'You'd be taking on three of us and a Nanny — no, not a Nanny, she's going to retire, but the children will have to have a governess. Susan's twelve now and William's nine. Quite a circus.'

He smiled. 'Delightful. A new, young family.'

'They'll scream and fight and rush up and downstairs, and invade your dressing-room while you're shaving and require endless games of hide and seek.'

'I should like that,' said Richard, meaning it.

'Where would we live?'

'It would have to be London. I'll find a house north of the Park — it's cheaper.'

'What will your son and daughter think?'

'I like to think they both want my eventual happiness, and have done, ever since their mother died.'

Virginia was deliberately asking him every question to which a snag might be attached. 'She was very beautiful — Lady Marjorie.'

'Yes.'

'Are you ready yet to give all your love to another woman? I don't mean that selfishly, Richard.'

'I am ready to remarry, Virginia, my darling, if you'll have me. That is, if you're ready too. It's not been very long for you, has it?'

'Nearly four years. I think Charles would have wished it. When war broke out he said that if he was — unlucky — I'd have to look round sooner or later for someone to be a father to our children.'

Richard nodded, remembering poor Lady Prue and her strong hints. 'Marjorie told her greatest friend the same about me. That she'd expect me to remarry, if . . .'

'People should. But not for convenience.'

Richard laughed aloud, startling a waiter. 'Oh, good heavens, no. You're not convenient, my darling, not at all.'

She joined in his laughter. 'No, I didn't think I was.'

'But I don't care how many screaming children you have, or that you once nearly got me the sack from the Admiralty, or that I took the most violent dislike to you the first time we met. I asked you, in writing, to marry me, Virginia my dearest, because I've fallen deeply in love with you. And I want you to think over very carefully the prospect of becoming my wife, but not let it spoil your dinner.'

She reached her hand across the table and took his. Her eyes were very bright with tears she would not let fall. 'I won't,' she said, 'I won't.'

Richard's face was alarmed. 'You won't what?'

'Let it spoil my dinner, Richard, because I don't have to think it over. I already have, and I accept.'

A very bright-faced Lord Bellamy appeared before his family next morning, having eaten a hearty breakfast and skimmed through the news, too happy to take in its significance. The others, who had taken their breakfasts on trays, were subdued, James and Hazel playing beggar-my-neighbour (James had lately taken to the games of his childhood) and Georgina, suffering from anti-climax, staring out of the window.

'Good morning, my dears,' he said. 'Well, this seems to be a suitable moment to tell you my news, with all the family gathered together in one room for once.'

James found a quibble. 'All the family isn't gathered. Elizabeth isn't here.'

'I wrote a long letter to Elizabeth last night.'

'What about? What *is* this, Father?'

'I believe I can guess,' said Hazel.

'They've made you Prime Minister?' suggested Georgina. He smiled, shaking his head. 'I want you all to know that last night I asked Virginia Hamilton to become my wife, and she agreed. There. That's my secret out.'

Hazel flew into his arms. 'Oh, Richard, how lovely — congratulations! She's so nice and you'll be very happy, I know you will. Oh, it's wonderful news.' Georgina echoed her, kissing him heartily; only James sat staring at his father, blank-faced. Richard was saying, 'We'll get married as soon as we can find a house and get settled in with the children. At least I shall no longer be a paying guest here — one less mouth to feed.'

'Oh, no!' cried Georgina. 'Oh, but we'll miss you terribly. What shall we do without you?'

'Well, I hope I shall see *something* of you. I'm not going off to Timbuctoo, only north of Hyde Park, if we can find somewhere.'

'All the same, the house will seem funny without you.'

'I hope not too funny. Well, I must go or my chief clerk will start worrying.'

Georgina got up. 'I must go, too. I promised to go and see Viola Courtney on my way to Selfridges. She lives in Manchester Square and she's down with this horrible Spanish 'flu.'

'Well, don't get too close to her. It's catching. You can come in my taxi if you like – I'll drop you at Hyde Park Corner.'

The two left behind felt the silence settling around them. Hazel went back to sit at the games-table and picked up the cards. James had lost interest.

'One, two and – oh, Jack. One, please.' She was trying to sound normal. He turned his head away. 'I can't see much point in this idiotic game.'

'So you want to stop?'

'What else is there to do?' His eyes were as bleak as his tone.

She put down her cards. 'I'm trying so hard, James, to . . .'

'To keep me amused?'

Hazel's temper, so long kept under restraint, flared out. 'Yes, I am. I'm doing my best. I know you still don't feel well and I know you're rather depressed, but I *do* think you might *try* and be a bit more cheerful.'

He sneered. 'Cheerful? God, with that stupid maddening woman fussing over me all day upstairs? I only come down here to get away from her. Then *you* start on me.'

'*I* start?' Hazel jumped up from her chair. 'Look, I'm trying to keep you as happy and comfortable as I can. Nurse Wilkins may be maddening and fussy, but you still need her, at least you say you do, if only to answer your bell in the night. If you really can't stand the sight of her I'll get rid of her – again.'

'I wish to God you would.'

Hazel's face was grim. 'Very well, I will. I'll pay her a week's salary and dismiss her, if it'll make you any happier. Anything, only please try to be a little more amenable.' She had reached the door. James turned, in surprise. He was so used to making wild statements that nobody was going to act upon.

'Where are you going?'

'To dismiss Nurse Wilkins,' she flashed back. 'Where do you think I'm going?'

'Oh, don't be so idiotic, Hazel. I didn't mean sack the woman.'

'That's what you said.'

'I didn't.'

'Yes, you did, James. You implied that you wanted me to dismiss her.' Hazel's control was rapidly giving way. 'Why must you go on and on being so unreasonable?'

He shouted at her. 'Oh, go away, if you're going to cry. I can't bear weeping women. Get out, if you're going to weep all over the place!'

She ran back to his side. 'James, what have I done wrong? Why are you being so cruel to me, why? Nothing I do seems to be right these days. You shout at me and curse me whenever I try to be helpful and loving and concerned for you . . .'

He swung his shoulder away from her touch. 'Leave me alone, Hazel. Just leave me alone, will you?'

She swallowed back the tears, then said, 'What do you want me to do about Nurse Wilkins?'

'I don't care. Yes, I do. Send her away.'

'Are you sure?'

James turned savagely back, his face flushed with temper. 'I said send her away. Didn't you hear me?'

'After all she's done for you.'

'Send her away!' he shouted. 'And leave me alone.'

Hazel stared at him in shock and bewilderment. Then, with a sob, she turned and ran out of the room, banging the door behind her. The angry colour faded from his face, leaving it white. Then he called 'Hazel! Come back.' But he knew she would not. He muttered to himself. 'I didn't mean that, Hazel.

I was only . . .' Getting up painfully, he limped towards the door, but instead of opening it stood, leaning against the back of a chair. After a moment or two he went into the hall. Hazel was disappearing round the bend of the stairs, Rose beside her, the maid's arm tenderly round the mistress's shoulder.

In the haven of her room Hazel was sitting at her dressing-table, her head on her arms, crying broken-heartedly, while Rose patted and soothed her. 'He doesn't mean it, madam. He's not himself, not yet. You mustn't be upset by it. There, madam.' She stroked the soft, tumbled chestnut hair. Hazel lifted her swollen face.

'Oh, dear Rose. You're so good and comforting. When I think about what *you've* suffered . . .'

'We've all suffered, madam. You've had the uncertainty, the worry of not knowing.'

'Yes, but the Major is safe, he's home and he's alive. I should be so thankful. But he's changed. He's not loving or glad to be safe. It seems almost — as if he'd rather be dead.' She began to cry again, in Rose's arms.

'It's the strain, madam — what he's been through, that's all.' She laid a cool hand against Hazel's wet face. 'Madam, your face is awfully hot, your cheeks are burning. Feel your skin!'

'Yes, I . . . it's being upset, I expect.' She blew her nose and tried to recover herself, but Rose was eyeing her worriedly.

'Are you feeling all right?' she asked.

'Just a little — feverish, perhaps. And a bit giddy. My back aches, too. Don't worry, Rose, it'll pass.'

But Rose was worried. 'Don't you think you should lie down for a bit? It feels to me as if you had a temperature. It's not normal to be that hot. Would you let me take your temperature — just to satisfy myself?'

Hazel nodded wearily. 'All right. If you insist, Rose. The thermometer's in the small chest. I must admit I do feel a bit wretched.'

Rose took her temperature in the professional way taught her by Georgina, who had said that in wartime anything might happen and it was as well to know one's First Aid.

With alarm she saw the reading on the thermometer. 'It's over 104, madam. I think you ought to get into bed at once, while I get Mr. Hudson to telephone for the doctor. You know what I'm afraid of.'

'That I've got the Spanish 'flu. What if I have? A little quinine or something, and a few days in bed, that's all it is.'

'That's right, madam. You get undressed while I go down and tell Mr. Hudson.'

'Rose, if you see the Major, don't mention to him that I'm not well.'

'He ought to know, madam.'

'Not just yet, please. I don't want him upset or alarmed in any way. Not in his present state of mind.'

'Very good, madam.' Rose darted out and down to the servants' hall, her face taut with anxiety.

Dr. Foley was busy, but he managed to get round within the hour. His examination confirmed Rose's suspicions. 'I'm afraid she *has* contracted this beastly influenza. Rotten luck. You'll have to get this prescription made up at the chemist, as soon as possible.' He handed it to Rose. A raucous noise near-by offended his ears; a scratchy gramophone playing a popular song. 'I love the moon,' ground out the singer.

'I love the wild birds, the dusk and the dew,
But most of all, dear I love you.'

Dr. Foley frowned. 'Who's playing that gramophone?'

'Major Bellamy, sir. Next door in his room.'

'Well, he'll have to stop, she needs absolute rest and quiet. Go and tell him.'

Rose hesitated. 'I — well, it wouldn't be my place to tell the Major to stop playing his gramophone . . .'

'No, I suppose not. I'll go and see him myself.' He set off briskly towards the dressing-room, Rose protesting behind him. 'Oh, sir, madam specially didn't want him told,' Rose said, and Hazel, lifting heavy eyelids, murmured, 'Please. Don't let him think . . . I'm at all ill.'

'Of course he must be told,' snapped the doctor. 'He's your husband.'

'But he's not well himself . . .'

'He's well enough to be told if his wife is ill, because you

215

are ill, Mrs. Bellamy, I'm sorry to say. We don't want to cause too much alarm and worry, but — your case is quite severe.'

James was shocked and contrite, and tried to persuade the doctor to let him see Hazel, in vain.

'Sorry, old chap. I don't want her disturbed. We must just keep her quiet and try to get that temperature down. I'll be back this evening after dinner. Meantime — no music, eh?'

In the evening Hazel was worse. Her head and body were fire-hot and she shivered uncontrollably in the racking bone-ache of influenza. Faces and voices came and went, blurred, sometimes recognisable, more often distorted by temperature into those of strangers. The doctor was there, and Rose more often than anybody, and then someone who might be James.

'How bad is it?' he was asking the doctor in a whisper.

'Holding her own. That's about all one can say. Breathing's bad. Don't let her talk too much.' Quietly he went out, leaving James by the bedside. Hazel's head was moving uneasily from side to side of the pillow. His face came out of the blur of heat and pain, faintly lit by the light that came from the landing through the open door.

'James,' she whispered.

'Yes, my darling.'

'It's . . . dark. What time is it?'

'Half-past five. How do you feel?'

'A little better . . . I think . . . but I ache all over . . . and my head aches . . . dreadfully.'

'Don't try to talk, the doctor says you mustn't. Try to get to sleep again.' Quietly he went out, closing the door behind him. Through the panels he heard her moaning. 'Oh God,' he said aloud. 'Oh God, what a brute I've been.'

In the morning-room Richard and Virginia were having tea. James looked at her blankly for a moment, at their happy faces, and felt like slamming out again. Then an instinct he would not have had earlier that day told him that he had behaved selfishly long enough, inflicting his own black humours on other people. He smiled charmingly and went to shake hands with Virginia.

'I'm so sorry to hear about Hazel, James. I wouldn't have come if I'd known.'

'Hudson tells me Dr. Foley's been,' said Richard. 'How is she?'

'A bit better now, but still pretty miserable, poor darling.' He turned to Virginia. 'You're going to be my stepmother, I believe.'

She made a comic face. 'Oh dear, that makes me feel ninety at least, and rather wicked. Stepmothers in stories always are.'

'Am I to call you Stepmamma?'

'Heavens, no, thank you.'

'Virginia, then.'

'Of course. Have a cup of tea. I feel an awful intruder doing this but Richard insisted on bringing me home. We've been looking at houses, one in Sussex Gardens and one in Clarendon Street.' She passed him the cup. 'Now I'm here, I want so much to go up and see Hazel, if it's allowed – perhaps read to her, if she feels up to it. Do you think I might?'

'That would be awfully kind,' James said. 'I shouldn't think at the moment . . . but it depends on what Dr. Foley says when he comes after dinner.'

'Heard the good news, James?' Richard asked.

'Only yours and Virginia's. Is there more?'

'Yes – the war news. The German armies are falling back on all fronts, and Austria-Hungary has asked for cease-fire terms. Lord Cavan's troops and the Italians have smashed the Hapsburgs for ever.'

James looked cynical. 'Really? Well, I can't believe Ludendorff will surrender on any terms. Northcliffe doesn't think so, nor do the troops. The Boche are still strafing our chaps out there.'

'But if Hindenburg's ready to surrender . . .' Virginia began.

'I wish I *could* believe it was nearly over. What was it? August 4th, 1914, to – what's today? October 28th, 1918. That's four years and two months. It seems more like forty.'

Dr. Foley's cheerful prognosis of not more than a week's illness for Hazel was proving wrong. On the sixth day after she had been stricken her temperature was still high and at times she was delirious.

'Talking all kinds of nonsense,' said Rose despondently. 'Didn't know me, nor the doctor either.'

'It always takes a few days to shake off a fever,' said Mr. Hudson.

'Pity that Nurse Wilkins left,' Mrs. Bridges said. 'Nice time to choose, I must say. We could have done with her. How's the Major taking it, Rose?'

'He sat with her all last night and he's still in there this morning. Not like him at all. Sorry now he shouted at her the day she took ill, I shouldn't wonder. Dr. Foley's coming again after lunch, and they're getting in a night nurse, because Dr. Foley says the Major's wearing himself out.'

Ruby came in from the kitchen. 'Some men have been putting straw down in the street outside – have you seen?'

'Yes. The doctor ordered it,' said Rose. Daisy elucidated, 'It's so's the traffic won't make too much noise going by, and disturb her. They do that when someone in the house is gravely ill.'

Mr. Hudson shot her a reproving look. 'All right, Daisy, less talk and get on with your tea.'

'I hear there's two cases of it next door but one, Number 169, one of the children and the nursery-maid,' said Mrs. Bridges. 'No knowing who'll get it next.'

That evening Virginia, who had been reading to Hazel, rejoined James. 'She's asleep now. I was reading Hardy to her, and he proved soporific. Richard's with her now.'

'It's very good of you, Virginia. Thank you.'

'Well, if you knew how kind she was to me the first time I came into this house – and then the other awful time when Michael . . . She's an angel.'

'I know she is. And I've been absolutely vile to her lately – treating her like a sort of whipping-boy, hurting her . . . We had a quarrel just before she was ill, and she said, "Why are you being so cruel to me?" And – do you know, Virginia, I *enjoyed* that, in an awful way. I don't know what's the matter with me. I must be going mad.'

Virginia touched his arm. 'I think she understands, James. She loves you very much. I know that, because she told me so just before she fell asleep.'

Richard came into the room, tense-faced, and went straight to the telephone. 'Hudson? Put me through to Dr. Foley's number, will you. As quickly as you can.'

James looked up sharply. 'What's the matter, Father?'

'I'm sure it's nothing to be alarmed about. But I think Foley ought to come round at once and look at her. She's breathing very noisily, with rather an effort. That damned night-nurse won't be here for an hour yet, will she? What a time Hudson's being . . .'

'The doctor's coming round after dinner, Father,' said James.

'I want him here now.'

An hour or so later the servants waited in the kitchen for news. Mr. Hudson was drowsing, the women, Mrs. Bridges and Rose, silently sewing. Daisy was out with Edward, who was home on leave. The ticking of the clock seemed very loud. 'Is he going to be here all night?' Mrs. Bridges asked of nobody. Then, at last, there were voices in the hall.

'That's the doctor going now,' said Rose. 'I'm going up to see how she is.'

Mr. Hudson stirred. 'It's not your place to go up, Rose.'

'I don't care. I'm going.'

She opened the pass-door a few inches and peeped through. Richard and the doctor, with grave faces, were talking quietly. Richard, seeing her, broke off.

'Excuse me, m'lord – it was just to enquire how madam's going on.'

Neither man spoke; then, after a moment, Richard said very quietly 'Mrs. Bellamy died in her sleep, Rose. About ten minutes ago.'

Stricken, unbelieving, she stared at him, then looked up the stairs. He followed her thought. 'Don't go up, Rose.

219

Perhaps you'd better just go down and tell the others, would you?'

The Armistice was declared on the day of Hazel's funeral, 11 November 1918. The family and Virginia and the servants, all but Daisy and Edward, had gone to the church in Wimbledon where she was to be buried. Daisy stood with Edward at the window of the servants' hall, listening to the guns of the Horse Artillery in Hyde Park, booming out the news of peace, and the clashing of church bells all over London.

'It's over,' Daisy said with a lump in her throat. 'It's all over, and my Eddie's safe.'

He gave her a squeeze. 'That's right. And all ready for a new life, eh? We'll show 'em. No more service for us. We'll make a nice pile of money and buy a nice little house with a garden, and you'll be standing at the gate every evening, waiting for your wealthy and successful hubby to come home for a nice supper.'

'Home from where, Eddie?'

'Eh? Oh, from the works, the factory, or maybe the bank or business firm where I'm employed.'

'I see. Then I think we ought to give notice tonight.'

Entwined, they stood, looking out into the future.

The 'Upstairs, Downstairs' Series

Here is the full story of the Bellamy family and of their servants from the early days of the twentieth century to the darker age of the First World War.

All are based on the internationally popular series of television plays starring David Langton as Mr. Bellamy and Jean Marsh as Rose.

UPSTAIRS, DOWNSTAIRS	John Hawkesworth	35p
ROSE'S STORY	Terence Brady and Charlotte Bingham	35p
SARAH'S STORY	Mollie Hardwick	30p
MR BELLAMY'S STORY	Michael Hardwick	35p
MR HUDSON'S DIARIES	Michael Hardwick	30p
IN MY LADY'S CHAMBER	John Hawkesworth	30p
THE YEARS OF CHANGE	Mollie Hardwick	45p

A Selection of Historical Romance from Sphere

VALENTINA	Evelyn Anthony	40p
FAR FLIES THE EAGLE	Evelyn Anthony	40p
THE GAME OF KINGS	Dorothy Dunnett	45p
QUEEN'S PLAY	Dorothy Dunnett	40p
THE DISORDERLY KNIGHTS	Dorothy Dunnett	60p
PAWN IN FRANKINCENSE	Dorothy Dunnett	75p
THE RINGED CASTLE	Dorothy Dunnett	85p
MADAME CASANOVA	Gaby von Schonthan	50p

A Selection of General Fiction from Sphere

THE BLACK WINE	Hal Bennett	55p
LORD OF DARK PLACES	Hal Bennett	40p
DANDO AND THE SUMMER PALACE	William Clive	40p
DANDO ON DELHI RIDGE	William Clive	40p
A CARD FOR THE CLUBS	Les Dawson	30p
BETTY	K. Allen Saddler	45p
GARDEN OF SAND	Earl Thompson	50p
THE COAST OF LONELINESS	Colin Willock	35p
THE FIGHTERS	Colin Willock	70p
KILLING ZONE	William C. Woods	30p